Also by Carolyn Brown

What Happens in Texas
A Heap of Texas Trouble
Christmas at Home
Holidays on the Ranch
The Honeymoon Inn
The Shop on Main Street
The Sisters Café
Secrets in the Sand
Red River Deep
Bride for a Day
A Chance Inheritance
The Wedding Gift

Lucky Cowboys
Lucky in Love
One Lucky Cowboy
Getting Lucky
Talk Cowboy to Me

Honky Tonk
I Love This Bar
Hell, Yeah
My Give a Damn's Busted
Honky Tonk Christmas

Spikes & Spurs
Love Drunk Cowboy
Red's Hot Cowboy
Darn Good Cowboy Christmas
One Hot Cowboy Wedding
Mistletoe Cowboy
Just a Cowboy and His Baby
Cowboy Seeks Bride

Cowboys & Brides
Billion Dollar Cowboy
The Cowboy's Christmas Baby
*The Cowboy's Mail
Order Bride*
How to Marry a Cowboy

Burnt Boot, Texas
Cowboy Boots for Christmas
*The Trouble with Texas
Cowboys*
One Texas Cowboy Too Many
A Cowboy Christmas Miracle

On the Way to Us

to Us

CAROLYN BROWN

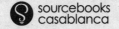

sourcebooks
casablanca

Published by Sourcebooks Casablanca, an imprint of Sourcebooks
P.O. Box 4410, Naperville, Illinois 60567-4410
(630) 961-3900
sourcebooks.com

On the Way to Us originally published as *For the Love of Mercy* in 1999 in the United States
of America by Precious Gem Romance, an imprint of Zebra Books. This edition based
on the paperback edition self-published by the author in 2007 as *An Old Love's Shadow*.

Love Struck Café originally published as an ebook in 2022 in the
United States of America by Sourcebooks Casablanca.

Printed and bound in the United States of America.
OPM 10 9 8 7 6 5 4 3 2 1

Dear Reader,

More than twenty-five years ago, I kicked off my writing career with four short contemporary romance novels. I had been trying to get my toe in the door of a publisher for more than twenty years at that time, and I thought someone was playing a joke on me when I got "the call" that an editor wanted to buy the two stories I had submitted to her. Then a few months later, she bought two more. *On the Way to Us* was one of those books. At the time, the title was *For the Love of Mercy* and later became *An Old Love's Shadow*. *On the Way to Us* is my favorite of the three!

I hope you enjoy *On the Way to Us*, the bonus novella, and the excerpt from *The Sisters Café* and enjoy reading them as much as I enjoyed writing each one!

Until next time,
Carolyn Brown

Chapter 1

"Sweet Jesus, but I hate this place," Mercy growled.

"I've told you and told you not to swear in front of me. It makes my heart cry," Jenny said as she pulled her light brown hair up into a ponytail.

"Your heart doesn't cry," Mercy argued. "It just lays in your chest and pumps blood in and out."

"Then it makes my soul cry, and my soul lives in my heart." Jenny used the tiny piece of broken mirror hanging on the bedroom wall of the small adobe hut to touch up her makeup.

"I don't know why you even bother with makeup," Mercy said. "Sweat will take it all off before we reach the church."

"I'll see Kyle before that, and he'll see that I went to some trouble to be pretty for him, even if it's only for a little while," Jenny told her. "I'm ready, so let's go."

"I'm never coming back here again," Mercy said as they walked out of the one-room hut that was furnished with only the barest of necessities. Two cots, a broken mirror above an old table with a washbowl and pitcher, and a bathroom with a toilet and makeshift shower.

Before they were halfway to the church, sweat was dripping off Mercy's face and running all the way down Mercy's neck to puddle up at the band of her bra. She pulled a paper towel from the pocket of her denim shorts and tried to stop the moisture at her forehead and upper lips, but it did very little good.

She waded through dust tornadoes that boiled up almost to her knees and wondered why she'd ever come here in the first place. "I don't know why I let you and Dr. Nelson talk me into using my vacation days to come here," she grumbled. "There's nothing but dust and sweat and work. I'd rather be back in the office making appointments and typing up reports."

"Yes, it's work, but it's also precious little kids who are so glad to get their teeth fixed and learn about God," Jenny scolded.

"That's the only good thing I've found in this place," Mercy said. "And I don't care if Dr. Nelson begs until his beady little eyes pop right out of his head and his gray mustache crawls up his face and tries to cover the bald spot on the back of his head, I'm not coming back another year."

"Oh, yes, you will." Jenny giggled. "I felt like that the first year, but I soon forgot the heat and only remembered the children and the good feeling in my heart that came from helping them. You will too."

"Not me," Mercy declared.

"You've sure changed since we came out here." Jenny picked up her pace. "You used to be kindhearted and sweet. Now, you do nothing but complain. Turn that frown upside down. You get to lead the singing tonight before we break into groups for Bible school. You have such a lovely voice. I bet there's angels in heaven who would give the feathers out of one of their wings to sing like you."

"You can stop with the compliments," Mercy said. "I meant what I said. This is my last vacation in this place. When I have time off, I'm going to the mountains or the beach, not to a desert place like extreme West Texas."

"Never say never," Jenny quipped.

Jenny had an extra spring in her step when she knocked on the door of another adobe house not far from the church. Kyle opened the door immediately and gave Jenny a kiss on the cheek.

"You sure look lovely tonight." He grinned. He was only a few inches taller than Jenny, and they both had round faces and brown eyes. He wore his thinning brown hair cut short, and the few extra pounds he carried hung around his midsection. That old saying about beauty being in the eye of the beholder had to have some merit, because Jenny thought Kyle was downright handsome. The way he looked at her, even that night, with at least half her makeup already sweated off, testified that he thought the same about her.

Mercy hung back as they walked to give them some alone time, but it wasn't a sacrifice. The church had no air-conditioning or even fans, so it would be just as hot in there as it was out on the dirt street.

That she had been the third wheel ever since they arrived with Dr. Nelson didn't bother Mercy as much as the extra dust stirred up every time any kind of vehicle passed them. She would need another shower after the evening services—a revival of sorts—at the mission. Dr. Nelson wasn't just a dentist; he was a lay preacher. He came to West Texas, to a little town out in the middle of nowhere, the first week of June every year so the local missionary could take his family on a vacation.

She wasn't eavesdropping, but she overheard Kyle talking

about hoping that he could come to that area when he started his missionary work. Jenny's voice sounded almost as excited as Kyle's. That was good, but Mercy wasn't out to save the world like Jenny and Kyle. No, sir, she just wanted to do her job back in southern Oklahoma as the office manager, go on a nice vacation once a year to a place where she could hear ocean waves lapping up on the shore, eat seafood, and read a good thick romance book. She slapped a mosquito the size of a Texas buzzard that had landed on her arm and tried to suck all the blood from her body.

"Next year, if I'm given an ultimatum between coming here or losing my job, I'll take the latter," she muttered.

"What was that?" Kyle turned around at the steps leading up to the church.

"I said I'll quit my job before I come back here," she said.

A spider big enough to provide a meal for three people ambled across the road between her and Jenny, and she stopped dead. That varmint was another reason she wouldn't be returning to this place. Spiders, mice, sweat, and dust topped her list of what she didn't like. Then there were the cold showers because there was no hot water, no air-conditioning, and Jenny's constant positive attitude. Put them all together and it was enough to fry the halo right off an angel's head and singe the pretty white wings—and Mercy was not an angel.

They can save the whole danged universe if they want to, and while they're at it they can take my name off the top of the list of those willing to follow behind them, she thought as she started up the steps behind Jenny and Kyle.

She felt like a giant wilted sunflower when she entered the church. God had made her too tall to be a pretty petunia or even a rose. She was just under six feet tall. If people were flowers, the smaller Jenny would be given a place among the coreopsis—they loved heat and sun and didn't grow tall. Mercy would be a sunflower, or maybe, if she was lucky, she would be one of those giant hollyhocks like the ones in her mother's flower garden. At that moment, she didn't care which floral genus she would be thrown into, she just wanted to shuck all her clothes, stand under the cold shower until she cooled down, and then stretch out on her cot and pray for a gentle breeze to find its way through the open window to her bedside. The last thing she wanted to do was lead a bunch of kids in singing hymns.

"What's got into you?" Jenny asked when Mercy sat down on the back pew in the mission.

"I'm grumpy, and I apologize for it, but you painted a

very different picture of what this was like when you talked me into coming down here with y'all," Mercy said.

"Apology accepted, as long as you try to adjust your stinky attitude," Jenny said.

"More than my attitude is stinky," Mercy grumbled.

"Think about the children," Jenny told her. "Doesn't it just make you feel wonderful to know you might be bringing one of those children and maybe some of their parents to the Lord by introducing them to the gospel story?"

"Not right now, but I'll try to work on it," Mercy answered. "Right now, I don't want to sing. I just want to be cool, and I don't want to smell dust. I want to wallow in a bathtub with bubble bath and I want to drink ice water and not think about it making me sick if I do."

"Well!" Jenny huffed. "That's really selfish of you. You knew when you came down here it was a working vacation. At least you get to work on a laptop all day. I have to sit on a hard stool and hand Dr. Nelson tools and suction out the kids' mouths with sweaty hands."

"If you think for one minute my hands aren't so sweaty that my fingers stick to the keys, you have rocks for brains." Mercy's finger shot up just inches from Jenny's nose. "But *you* failed to tell me about spiders and heat and the fancy shower that is nothing but a garden hose connected to a coffee can with holes in the bottom of it."

Jenny slapped Mercy's finger away. "We've got five more days, so suck it up, my friend. I hear folks coming in, so get ready to lead a few hymns and read the verses that the children will be learning about in their individual classes this evening."

"What I'd like to lead is an exodus out of this place." Mercy got to her feet and headed up the center aisle to the front of the church to sit on the bench beside Dr. Nelson. How on earth that man could stand to wear a long-sleeved shirt was a total mystery. Mercy had paired khaki shorts with a bright blue tank top and wore sandals and was still sweltering.

"Mercy." Dr. Nelson acknowledged her with a nod.

His silver-gray hair was feathered straight back, and his dark blue eyes looked tired. "I'd forgotten how much work this is, but I'm glad that I came this year. I'll be retiring before Christmas, so this is my last year. I probably shouldn't spring this on you like this, and please don't tell the rest of the staff. I'm going to make the announcement when I get back."

"Is someone else coming in to take over the practice?" Her mind went in circles—where would she find another job?

Should she start getting her résumé ready? Would she and Jenny still be working at the same place, or even in the same area? Would they need to find different roommates?

"I've sold the practice, but I'll give the staff at least three months' notice and a nice severance package," Dr. Nelson said.

The heat took a second place to the news that she would have to find a new job. She'd worked at that clinic ever since she was a teenager, when she helped make appointments and did filing jobs after school and in the summers, and had continued working there while she got her degree in business.

The pews filled up, and all the little kids that she'd been working with, both in the dentist's office and then in the evenings in Bible school, smiled at her like she was an angel. A guilt trip over the way she'd been feeling floated down from the bare rafters above her head and settled on her shoulders. She could go home to an air-conditioned house with a real shower, and these little children had to stay right there, possibly with no hope of anyone coming the next year to check their teeth or teach them Bible lessons.

The first hymn was "Abide With Me," which was the theme of the Bible school classes that year. Mercy started it off, then toned her voice down to listen to the children and parents sing.

As she sang the words to the familiar song, her thoughts wandered back to her roommate. Jenny had told Mercy to spend more time on her knees, asking God to lead and direct her life. She was sure that Jenny would do just that when Dr. Nelson delivered the news of his retirement.

What Mercy would like to pray for the Almighty to direct right now was a vehicle—plane, train, or even Rollerblades—to take her home, and she didn't even feel guilty about that like she did about complaining about her situation. For that matter, Mercy wasn't asking God for much, because when Jenny had prayed for God to send a good Christian man into her life, she had met Kyle. Mercy did not want a guy studying to be a missionary in her life, so she wasn't about to utter that prayer. She also didn't care if Jenny fell down and kissed Mercy's bright red toenails, she wasn't going out with Kyle's friend, the ultrareligious, over-weight, under-tall Brent, with the baby face and mushy lips. Mercy had sworn, years ago, that she would never go out with someone she had to bend down to kiss, and she wasn't changing her mind.

Somewhere in the middle of the third verse she couldn't hear the children anymore. The *thump, thump, thump* that sounded like a full-scale mariachi band drowned out the singing. She hoped whoever was driving down the street with their music turned up to the point of being deafening would hurry on past, so they could finish the hymn and she could read the devotional. She raised her hand to indicate they should sing louder and ignore the music outside that could probably be heard all the way back to her hometown of Marietta, Oklahoma.

Everyone sang louder, almost but not quite drowning out whatever was going on out there on the street. Then whoever was just outside the mission's adobe walls turned up the music even more. Mercy leaned into the microphone, finished the last chorus of the hymn, raised her voice to read the devotional, and then stomped down the middle of the two rows of pews. Whoever was outside the small church would do well to drive away as fast as his vehicle would go, because he was about to face the wrath of Mercy Spenser. She might not want to be wallowing in a sweat bath and standing in front of a bunch of kids, but they all had a right to sing spiritual songs if they wanted—and to do so without being disturbed. Did the person playing loud music have no respect for God? The rusty hinges on the double doors creaked as she threw them open, and she expected to see the culprit parked on the church steps with his music turned all the way up to the maximum volume, but no one was there. She closed the doors behind her, and the music continued to blast away, and now loud conversations and laughter were added right in with it. She bit her tongue to keep back a string of cusswords and then realized where the noise was coming from—right next door at Sancho's Cantina. What she had been hearing was a jukebox blaring away so loud that it was a wonder the dead didn't rise right up out of the cemetery on the west side of town and protest.

"Well, dear hearts, it won't be playing long!" Mercy declared in a vengeful tone and covered the distance between the front of the church and the cantina with long strides. When she blasted through the swinging doors, she almost ran right into a long strip of sticky paper spiraling from the ceiling. It was covered with the remains of dead flies and a few mosquitoes. She thought of the one hanging above her cot in the place where she and Jenny were staying.

Every man in the place stopped talking when she crossed the bare wood floor.

A young man whistled loudly, and several others stared at her as if she had an extra eye in the middle of her forehead.

"I'm looking for Sancho!" she yelled about the time jukebox went silent.

Everyone in the place either chuckled or laughed out loud.

"Where is he?" She lowered her voice slightly, but she got nothing but more laughter.

"What can I do for you?" A tall, dark-haired man came from a back room and set a case of beer on the bar.

"Are you Sancho?" she asked.

"Hell, no!" The man started at her sandals and eyed her all the way to her limp blond ponytail. "If you're looking for old Sancho, you're about fifty years too late. That's how long I think he's been dead anyway."

"Well, who are you?" she asked.

"Doesn't matter who I am. Why are you looking for Sancho?" the bartender asked.

She popped her hands on her hips and said, "I'm Mercy Spenser, and we're trying to have Bible school next door. Can you keep this music down?" she asked.

"I don't think so. These men come in here after a long day at work, and they want a beer or a little tequila or mescal and music from the jukebox. What they don't want is a kids' choir singing 'Rock of Ages' to them." His gaze met hers in a challenge.

Mercy took a step forward and leaned across the bar. "I'm only asking for one hour, two at the most. If you are any kind of man…"

Without blinking, he shook his head. "Don't question whether I am a man or not, Sister Mercy. You can sing your hallelujah songs in the daytime when these good men are at work. I've got a business to run, not a church."

"I'm not a sister!" She clenched her fists to her side.

"Well, then have a beer on the house, and enjoy the cantina." He took a bottle from the case and held it out to her. "It will cool you off and take the anger from those pretty blue eyes."

He was more than six feet tall, and his eyes were sparkling green. He combed his light brown hair back with his fingertips, and the muscles in his arms stretched the material in his snowy white T-shirt.

"I'm just Mercy, not Sister Mercy."

"If you're not a nun, then just go back over there and tell them they can sing all they want to during the day. And leave the nighttime to the men who want to have a cold one," he said.

Mercy ignored the beer he was offering and slowly moved even closer to him and didn't stop until they were nose to nose. "We'll sing when we damn well want, and you should at least respect a church. We are only there for an hour."

"Easy there, Miss Mercy. I'm not ready to dodge the

lightning bolts that might get sent down here meant for you for cussing. But know this, darlin', I'm not losing an hour's business just so you can do some preachin', so it looks like we're at a standstill." He kept staring right into her eyes.

"Way to tell her, Hunter." A guy at the end of the bar held up a beer in a toast about the same time that someone plugged coins into the jukebox and the music started again.

Hunter Wilson hadn't seen many women in his life who could look him right in the eye without standing on tiptoe, and none that would get right in his face and dare him to contradict her. In another place or time, he might even sing hymns with the beautiful blond, but not in his best friend's cantina. It would probably be easier to try to talk the habit off a real nun than to try to talk sense to the woman staring him down.

"You are horrible," she muttered.

"Go on back to your Bible studies, sweetheart," Hunter whispered. "I will not turn down the jukebox, but I will turn it up if your singing causes me to lose customers."

"You are…" She struggled for something horrible to call him. "Have you no reverence for God?"

"Of course I do." Hunter smiled. "I've got a deal with Him. I don't sell beer in His building, and He don't expect me to sing 'Amazing Grace' when I pour a shot of tequila in here."

"You...you..." She stomped her foot on the wood floor hard enough to rattle the bottles behind the bar. She drew back her hand but before she could slap him, he grabbed it in a vise grip. The sensations he felt from touching her sent sparks dancing around the whole bar.

"Sister Mercy, you must learn to control your temper," he said. "I don't think they allow wrath up in heaven. Now, get on back to your mission of righteousness, and keep the noise down, darlin'." He released her arm and stepped back out of her reach.

"Go to hell!" Mercy sputtered.

"Not if you're going to be there," he threw back over his shoulder.

The men howled with laughter just as she reached the doors, and Mercy blushed from the end of her toenails all the way up to the top of her head. She didn't see Hunter turn abruptly from the bar and put his hand up to quiet them, and she didn't hear him speak in Spanish telling them to keep the jukebox turned just high enough so they couldn't hear the music next door.

Hunter hadn't wanted to go to Acala, a little town in West Texas, for two weeks. He didn't mind running the cantina for his friend, Mickey, but he would have preferred to do it in the middle of the winter. However, Mickey's fiancée had her heart set on a full-fledged Mexican wedding right smack in the middle of the summer, followed by a honeymoon in Alaska. Since Hunter couldn't talk Mickey into letting him be the third wheel on the honeymoon, here he was in the hottest, noisiest place on the whole earth serving tequila and beer— while his best friend from college spent two weeks in Alaska.

Everything had been rather routine until Mercy came storming into the cantina with fire in her eyes. He was the bartender and short-order cook from just after five o'clock until well past midnight. Then he slept until noon, read a good book through the hot afternoon, and opened the bar again. Hunter didn't know just what forces dropped that gorgeous blond amazon on his front porch, but he would sure like to thank them. That was the most fun he'd had in years, and when Mickey called in to check on the bar, he would have a story to tell him. The way new bride and Mickey were enjoying Alaska, Hunter wouldn't be surprised to get a phone call telling him to shut down the cantina and fly to Alaska to help him build a twelve-room igloo.

He dried a dozen shot glasses, polishing them until they shined and wishing Sister Mercy would come busting back in for another round. His hands itched to turn the jukebox up as far as it would go again, but he'd probably teased the

Almighty enough with his ribald remarks for one night. And he was not fast enough to dodge lightning bolts at the ripe old age of thirty.

━━━━━━

Mercy hurried back to the church in time to catch a frown from Jenny as she made her way to the back corner where her little group of children waited for their Bible school lesson. The whole time she taught it, she expected to hear the blast of the jukebox, but the rascal next door kept it at a low drone the rest of the evening.

Jenny had said that she would get stars in her eternal crown for coming to this godforsaken place and helping out for a week, but after the anger she'd felt in the cantina, Mercy didn't think there was the hope of even one star in her crown. If she had to deal with Hunter and that cantina every day she was here, when she took her last breath on this earth all she'd have waiting in Heaven would be a pasteboard crown covered with tinfoil.

When she finished the lesson, all the people gathered into a small room off to one side where they had cold juice packs, a bowl of fresh fruit, and a platter of individually wrapped cheese and crackers set out for evening snacks. After the fellowship there, she helped clean up the room and straighten up the sanctuary. Then she, Jenny, and Kyle walked back to the places they had been given.

The sunset put on a beautiful show with brilliant oranges, yellows, and shades of pink and purple. No spiders crossed the road, and she didn't see so much as a hint of even a mouse or rat scurrying off between the buildings. A soft breeze rustled through the live oak tree beside the place where Jenny and Mercy stayed, but she just felt the effects of the wind. She couldn't hear the leaves brushing against each other, because the noise of the cantina drowned that little pleasure out.

They reached Kyle's place first, and Mercy hurried on ahead to give Jenny a moment of privacy with her boyfriend. She went inside the tiny one-room building and wondered what it was used for when the missionaries weren't in town. Did the owner rent it out like a hotel room?

"So, did you get over your snit?" Jenny asked when she came through the door.

"Not yet, but I'm working on it," Mercy answered.

"What happened when you stormed out of the church?" Jenny asked. "I thought you might have packed your bags and hired someone to drive you to the airport."

"I didn't think of it at the time, or I might have done just that." Mercy stripped out of all her clothing, wrapped a towel around herself, and went to the shower. Located in the corner of the room, it had a plastic curtain on a circular rod and a hole in the concrete floor to drain the water. She turned on the faucet, and a green garden hose took water up to the coffee can. She stepped around the curtain, hung her towel on a rack outside the makeshift stall, and grabbed the bar of soap. "I got to yell at that fool next door at Sancho's Cantina, so that helped." She raised her voice so Jenny could hear her. "That made me feel better."

"So, you met Mickey?" Jenny asked.

"Who?" Mercy finished her quick cooldown shower, wrapped the towel back around her, and stepped out. "Your turn. I tried to leave you some warm water."

Jenny giggled. "Mickey owns Sancho's. He usually keeps things pretty quiet until after church services. He's built a lot like Kyle. Kinda overweight, but a real teddy bear." She crossed the room, stepped behind the curtain, and hung her towel on the rack.

"That's not who I locked horns with. This fellow looked like he belonged on a movie set. Lord, he was good-looking!"

"Don't use the Savior's name in vain." Jenny stuck a hand outside the curtain and wiggled her finger.

Mercy dried off her body, hung her towel over the foot of the cot, and pulled on underpants and a faded nightshirt that barely reached to mid-thigh. She didn't bother turning back the covers, but just stretched out on top of them and let the night breeze blow over her body.

"Are you asleep?" Jenny whispered when she stepped out of the shower.

"Nope," Mercy answered.

"Then let's kneel beside the bed and say our prayers." Jenny dropped down on her knees beside her cot.

"I'm about to fall asleep." Mercy yawned. "This heat fries a person. I'll pray double tomorrow night."

"Mercy!"

"Oh, all right." Mercy laughed. "I already said prayers while you were in the shower. I was just kidding." She crossed her fingers behind her back. Just three more days, and she could load her little suitcase on the bus and go home to Oklahoma. Three more nights of this unbearable heat and no water fit to drink. Suddenly, she had an overwhelming craving for just one shot of the tequila that good-looking hunk of a man was pouring at the cantina, or even a few sips of the beer he offered her.

I'd better seriously think about dating Brent when we

get back, she thought and then shivered. *No, I will not. I'm not attracted to him, and he's shorter than I am. I'm not desperate.*

Chapter 2

MERCY WAS STILL AT ODDS WITH HERSELF WHEN THEY returned to Oklahoma. She had no idea why Dr. Nelson had trusted her with his plans, but the idea of hunting another job, plus the unsettled feeling she had in West Texas, hung on to her like goat-head stickers from a cow pasture.

That evening, she slung the hangers from one end of the rod to the other in her closet. Of all the places she didn't want to be tonight, it was sitting across the table from Brent and watching his hungry eyes look her over as if she were a medium-rare T-bone steak. She pulled out a sleeveless denim minidress and held it up to her. It showed at least half an inch of cleavage. Jenny would climb up on a soapbox and preach a hellfire and damnation sermon if Mercy decided to wear that particular dress. She was in the process of returning it to her closet when Jenny opened the door without knocking and stopped in her tracks.

Jenny's forefinger came up so fast it was just a blur, and she gasped. "You. Are. Not. Wearing. That. I told you I wasn't going anywhere with you if you ever wore that again. I can't believe you even still have it in your closet. It looks like something a woman would walk the streets in, not wear to dinner with a respectable man."

Mercy laid the dress on the bed and stared at it. She'd let Jenny dictate her life long enough, from telling her what to wear to talking her into going to that hot desert place a few weeks ago. "Yep, I am wearing it." Mercy shook her blond hair out of the ponytail and let the thick mane fall past her shoulders in big curls. "It's hot tonight, and you said we'd be eating out on a patio," she said as she applied more makeup than she usually wore.

"Why do you want to look like a hussy?" Jenny asked with one of her special guilt-trip sighs. "Brent is such a good guy. Are you trying to run him off?"

"I've told you like a million times that I am not attracted to him. I'll go to dinner with y'all, but this is not a date," Mercy answered. "You'd do well to wear something cool since we'll be seated outside."

"What's the matter with what I'm wearing?" Jenny asked.

"Not one thing if you are fifty years old on the way to a Sunday school social," Mercy answered. "Take off the jacket. Be brave and let your shoulders show."

"This is an important night, and I want to look nice for Kyle. Maybe I want to be modest like a missionary's wife should be." Jenny slapped a hand over her mouth. "You made me spoil our secret. We have decided to get married. We were going to tell you and Brent about it at the same time."

"And what's that got to do with me looking like a hussy?" Mercy asked.

"You just don't get it," Jenny told her bluntly. "Since we got back from our vacation, you've been edgy, hateful, and mean."

Mercy should have felt like someone kicked her in the chest, but instead she felt a sense of relief. "Well, thanks so much for that honesty. I admit I'm in a mood, but I'm figuring out that living with you with all your righteousness isn't easy. And that was not a vacation—it was torture."

"Well, let me tell you something, Mercy Spenser, you aren't easy to keep on the right track either. You used to be a good girl, and now you've turned rebellious. Kyle has noticed it too. He wasn't even sure he wanted you and Brent to double-date with us tonight. I stood up for you and said that you would be good for Brent, and God only knows, he would sure enough be good for you."

"Hey, don't do me any favors. I don't want to go out with Kyle's creepy friend anyway." Mercy slipped her feet into a pair of wedges that made her well over six feet tall.

"What happened to you?" Jenny looked up to her. "We were college roommates and have lived together ever since we graduated, and you've never acted like this."

"What happened to me? Guess I'm getting tired of being run like a little toy train," Mercy told her. "It's been easier to just go along with whatever you wanted. Church three times a week, devotionals every morning before we left for work—"

"You hypocrite," Jenny growled. "You never have been a true Christian."

"I believe that would fall under the umbrella of judging, my friend," Mercy said. "But I don't want to fight with you on your special night. Let's talk about a wedding, rather than the fact that you and I are growing apart. Mama would say that it's for the best so that neither of us will grieve when the other one goes on their own special path, which means marriage for you and who knows what for me. We can still be friends even if we don't agree on everything."

"We haven't agreed on *anything* lately," Jenny said with another of her loud sighs. "Kyle and I have decided to get married in two weeks. Just a simple little ceremony in my folks' backyard. We think a big hoopla goes against our principles as missionaries," Jenny explained. "It's time for you to look for another roommate or else you'll have to pay all the rent on this house by yourself."

"Where are you two going to live?" Two weeks? That wasn't very long. Was this an omen for her to find another job and an apartment of her own—maybe in another location?

"In Acala," Jenny almost sneered. "Where else? That's where we feel we've been called to start our missionary work, and there's an opening for us right where we were this summer. The pastor of that little church is retiring, and we've been offered the job of taking over there. A small parsonage comes with it. We are going to be so happy."

Mercy stood up and bent to hug Jenny. "I'm happy for you, and hope that you and Kyle have a happy life over there in that part of the world. I'm ready, and I'm not wiping off my makeup or picking out another dress. This right here is what I'm wearing. Like I said, we'll have to be friends in spite of our differences."

Jenny raised her chin a notch. "I'll pray for your attitude."

"Thank you." Mercy laughed. "It can use all the help it can get."

The drive from Marietta to Ardmore where the restaurant was located took all of twenty minutes. Mercy drove, because they were meeting the guys at the restaurant, and Kyle would bring Jenny home after they had eaten. She turned on the radio and listened to her favorite country music station the whole way to Ardmore. When she stopped at the traffic light crossing the major highway, she looked over at the cowboy in the truck next to her and could have sworn she was staring right at Hunter from the cantina. Then he turned to face her, and she realized that he wasn't nearly as handsome or sexy as Hunter had been.

"You look like you just saw a ghost," Jenny said.

"I kind of did, but it's gone now," Mercy said. "It's just now hitting me that you and Kyle are getting married so fast. Are you…"

Jenny blushed and held up a hand. "I am not pregnant! We haven't even…" The blush deepened, and she turned to look out the window. "We are both saving ourselves until our wedding night."

"Are you serious?" Mercy asked.

"Yes, I am," Jenny answered.

"But you've been dating two years…" Mercy started.

"We agreed in the beginning that we would wait," Jenny butted in before Mercy went any further. "Like you said, you and I"—she gave Mercy a scathing look—"are very different."

"More than I ever imagined," Mercy said as she pulled into the parking lot and snagged a space right in front of the door.

Kyle and Brent were waiting at a table for four on the patio when they arrived, and Mercy hadn't realized she was holding her breath until it all came out in a whoosh.

"What's that all about?" Jenny asked.

"I'm glad we've got a table and not a booth. I don't want to have to sit snuggled up beside Brent in a booth," Mercy answered.

"That's mean," Jenny said as she got out of the car and waved at Kyle.

Kyle's eyebrows raised when he saw them coming toward the table, and Jenny shook her head. Neither gesture got past Mercy, but then neither did the look in Brent's eyes when he saw Mercy. His expression told her he'd gladly ignore his religious convictions if she'd be willing to aid and abet in his sinning. His gaze started at the toes of her sandals and traveled up her long legs to the hem of the minidress, stopped a moment longer than necessary on the cleavage, and finally scanned her face. He could look all he wanted, but if he thought about planting even a chaste goodnight kiss anywhere on her face, he'd better think again.

Kyle stood up, and Brent followed his lead. When they'd seated the two women, Kyle leaned over and kissed Jenny on the cheek. "You look beautiful tonight, darlin'."

"Thank you." She smiled over at him. "Are we ready?"

"I believe we are." Kyle took her hand in his and held it on the tabletop. "I've been offered a missionary job in Acala, Texas, in the very little town that we were at a few weeks ago, and we've decided to get married in two weeks."

"How exciting." Brent clapped his pudgy hands together like a toddler.

"Congratulations," Mercy said. "I'm happy for you both, but I'll be a little sad to lose my roommate and best friend."

"Thank you both," Kyle said. "I want you to be my best man, Brent. We aren't having a big wedding. Just a small affair at Jenny's folks' place over in Madill. So, I'll have just one attendant and so will Jenny."

Mercy waited, knowing what was coming next, and dreading it. That would mean she and Brent would be thrown together at all kinds of pre-wedding events for the next two weeks.

"And"—Jenny smiled across the table at Mercy—"I've asked our preacher's wife to be my matron of honor. I was going to ask you, Mercy, but you're so tall, and we're all so short, you'd look out of place. I would like you to sit at the guest book. When you're sitting down, you don't look so much like a giant."

For just a split second, anger rose up from Mercy's sandals to her blue eyes. Then she realized that she didn't have to give bridal showers; she didn't have to help dress the bride; she didn't even have to be in the same room with Brent for the next two weeks.

"Thank you!" Mercy smiled at Jenny. "That's a perfect job for a giant. I'll be there an hour before the wedding, and I'll even buy a new dress in whatever color you choose."

"That's sweet. I'm using baby pink for my bouquet, so a dress in that color would be good, and it needs to have sleeves and reach your ankles," Jenny said.

"Yes, ma'am." Mercy held her hands in her lap to keep from saluting, but just thinking about wearing a dress like that to an outside wedding in July made her hot.

"Two weeks isn't very long to plan a wedding. I bet your mama is ready to string you up, Jenny," Brent said.

"Not really." Jenny flashed a brilliant smile across the

table. "She's actually relieved that I want something simple. She's altering her wedding dress for me, and you guys are wearing black slacks and white shirts. We don't want a big show."

"We want a solid marriage, not a long engagement or a fancy wedding," Kyle added.

"What better way to start off than a million miles away from both sets of parents," Mercy said. "You'll have to depend on each other for everything, and that will make for a strong marriage."

Jenny shifted her focus from Brent to Mercy. "You are so right. I'm glad to see you with a more positive attitude."

The waitress finally made her way to their table. "Are y'all the group who asked for a bottle of chilled nonalcoholic champagne?"

"Yes, we are," Kyle said. "We're celebrating our engagement and marriage in two weeks."

"Oh! Now I understand why you want nonalcoholic." The waitress winked at Jenny.

"It's not for that reason." Jenny blushed. "We don't believe in drinking. We are missionaries."

"I see," the waitress said with a smile. "Good for you and congratulations. I'll have that right out. Y'all ready to order or do you need a few minutes?"

"Give us a little while," Kyle answered.

Thinking even of nonalcoholic champagne took Mercy's thoughts back to the cantina when Hunter whatever-his-last-name-was offered her a cold beer. When she got engaged, she intended to have a big washtub full of ice and bottles of beer to celebrate, not nonalcoholic champagne.

Brent leaned over and whispered, "What are you thinking about? You had a faraway expression that tells me you'd like to catch the bouquet at the wedding and be next to get married."

He smelled like he had taken a bath in cologne and chewed six sticks of wintergreen gum before coming to the restaurant. Both scents gagged Mercy, and she leaned over to one side and got a dirty look from Jenny.

"I was thinking about my wedding and how I plan to have a washtub full of iced-down beer at it." Mercy picked up the menu and focused on it. "But that won't be for years and years. I'm not ready to get into any kind of serious relationship."

Brent not only leaned back into his own space but scooted his chair over a few inches. "Then I guess you won't be fighting the other ladies for the bouquet?"

"Nope. I'm going to be the one in the back of the yard

with my hands in my pockets," Mercy answered. "That reminds me, Jenny. When we go shopping for my dress, it has to have pockets."

"Why does it need pockets?" Jenny asked. "Oh, I get it. That's so you can put your hands in them when I throw the bouquet, right? What happened to you in Texas anyway?"

"I guess the heat got to me," Mercy answered with a shrug. "I'm sorry if I'm ruining your night. I'll be nice the rest of the evening."

"That would be good," Jenny said, "or else you'll be lucky to be invited to our wedding. Jesus says I have to love you, but here lately I don't like you so much."

Mercy opened her mouth to return the sentiment, but clamped it shut. "Again, I apologize. It must be what I told you about what Mama said. We have to go through this so the pain of separation won't hurt so badly."

"Brent and I haven't had arguments," Kyle said.

"But you don't live in the same house with him," Mercy said with half a smile. "Jenny and I are more than friends. We're roommates, and we've shared everything…"

"From tears to prayers." Jenny finished the sentence. "I'm sorry I've been so catty."

"Me too," Mercy told her.

The waitress set a galvanized milk bucket filled with ice and a bottle of fake champagne in the middle of the table along with four plastic cups. "Want me to pour for you?"

"I can do that right after we order," Jenny answered and told the lady what she wanted.

When everyone had put in their order, Jenny removed the bottle and twisted the lid off. Mercy would have chosen a bottle with a cork to make it a bigger ceremony, but this wasn't her party. Jenny filled four cups and passed them around.

Mercy held hers up first and said, "To my friend Jenny and the love of her life, Kyle. May all the roads you take lead to happiness."

The cups didn't make a tinkling sound when they touched them, and even though the drink was cold, it didn't have much taste. Mercy hoped that wasn't an omen for the upcoming marriage.

"That was so sweet of you, Mercy," Jenny said after she'd taken a few sips.

"I meant every word." Mercy downed what was in her cup.

Sitting through the next hour was a chore, but Mercy managed without even getting another dirty look from Jenny, which was a big accomplishment. She capped it off by picking up the bill for dinner. She thought Brent might at least offer to add the tip, but when he didn't speak up, she took care of that too.

"I hate to leave good company, but I should be getting home. I'll see you later, Jenny. Don't keep her out past midnight, Kyle," she teased, "or she might turn from Cinderella into a cleaning lady."

"She would still be beautiful if she did," Kyle said.

"I'm so jealous," Brent said.

"See all y'all later," Mercy said as she pushed back her chair and headed across the room. She stepped off the patio into the hot summer night and walked right into what felt like a brick wall. One second she was going forward, and the next she was slammed into something solid that didn't budge.

"Excuse me!" Someone gripped her arm to keep her from falling.

"I'm so sorry. I wasn't watching where I was going." She looked up into Hunter's green eyes.

"Sister Mercy, we meet again." Hunter grinned but didn't let go of his grip on her arm.

"I told you, I'm not a nun." She couldn't believe her eyes, but the sparks dancing around the porch were just as hot as they had been at the cantina a few weeks before.

"That's right, you did," he said. "What are you doing in Ardmore?"

"Eating a steak," she answered. "What are you doing here? I thought you lived out in West Texas."

"Nope, I just vacation there occasionally. I live between Gainesville and Denton, Texas. And you?" he asked.

She pulled her arm away. "I live south of here," she answered.

"Well, nice seeing you again, Mercy." He tipped his cowboy hat and stepped around her to go inside the restaurant, then noticed that she had dropped her scarf on the ground.

Hunter grabbed it and turned around to yell at her, but she was already in her car and pulling out of the parking lot. He raced back to his truck and caught sight of her little blue vehicle when it took the ramp to catch Interstate 35 south.

While he was still managing the cantina for Mickey, he'd done his best to find out where she was from. He'd asked the men in the cantina, and finally one of the men asked a teenager, who knew her name and that the church people that she'd come out there with were based in Ardmore, Oklahoma.

He found Mercy Spenser on social media, but no amount

of digging could turn up a phone number, and she hadn't listed her hometown on her Facebook page. He'd driven up from Denton two weekends in a row and walked through the mall in Ardmore, but that proved useless. Figuring he'd never see her again, other than haunting his dreams almost every night, he finally gave up on ever finding her.

Then there she plowed right into him in front of the restaurant where he'd planned to eat that night, and dropped her scarf almost at his feet. That was pure karma—and a big favor from the universe—to his way of thinking.

She turned off the highway at a sign pointing toward Marietta. Then she made a few turns and drove down Main Street, crossed the railroad tracks, and made a right turn into a residential section. She pulled into a driveway in front of a small white frame house with red roses twining up the porch posts.

He parked half a block away and watched her get out of her car, slam the door, and march up to the porch. She went inside and then the porch light came on. That meant she was expecting someone—a boyfriend, a husband, a roommate?

Light filtered through the window and out on the porch. He sure didn't want for her to think he was a stalker, so he got out of his vehicle, walked over to her car, and draped the scarf over the door handle.

When he was back in his truck, he drove back down Main Street until he reached a gas station. He filled up the tank and went inside to get a cold root beer.

"That'll be forty dollars for the gas and three eighty-nine for the soda pop," the old guy with "Ernest" embroidered on the pocket of his shirt said.

Hunter pulled out a bill and handed it to him. "Would you know a girl named Mercy Spenser?"

"Sure," Ernest answered. "Knew her granddaddy and her daddy, and I even went to her folks' wedding, so yep, I know her. Why are you askin' about Mercy?"

"I met her down at the mission when she traveled down there with her church. I ran into her in Ardmore this evening. I just wondered if you might know her," Hunter answered.

Ernest eyed him for a few seconds. "She's lived here all her life. Her folks moved somewhere down around Austin, some little town named Flowers." He rubbed his chin. "No, that's not right but it sounds like that. Anyway, they moved south a few years ago to be closer to their other two daughters, but she stayed here. She's got a roommate, named…doggone it, I can't ever remember that name. Self-righteous as hell. I attend the same church with her and…and…Jenny." He snapped his fingers. "That's it. Jenny Mathison! That woman acts like she invented the Pearly Gates and God only lets anyone get into heaven that she approves of. I knew I'd think of it if I kept talking."

"Where does Mercy work? I thought she might be married to a preacher."

"Lord no!" Ernest chuckled. "She ain't preacher's wife material. Jenny might be someday. She's been cozying up to Kyle, who wants to be a missionary. But I don't see Mercy ever marrying a preacher."

"Why would you say that?" Hunter asked.

"She's a big girl. Kind of intimidatin' to most men," Ernest whispered.

"Big?" Hunter asked.

"I guess the word should be tall, or maybe beautiful. That combination kind of makes a man be afraid of rejection," Ernest said. "So, you met her when she went with the church to do missionary work?"

"Yes, I did. She came in the cantina where I worked to yell at me about having the jukebox turned up too high."

Ernest chuckled again. "That sounds just like her. She speaks her mind for sure." He leaned over the counter and whispered. "I think there's a landline in her house under Jenny Mathison's name. I probably shouldn't even be telling you that."

"Thank you, and I promise I'm not a stalker," Hunter said.

"You better not be." Ernest straightened up. "Or Mercy will shoot you, and I'll help her drag your body to the river."

═══════════

The landline seldom rang, and Mercy had argued with Jenny about paying half the bill every month on something they didn't use very often. Jenny's argument was that she was so lackadaisical about keeping her cell phone charged that she needed the landline at times. Mercy figured it was because she just liked the look of a pink Princess phone sitting on the kitchen counter.

When it rang that evening, Mercy sent up a silent prayer asking that Jenny wasn't bringing Kyle and Brent to the house for a movie that evening. She finally picked up the phone on the third ring.

"Hello?"

"Mercy Spenser?"

"Yes. Who is this?" she asked.

"Hunter Wilson. You wanted me to shut down the cantina, and you tried to knock me down less than an hour ago," he answered.

"How did you get my phone number?" she snapped.

"A kind gentleman named Ernest at the service station in town told me that you had a landline under the name Jenny Mathison," he answered. "Don't be mad at him, though. I told him that I wasn't a stalker. I would like to take you to dinner tomorrow night," he said. "We seem to have gotten off on the wrong foot, but when you bumped into me tonight, I thought maybe it was a sign I should get to know you better."

She was stunned and more than a little flattered that he would go to that much trouble to call her.

"Mercy?" he finally asked.

"Tell you what, Mr. Hunter Wilson. There's a church social tomorrow night. A fundraiser for our missionaries. It's a box supper. Ever been to one?" she asked.

"Nope," he said. "But I know what they are. The men bid on the supper brought in by the women, and the top bidder gets to eat with the woman whose fried chicken he purchases. Right?"

"Right," she said and gave him the address of the small church she and Jenny attended. "It's not hard to find, and I'll be there. If you want to have supper with me, buy the wicker basket with a pink bow."

"I'll be there," he said. "Good night, Miss Mercy, and sweet dreams."

"Yeah, right," she muttered as she headed down the hallway to draw a bath. "As if I'll dream about anything but your deep drawl, Hunter Wilson."

Chapter 3

MERCY AND JENNY USUALLY SHARED EVERYTHING, BUT Mercy didn't tell her about Hunter's call or that she had invited him to the church social. Jenny would have preached at her for at least an hour and then prayed out loud for her another hour. Besides, chances were that Hunter wouldn't even show up.

She and Jenny took their own vehicles that evening, and Mercy was one of the first ones to sit her basket on the long table in the fellowship hall. Chairs had been set up with a center aisle, and Milton, an elderly deacon in the church, was ready to hand out bidding numbers. Jenny came inside with her basket and set it beside Mercy's, and then made sure that Kyle and Brent both had their bidding numbers ready.

"Bossy, aren't you?" Mercy said. "They're grown men. They should know to get a number."

"I just want to be sure that Brent is ready to bid on your basket. I told him which one was yours. I'm not giving up on you two," Jenny said.

"Then you are going to be sorely disappointed," Mercy told her and moved to the other side of the room.

Ernest held the door for a couple of ladies and then went straight to Kyle. He slipped a folded bill into Kyle's hand when he shook with him, but evidently Brent was on his own, because Ernest didn't help him out.

"Bless your heart, Ernest," Mercy muttered.

"Did I hear my name?" He turned around, and almost ran smack into Mercy.

That reminded her of the night before when she'd plowed into Hunter. It didn't look like he was going to show up, but then she hadn't given him a time, so maybe he would get there too late to bid anyway.

"Yes," Mercy finally said. "I saw what you just did."

"Shhh…" Ernest said. "It's the same as me bidding on a box supper. The money all goes to the same place so I could just donate it, or I can help Kyle. Those kids are going to need all the help they can get, just startin' out as missionaries and all."

"Then double bless your heart." Mercy smiled.

Jenny walked up and laced her fingers into Kyle's. "What are y'all talking about?"

"How that I intend to give Brent a run for his money," Ernest teased. "I'm going to run that bidding up so high, we'll just see who gets to eat supper with Miss Jenny or Miss Mercy."

"I brought along my piggy bank." Kyle grinned.

"Oh, come on, you two." Jenny giggled. "You are making me blush."

Ernest turned to Brent. "Who you going to eat with?"

"I'm bidding on Mercy Spenser's basket." Brent looked over his shoulder and winked at Mercy.

"Good luck," Ernest said.

"You are going to need it," Hunter said.

Mercy recognized his voice and whipped around to look him right in the eye. "Well, hello. I really didn't think you'd show up here."

"Here I am," Hunter said, "and ready to bid."

"You'll have to outbid me," Ernest teased, "and this young man right here." He pointed toward Brent.

"I brought two whole dollars," Hunter said. "Think that might be enough. Are we the first ones here or the only ones?"

"First ones, and two dollars won't even start a bid," Brent growled.

"When does the bidding begin?" Hunter ignored him and kept his focus on Mercy.

"In about half an hour. The womenfolk will come trailin' in here in a few minutes with their boxes. Mercy and Jenny volunteered to help get things set things up, so they're here early. This here is Kyle, Jenny's fiancé, and this guy"—Ernest pointed toward Brent—"is here to bid on Mercy's dinner. The auctioneer is supposed to be here soon. Did you just come to bid on the supper and eat with Mercy?"

"I did," Hunter answered.

"Mercy and I've got some more work to do, so we'll leave you guys to count your pennies." Jenny grabbed Mercy's arm and pulled her over toward the lectern where the auctioneer would do his job.

"Who is that man?" Jenny whispered.

"That's Hunter Wilson, the guy from the cantina. Remember when I went over there and fussed about the noise?" Mercy glanced over her shoulder in time to see Brent glaring at Hunter.

"Oh. My. Goodness!" Jenny gasped. "What's he doing in Oklahoma?"

"He lives somewhere near Denton, and I ran into him—literally ran right into him—outside the steak house last night," Mercy explained. "Then he called me and asked me out to dinner, and I told him to…" She paused to catch her breath.

"Come to this event," Jenny finished for her. "What were you thinking? I was hoping that you and Brent were…"

Mercy threw up a palm. "Get that out of your head. No amount of throwing us together is ever going to make me like him. There are no sparks, no vibes, nothing, zilch."

Jenny crossed her arms over her chest and raised both eyebrows almost to her hairline. "And there are with that stranger who worked in a cantina that is nothing but a beer joint?"

"No," Mercy said with a sigh. "Maybe. I'm not sure. Could be."

"Make up your mind," Jenny scolded.

"I'm trying to decide when it comes to Hunter," Mercy told her, "but anything with Brent is not going to happen, so stop pushing. I'm not attracted to him—not one single, solitary bit."

Jenny took a step forward, stood on her tiptoes, and hugged Mercy. "I just want the best for you, and Brent adores you."

Mercy wrapped her arms around Jenny and said, "But we have to adore each other, like you and Kyle, for it to work out."

"That's sweet of you to say," Jenny said, "especially after the way you've been acting lately."

Mercy took a step back and pointed toward the door. "Look, more and more people are coming in, and the table is filling up with boxes."

"This is so exciting!" A smile lit Jenny's face. "I'm so thankful for the support our church is giving Kyle and me for our mission work."

"I wasn't aware this fundraiser was for y'all," Mercy said.

"Neither was I, until Preacher Don told Kyle earlier today," Jenny said. "We should go mingle and greet the other ladies."

"I'm going to make a trip to the bathroom before the bidding starts," Mercy said.

"See you at home tonight, if not before," Jenny said with a nod. "Brent might win your basket after all. I'm still going to pray that you change your mind about him. He can be very charming."

"Ain't goin' to happen," Mercy said, and then headed to the back of the fellowship hall.

"God can make miracles happen," Jenny called out.

Mercy needed a moment of quiet before the bidding began, so she was glad that she was the only one in the ladies' room. She wet a paper towel with cold water and held it against her forehead, thankful that she hadn't bothered with anything other than a little lipstick that evening. She had vowed that she would be nice to Brent if he won her fried chicken supper. She sure didn't want to ruin the whole evening for Jenny and Kyle, but she didn't intend to let Brent think there was hope for them either.

She checked her reflection in the floor-length mirror on the back of the bathroom door. She hadn't wanted to argue with Jenny again, so she had chosen a multicolored skirt and tucked a blue T-shirt into the waist for the event. She had put on a wide belt with a rhinestone-studded buckle and conchas. That had brought a few aggravated looks from Jenny, but she hadn't fussed at Mercy.

She was about to open the door when Lisa Payton rushed inside. Lisa taught kindergarten at one of the local elementary schools, and had been flirting with Brent for months. She stopped in her tracks right inside the door and glared at Mercy.

"Hello, Lisa. Who do you hope gets your basket tonight?" Mercy asked.

"I want Brent to win it, but..." She shrugged. "I've been in love with him since I was twelve years old, but he's only got eyes for you. Why don't you just tell him to get lost so I can have a chance?"

Mercy rolled her eyes toward the ceiling. "Lord only knows how hard I've tried. I wish you would flirt with him, just so he would go away."

"Why wouldn't you want to date him?" Lisa turned to face the mirror and tucked a strand of red hair up into her messy bun. "He's funny, cute, and so sweet."

"No sparks," Mercy told her, and slipped out the door into the fellowship hall.

There might not be chemistry between her and Brent, but sparks danced around the fellowship hall like fireworks on the Fourth of July when she caught sight of Hunter standing against the far wall. She quickly looked away, but not before she saw him tip his cowboy hat and smile.

"Miss Mercy," Ernest called across the room. "We've been waiting for you so we can start the auction. The auctioneer had a last-minute family emergency, so I'm standing in for him tonight. I understand you are the one who is going to bring the baskets from the table over there"—he pointed with the gavel— "and put them in front of me so folks can see them better. Bring the first one, and let's get this show on the road."

Mercy picked up one with a purple bow and pretended that it was so heavy she had trouble carrying it. "Looks like whoever gets to open this box might find a whole pie or cake in it," she teased.

"You know the rules. The highest bidder gets the basket and the girl for the evening. Let's get going." Ernest held up the first basket so everyone could see it. "Purple bow, and I believe I smell a spice cake in here. If I wasn't the auctioneer, I'd bid on it myself."

"Five dollars," a guy from the back of the room yelled. "My granny used to make spice cake at Christmas. I haven't had one in years."

Mercy was very aware of Hunter making his way across the room to stand beside her at the end of the long table holding the box dinners. The scent of his cologne—or shaving lotion—wafted over to her. Something woodsy with hints of vanilla and leather. Between that and the way her hormones were screaming, her chest tightened, and her pulse raced.

"I didn't think you'd show up." Her voice was so breathy that she hardly recognized it. "I figured an event like this would scare off the proprietor of Sancho's Cantina."

"I don't own the cantina. I was only there for two weeks while the real proprietor of Sancho's Cantina took his beautiful new bride on a honeymoon to Alaska. Like I told you last night, I've got a little spread just over in North Texas and an office in Gainesville. I'm an outdoors person, so I don't spend much time behind a desk," he said.

Brent stepped out of the crowd to stand on Mercy's other side, and whispered, "I intend to win your basket."

Mercy felt the sting of Lisa's stares and turned to find her standing right beside Jenny on the other side of the room. She touched Brent on the arm—no vibes, not even a little tiny spark—and whispered, "Lisa Payton has a big crush on you. Why don't you bid on her basket?"

"Lisa is out of my league," Brent said with a long sigh. "She could date anyone in the whole church."

"Maybe so, but she confided in me that she's liked you since y'all were in middle school," Mercy told him, and then wondered what he considered her to be—chopped liver?

"Well, how about that," Brent said and waved across the room.

Both Jenny and Lisa waved back.

"I'm still bidding on your basket," Brent said and then

gave Hunter a dirty look "But if I don't win it, I will bid on Lisa's. Are you sure you're telling me the truth about her, or is this a cruel joke?"

"I'd say from the looks she's giving you that Mercy is most definitely right about that lady," Hunter said.

"I'm going to talk to Kyle. He'll be honest with me," Brent said.

Mercy laid a hand over her heart. "I'm hurt that you think I would lie to you."

"After the way you've been acting since you came home from our Acala summer vacation, I wouldn't put it past you," Brent said.

The bidding stopped at twenty dollars for the first dinner. "Now on to the next one. Hand me another one, Mercy."

She chose Jenny's box, hoping that she and Kyle would go on outside and give Lisa some time alone with Brent. Mercy had never played matchmaker, but she was willing to give it her best shot if it meant getting Brent to look at someone else.

"Look at this beautiful box, or maybe I should say basket, since it's all fancy. I smell chocolate coming from it, and maybe some potato salad. Who's going to start the bidding? Do I hear five dollars?" Ernest asked.

Mercy went back to her place at the end of the table.

"Do you have history with Brent?" Hunter asked. "I don't plow in another man's field."

"To begin with, I'm not a field, and to end with, I do not belong to anyone," she said. "Brent, Jenny, Kyle, and I have known each other since college, but believe me, I am not interested in him for any more than barely a friend."

"Ernest was right. You do speak your mind." Hunter chuckled.

"Yes, I do," she replied.

"I'm not complaining." He raised his hand to bid on Jenny's basket.

"Don't bid on that one. It's Jenny's, and she wants to share it with her fiancé," Mercy whispered.

"One hundred dollars," Milton, the elderly deacon, yelled from the back of the room.

"I've got a hundred. Do I hear a hundred and five, just five more," Ernest rattled off his pitch, but there were no raised hands.

"Sold to Milton James," Ernest said.

Jenny looked like she would burst into tears, and then Milton made his way through the crowd to the front of the room and handed the basket off to Kyle. "I never was very fond of chocolate, so I'm going to give this to Kyle. I think he'll enjoy having dinner with his fiancée."

The whistles, whoops, and applause were probably heard all the way to the fire station down on Main Street.

"That was a sweet thing to do," Hunter said.

"Yes, it was, but Milton is a good person." Mercy picked up her basket next and carried it to Ernest.

"I do believe I saw Miss Mercy carry this basket in here. Let's start the bidding at ten dollars," Ernest said in his auctioneer's fast talk.

Jenny and Kyle had made it across the room, but before they went outside, they stopped in front of Mercy. There was no mistaking the expression on Jenny's face. She was definitely not happy with Mercy even standing beside Hunter, and she would crawl up on her soapbox and do a fair amount of preaching when she and Mercy got back home that evening.

"Brent is flirting with Lisa. You better wake up," Jenny snapped under her breath.

"Lisa is in love with him. Go play matchmaker with them, and leave me alone," Mercy whispered.

Jenny set her mouth in a firm line and stared up at Hunter, "Are you going to join our church?"

"No, ma'am," Hunter answered. "I'm not much of a churchgoer. I just came for the supper."

The bidding started, and Jenny smiled across the room at Brent.

"Come on, fellers, ten dollars to have supper with the lady who owns this box dinner. Don't make me drop the bid down to five dollars," Ernest said.

"Ten dollars," Brent said.

"Fifteen," Milton shouted.

Milton was one of the wealthiest men in the church, and he would bid until he won. Then, Mercy had no doubt, he would give the dinner to Brent.

"Twenty," Brent said.

Lisa gave her a nasty look at the same time.

"I hear twenty...do I hear twenty-five," the Ernest rattled.

"Fifty," Hunter yelled.

"Fifty, I've got fifty, do I hear fifty-five?"

Silence reigned for a minute while everyone turned to look at Hunter.

"Fifty-five," Milton yelled.

Mercy could have told Hunter that the church family was a close-knit community and it took a while for newcomers— even those who just came for the fundraiser to be accepted.

"One hundred dollars," Hunter said.

The room went silent, and folks began to look from Milton to Hunter and then to Brent to see who would win Mercy's dinner.

"One hundred ten dollars," Brent yelled.

"Looks like we got a hot item here," Ernest said. "Do I hear one hundred and twenty... Is it going...going..."

"Five hundred dollars," Hunter said.

"Did I hear you right, son?" Ernest asked.

"Yes, sir," Hunter pulled his wallet out and walked to the podium.

"Anyone here want to top that bid?" Ernest glanced over at Brent and then back at Milton.

Both of them shook their heads.

"Then sold to the cowboy!" Ernest said. "And we thank you for your generosity to our missionaries, son," he said as he took the bills from Hunter's hand.

"Who have you gotten mixed up with, Mercy?" Jenny hissed.

"I'm not sure. Maybe the Mafia," Mercy answered.

"Now, can we go wherever it is that we share whatever is in the basket?" Hunter asked.

"I hope you enjoy the supper, and you'd be welcome to join us for Sunday services anytime you are in town," Ernest said.

"Thank you for the invitation." Hunter took the box and carried it over to where Mercy was standing.

"Lisa, darlin', will you take over Mercy's job?" Ernest said. "Maybe Brent will help you."

"Sure thing," Lisa agreed.

"What's the next step?" Hunter asked. "I noticed that folks were leaving when they won a bid. Do we follow them to a different room?"

"No." Mercy was a little breathless at Hunter's bid, a whole lot relieved that she didn't have to share supper with Brent, and very wary of some guy who could spend five hundred dollars on a woman he hardly knew. "We will pick up a quilt from my car and take it around back to have a picnic under the shade trees."

"Then I'm glad it's cooled down a little and that it's not raining." Hunter smiled.

"Me too." Mercy led the way outside, but knowing that she would be sitting on one of her grandmother's wedding ring quilts with Hunter sure didn't do much to cool down the heat inside her.

Mercy spread the big quilt out on the other side of the yard from Jenny and Kyle. "Why did you pay so much money for this?"

"Man has to pay for a good supper." Hunter sat down in the middle of the quilt. "I could tell you didn't want to share your supper with Brent, and it was pretty evident that the elderly guy was going to run the bid up and then give your dinner to Brent. So, I thought I might win some points with you if I ended the bidding, and, besides, the money is going for a good cause. I hope that's really fried chicken I smell. It's my favorite food. Got any potato salad in there?" He opened the box and inhaled deeply.

"Yes, right along with the fried chicken and plates, napkins, spoons, and two glasses for iced tea, but no tequila at a church social." She pulled out the picnic supplies. "Potato salad, hot rolls, and homemade brownies for dessert."

"Can I have both legs, or is that the piece you like?" Hunter asked.

"For five hundred dollars, Mr. Wilson, you can eat the whole chicken," she answered.

He loaded a plastic plate and lounged back at his ease. "My, my, Miss Mercy, did you cook all day?" He put on his best Texas drawl as he scooped a spoonful of food into his mouth. "Why, I just bet all the men in these parts are waiting in line for you to break their hearts."

"As big as I am, I'd probably break their backs instead of their hearts," she said.

"You certainly are tall, darlin'," he said when he'd swallowed a sip of tea.

"I was always the tallest kid in class, and there were only two boys taller than me in our graduating class." She smiled.

"Don't let anyone ever put you down for being tall." Hunter pointed a chicken leg at her. "Being tall is not immoral, and it's not against the law. And it's damn sure not a sin."

"Careful with those cusswords," Mercy whispered, liking the fact that Hunter was taller than she was—she could probably even wear high heels with him if they ever had a real date.

"Why?" Hunter asked. "We're not in the church house, so lightning shouldn't come down and strike me."

"Because Jenny will come over here, drop down on her knees, and pray for your soul."

"For real?" Hunter asked.

"Oh, yeah," Mercy whispered. "She's prayed for me too many times to count."

"Why do you live with her?"

"She's my friend," Mercy answered.

Brent carried a basket and blanket out while Lisa hung on his arm, looking up into his eyes like he had just hung the moon. He looked like a cornered rat but stopped when he and Lisa were at the edge of Mercy's quilt.

"Looks like the best man won both of these dinners," Brent said.

"I believe we did." Hunter nodded.

"Let's go over there." Lisa pointed toward a secluded, shady corner. "It's nice and private. Did you know that I'm going back to West Texas for Christmas break? I was hoping you'd planned to go also."

"If I can get the time off work, I would love to go back," Brent said.

"Now that's a good match," Mercy mumbled.

"Yep," Hunter said. "Maybe there will be a double wedding when your roommate gets married."

"That would be a wonderful miracle," Mercy agreed.

Later that evening, Hunter walked Mercy to her car and kissed her gently on the cheek. "I enjoyed this evening very much, but I would still like to take you to dinner next weekend—that is, if I passed the test."

"What test?" Mercy asked.

"To show you that I'm not a stalker and that I'm serious about getting to know you," he answered. "If I did, can I have your cell phone number?"

"If you will go to church with me tomorrow morning and sing in the choir, I will consider a date," Mercy answered. "But give me your phone, and we'll exchange numbers. I'd rather you didn't call the landline."

"You're a hard woman, Mercy Spenser." Hunter shook his head seriously. "What time do I pick you up and where do you live? And why don't you want me to call the house phone?"

"Ten thirty," she said. "Services start at eleven. We'll skip Sunday school and just go to morning worship. Jenny has calluses on her knees already from praying for me. If you called the landline, she could overhear our conversations, and she would get on her soapbox—again."

He handed over his phone. "Again?"

"I'll hear about this tonight, believe me," Mercy said.

"Was it worth it?" Hunter asked.

"Yes, it was, and I will remind her that the money you donated will go a long way for the missionary work that she and Kyle will be doing," Mercy answered. "I live at..." she rattled off the address. "Need me to write it down?"

"No, I can remember that," he answered. "Ten thirty tomorrow morning, then next week you're at my mercy for a date. No pun intended." He whistled all the way to his truck.

Mercy recognized the tune as one of Blake Shelton's songs, "Honey Bee." Brent's eyes had seemed to roam over her body like she was a prize heifer at the county fair and had done nothing but aggravate her. Hunter had made her feel like she was the queen of the whole evening just by a sweet kiss on the cheek.

The words to the song ran through her mind as she drove back to Marietta. In the song, the woman was a honeysuckle and the man a honeybee. She was still humming the tune when she reached the house, but her mood changed when Jenny came out of her bedroom, crossed her arms over her chest, then plopped down on the sofa.

"What have you got to say for yourself?" she demanded. "I suppose you already know that Lisa is beating your time with Brent, and I thought we promised back in our college days that we wouldn't go out with any more bad boy types after what happened with you and Liam Barton."

Mercy's mood dropped into the gutter at the very mention of Liam's name. A star football player, he had dated Mercy for about two weeks—long enough to talk her into bed a couple of times. Then she found out that she was the subject of a bet he'd made with his team members. If he could bed her in two weeks, then he'd win the money they'd all thrown in a pot. If not, he had to buy the beer for the graduation party.

"I remember." Mercy went to the freezer and took out a pint of rocky road ice cream. "One or two spoons, and what makes you think Hunter Wilson is a bad boy?"

"Don't bring a spoon for me." Jenny shook her head. "I can't gain a single pound, or Mama's wedding dress won't fit me, and, FYI, *you* don't need all those calories."

Mercy opened the container and scooped up a spoonful. "I'm not getting married, so I can eat what I want."

Jenny scowled. "If you ever get fat as well as tall, you'll really be a giant, and no guy will ever want to date you."

"Who are you going to belittle when you get to the mission?" Mercy asked. "I feel sorry for Kyle if he's on the other end of whatever this is. I'm supposed to be your best friend, and I can't do one thing right anymore."

"If I didn't care about you, I wouldn't try to help you." Jenny pouted. "I just want you to be as happy as I am with Kyle, and I think that Brent could—"

Mercy butted in before she could finish. "I wish you would care less about me and trust me more. I'll make my own decisions and live with the consequences of them."

"Okay! Okay!" Jenny's voice went high and squeaky

when she was angry. "Live your own life, but don't come running to me when it all falls apart. I *will* say 'I told you so.' You're traveling down a dead-end road to heartbreak just like you did with Liam."

"I haven't even been out on a real date with Hunter, but I plan to remedy that next week. And Jenny, it's my dead-end road, and it's my heart," Mercy told her and scooped another bite of ice cream into her mouth.

Chapter 4

THE CHOIR ROOM HAD BEEN FULL OF PEOPLE THAT SUNDAY morning, but they'd all claimed a robe and disappeared to get settled into the section behind the pulpit. Mercy flipped through what was left of the robes and handed one of the longer ones to Hunter. He slipped it over his white shirt and zipped it up as if it was old hat to him.

"Do you sing in the choir of whatever church you attend?" Mercy asked as she adjusted the white collar on her robe.

"I used to, but God and I had a disagreement a while back, and I haven't been visitin' with him much here lately." He reached over and tweaked her collar so that it was perfect.

When his fingertips brushed her neck, desire shot through her whole body, but evidently, Hunter wasn't affected like

Mercy was, because he took a step back and opened the door for her.

"Ready?" Hunter asked.

"Yes, I am," Mercy said with a nod, and then stopped when she heard voices coming through the vent from the nursery in the next room.

"I don't care what Jenny says about that man," an elderly lady's voice that Mercy recognized as Hattie Dailey's said. "He contributed five hundred dollars for our missionaries, and Jenny is the very one that money is going to help. Seems to me like she's biting the hand that feeds her."

Mercy blushed.

Hunter smiled.

"Oh, Jenny's just jealous," Ola Fay, another older lady, said with a giggle. "She probably looks at that good-looking hunk and gets the flutters, then feels guilty because Kyle can't make her heart pump that fast. Lord knows if there was a flutter left in my old bones, Mercy's man could make it work overtime. You girls see the way he filled out them jeans? If I was forty years younger, Mercy would have some competition."

"Honey, you'd have to be sixty years younger." Hattie joined her in laughter.

Mercy's blush deepened.

Hunter chuckled under his breath.

Two different elderly ladies came out of the bathroom and stopped in the hallway. "Mercy, we're running late. Would you and your boyfriend help us with our collars?"

"Sure." Mercy headed back to the choir room. "But..."

"But," Hunter butted in, "I'm better at fixing collars, so I'll do it for you ladies."

"I'm Hilda, and this is Iva Nell," the shorter one of the two made introductions.

"We know who you are." Iva Nell rushed into the room and grabbed a robe. "You are Hunter Wilson. Mercy met you last summer, and you donated a lot of money to the missionary fund last night."

"Small-town rumors," Mercy muttered.

"Well, I'm mighty pleased to meet y'all," Hunter drawled as he adjusted their collars.

Hilda, who was almost as tall as Mercy, nudged her on the arm and whispered, "He's a keeper. Don't let him get away."

"We had better get going," Iva Nell said. "We're going to have to sit on the back row as it is, and y'all know I can't carry a tune without folks around me."

"I'd forgotten how much I miss this," Hunter whispered.

"You can always come back. What made you and God argue, anyway?" Mercy asked.

"Long story for another time," he answered.

As luck would have it, or maybe as bad luck did have it, Mercy sat right beside Jenny in the choir section, and her thoughts went back to when she'd met Jenny in English 101 class at Murray State College in Tishomingo, Oklahoma. MIT, they had jokingly said when folks asked them where they went to school—Murray in Tishomingo.

They'd been roommates there, and when they had finished at the junior college, they shared a room at Southeastern Oklahoma State University in Durant. It seemed right that they move in together when they finished their education and went to work for the same dentist, Mercy as the office manager and Jenny as the dental hygienist. For the first time, though, Mercy realized just how much control she'd let Jenny have over her life, and suddenly she didn't like it. It made no difference that they were sitting in the choir loft listening to a sermon on humility. She had trouble controlling her temper. Little by little, Jenny had taken over Mercy's life. In just four short years, Jenny had become the equivalent of Mercy's mother—or even worse, because Mercy's mother didn't try to control her life.

Sitting in the choir loft that Sunday morning with Jenny on one side and Hunter on the other was like being between two opposing forces. With Jenny, she had to control her temper and her tongue. With Hunter, she could be who she was and not worry about his opinion of her.

She was tired of letting Jenny make all the decisions, including telling Mercy how to dress and wear her hair. Something had snapped when Mercy plowed into the cantina earlier in the summer. The incident seemed to wake Mercy up to the fact she had lost herself, and it was time to take back the power she'd let Jenny have for so long. There was a song that Mercy could relate to, and it had nothing to do with those in the hymnal. In her song, "Miss Me More," Kelsea Ballerini sang about a woman who had let a man control her, but now she missed herself more than she missed him when he was gone.

Mercy sighed, and Jenny poked her and gave her a nasty look.

Hunter leaned over and whispered, "Are you having trouble listening too?"

She nodded at Hunter and turned to face Jenny. "Evidently you aren't listening either."

Jenny frowned so hard that her eyes disappeared. Mercy told herself that in two weeks Jenny would be doing her missionary work where she could lecture anybody, anyplace, and at any time she wanted to do so. She could preach against the wiles of the devil all day and then test the springs of the marital bed with Kyle at night.

"And now I'm going to ask Ernest to give the benediction," the preacher finally said. "Remember that we'll be having a bake sale before Wednesday-night service. All the proceeds will go to help our own new missionaries, Jenny and Kyle."

"Isn't that nice?" Jenny whispered.

Mercy nodded and bowed her head. When Ernest quit praying, she stood up too fast, stumbled over her own two feet, and fell forward. She grasped at anything to break her fall, but got nothing but a handful of air. The next second, Hunter had wrapped her up in his arms, and their hearts raced together in unison.

"Thanks," she muttered. "Grace might be a virtue, but I was chasing butterflies when it was passed out."

"Anytime." He smiled at her. "It was catch you or else about half of us were going down with you—kind of like a row of dominoes. And honey, as beautiful as you are, it would be a shame if you were graceful too. You have to leave something for the less fortunate."

"One never knows. I thought you were being my knight in shining choir robe," she teased as she took a step back.

"Grace is not her middle name," Jenny smarted off.

Hunter raised a dark eyebrow. "Mercy Grace just doesn't sound like it goes together like Mercy Beautiful."

Mercy could have kissed Hunter right there in front of Jenny, the whole choir, and God Himself. Even if she never went out with him again after that day, she would always remember the look on Jenny's face.

The small, crowded restaurant they went to for Sunday dinner was so loud they could barely hear each other talk. So they left before ordering, and Hunter led the way back to his truck with his hand on Mercy's lower back. "Do you have to go home right now? We could get a burger and take it to the park so we could talk more. If not, can I see you again later this week?"

"I don't have to go home right now, and I'll think about another date, but right now I know a little spot down near the lake that's nice and quiet," she answered. "And we can grab a couple of burgers at the Sonic on the way."

"I'll drive, and you can navigate," he said with a smile. "I've even got a blanket in the back seat that we can spread out."

Her favorite spot was a place that she hadn't even shared with Jenny—not ever. He parked, got the blanket, and followed her to a weeping willow tree near the Red River. It wasn't clear and pretty—it got its name from the rusty red color of the water. That day there were a few ducks floating on it, and occasionally a catfish would flip up out of the steady flowing stream. She pushed back the limbs that reached all the way to the ground to reveal a grassy bit of ground, and then together they spread the blanket out.

Hunter sat down, and Mercy eased down beside him.

"Is this quiet enough?" she asked.

"It's awesome," he answered as he opened up the bag of burgers, fries, and milkshakes.

"What are you thinking about?" Hunter asked as he divided the food.

"Lots of things." Mercy smiled.

"Name one," he said as he dipped a french fry in ketchup and slowly headed toward her mouth with it.

"The fact that you put Jenny in her place when you said my name was Mercy Beautiful." She opened her mouth.

Women in her generation didn't swoon, but she almost did when his fingers brushed ever so softly against her lips.

"I was just stating a fact, darlin'. Do you always let her make fun of you like that? The way you stood up to me in the cantina, I figured you were a stick of dynamite with a lit fuse."

Mercy shrugged. "I was before I met Jenny, and…" She paused and stared out over the lake at the ducks. "It was just easier to let her have her way about everything, but things have changed here lately. She doesn't like the new me so well, but she will be leaving in a couple of weeks, so I don't guess it matters all that much."

"I understand about it being easier to let someone you are living with have their way," Hunter said. "Been there, done that, and got the scars to prove it."

"Want to talk about that?" Mercy asked.

"Nope, but I wonder if I kissed you goodbye when I take you home if she would come out of the house and scream at me like a fishwife telling me to go to hell. I really hope that fiancé of hers doesn't care who wears the pants. He seems like a good man, but, in my opinion, for what it's worth, he's got his job cut out for him."

"You, sir, are preaching to the choir," Mercy agreed. "But I don't think she'd be so brazen as to come out on the porch and scold me. She'll wait until I'm in the house. And she sure wouldn't tell you to go to hell. That would be cussin' in her world, and Jenny does not swear."

"Let's test that theory." Hunter grinned. "I'll walk you up to your door and kiss you. We'll see what happens. That is, unless you want to go to the ranch with me and help feed cattle this evening. I could have you back in time to go to work tomorrow morning."

Mercy shook her head. "Thanks for the invitation, but I'd better get home and give Jenny a chance to lecture me for a while. She's going to miss getting to boss me around when she leaves."

"Are you going to miss it?" Hunter asked.

"Not no, but hell no!" Mercy declared. "But we don't have to leave right now. We've got about an hour before I should be getting home."

Hunter teased. "What shall we do with it?"

"We could finish our lunch, then lie back on the blanket and figure out what the clouds are shaped like," she said.

"I was thinking of something a whole lot more fun, but then looking at the clouds with you sounds like fun. If we both guess the same thing three times in a row, I get a good-bye kiss at the door."

"Deal," Mercy agreed, then eased back on the blanket and pointed up to the sky. "That is a…"

"Cat," Hunter said.

"Guess that's one." Mercy smiled.

They laid side by side for several minutes until finally Hunter raised a forefinger. "See that one over the top of the tree. It's a sailboat."

"No, that one is a goat," Mercy argued.

"Then that one is a…"

"Marshmallow," Mercy butted in.

"Yep," Hunter agreed. "The dark around the edges makes it look like one that has been toasted perfectly for a s'more."

For the next hour they disagreed on every cloud that floated by, and then finally when they were folding up the quilt, Hunter pointed up, and said, "Look."

"It's a heart." Mercy smiled. "Did we just agree on a third one?"

"I believe we did." Hunter grinned. "Are you ready for your soapbox sermon?"

"Yep, I am," Mercy declared and decided that she was going to stand her ground with Jenny—even more than she had been doing.

The short drive back to the small house she and Jenny shared took only ten minutes. On one hand, Mercy dreaded the confrontation with her best friend. On the other, she was eager to get it over with.

Hunter parked in front of the house, hurried around to open the door for her, and then walked her up onto the porch. "Think she is watching?"

"Never know." Mercy looked up into his eyes—something that she didn't do often with guys.

He leaned in closer and whispered, "Want to make a wager on it?"

His warm breath on her neck sent tingles traipsing down her spine. She moistened her lips with the tip of her tongue. "What are the stakes?"

"If she opens the door, you go out with me again. If she doesn't, you go out with me again, and this time it doesn't involve church," he said.

"Sounds like a win-win situation," she murmured.

"I believe it might be," he said as his eyes fluttered shut, and his lips found hers.

When the kiss ended, he took a step back. "Door hasn't opened yet, so this time when we go out, it won't involve the church. I've planned a ranch party at my place this weekend.

Would you come to it? I can come and get you or meet you there."

"I would love to come to your party, and I'll drive myself." Mercy was so breathless that she was surprised words came out of her mouth.

"Do you think Jenny's loading a shotgun?" Hunter asked.

"No, but she will be getting ready to lambaste me with words," Mercy answered.

"I'll call or text later," Hunter said as he headed for his truck.

"I'll be tied up with Jenny's wedding shower on Friday," she called out. "When is your party and what time?"

He opened the door and turned to face her. "Party is Saturday night. Supper is served at six thirty. I'll text you the address and directions. I'll be looking forward to seeing you there, but we'll be talking before then. I enjoyed the day with you so much," he waved over his shoulder.

"I've had a wonderful time," she said and waved back at him.

She opened the front door and just stood inside the room staring at the empty space. Nothing was there but a gliding rocker she had bought last Christmas with her parents' holiday check. There was a folded note sitting on the chair with her name on the outside. She picked it up and sat down to read it.

Dear Mercy,

I'm leaving. I can't stand sharing this house with you for one more second. You used to be a good girl with values, but lately I don't know who you are. By the way, I've decided that Lisa Payton should sit at the guest book. Of course, you are still invited to the wedding. You are free to bring a guest if you like, but I hope you don't. Brent isn't interested in you anymore. He is with Lisa now. You'll never know what a good man you threw away to chase that bartender. When you are a lonely old woman, just look back and remember that you could have had an upstanding Christian husband who adored you. Lisa realizes his worth, and maybe someday things will work out for them. I certainly hope so.

I'm taking all the things that belong to me. You'll be surprised to see how much I had invested in our friendship when you notice how many things are gone now. My bedroom is already cleaned out, so you can let whomsoever you please move in to help you pay

the rent. If you choose not to come to the wedding, I
shall send you a card with our new address, so you'll
know where we live, in case you come to your senses
by next summer when the church comes back to do
mission work.

Sincerely,
Jenny

Mercy stood up, looked around at the more than half-empty house, and wandered into Jenny's bedroom. "How did you get all this out so fast? Church was only over three hours ago," she muttered.

All that was left in what had been a pristine pink-and-white bedroom was a hair barrette in the corner. She bent and picked it up, held it close to her chest, and then remembered that Jenny had borrowed it from her to wear on her first date with Kyle. Sunlight streamed through the spotlessly clean windows where white eyelet lace curtains used to hang. The closet doors were open, and not even a speck of dust remained on the floor.

She went back to the living room and pulled her rocking chair over to where the sofa used to be. She sat down and took stock of what was left—a TV and one end table with a lamp. One window had curtains, and the other was bare.

"That's right," she said to the empty room. "We shared the cost of those drapes, and bought matching lamps and end tables, so it's only right that she took her half. I'm glad we never got the cat that we talked about, or she might have taken half of it. The old tomcat that begs for food at our back door better be glad that she didn't think of him."

After a few minutes she pushed up out of the rocking chair and went to the kitchen. The stove and refrigerator were still there, but the table and chairs were gone. Jenny had bought them at a church auction, so they legally belonged to her.

Mercy opened the cabinet doors to find one plate, one bowl, and one coffee mug. "Is this what a divorce feels like?" Mercy asked herself. "If so, it's a strange feeling. Sad on one side, and complete joy on the other. I don't have to listen to Jenny fuss at me, but I will miss her."

On a trip through the bathroom, she found two towels and no bath mat, but Jenny had left the shower curtain.

She went to her bedroom, and it was just like she left it, except that a crocheted throw that Jenny had made for her last Christmas was missing.

"Hey, now, that was a gift!" she said.

She picked up a notepad and wrote: *Monday morning: 1. Call telephone company first thing and if she hasn't already done so, start a new plan just for me. 2. Go to grocery store for things I like (i.e., ice cream and honey-roasted peanuts). 3. Buy a new shirt to wear to the ranch party. 4. Never entertain notions of having another roommate. 5. Enjoy the wonderful feeling of being my own boss.*

Then she dug her phone out of her purse and called her mother.

"Hello, Mercy, what's going on in your part of the world?" Deana asked.

"Sit down, Mama, it's a long story," Mercy said and went on to tell her what had happened in the last few days.

"I've been expecting you and Jenny to part ways for a long time now," Deana said, "and to tell the truth, I'm glad. She's been stealing my daughter a little at a time, more so this last year since she's been dating Kyle."

"Why didn't you say something?" Mercy asked.

"You are a full-grown woman. You need to make your own decisions," Deana answered. "I'm sorry that you and Jenny parted this way when she's leaving so soon, but maybe it's for the best. Now, tell me more about this young man."

Chapter 5

MERCY WAS GLAD FOR HATTIE AND IVA NELL AND OLA FAY, who sat with her at the wedding shower on Friday night. Lisa took care of Mercy's former job of sitting beside Jenny and Kyle and writing down all the gifts as they were opened.

"What happened?" Iva Nell whispered.

"We got a divorce," Mercy answered out the side of her mouth.

"About time," Hattie muttered.

The whole evening was awkward, and Mercy was glad to finally feel like she could sneak away. She had barely gotten into her car when her phone pinged. She fumbled in her purse until she found it, and smiled when she saw that the three-word text—Did you survive?—was from Hunter.

Her thumbs flew as she typed in: Barely. On my way home.

A smiley face appeared in minutes with a message: Can't wait to see you.

She sent back a thumbs-up emoji and called her mother. When she parked in front of her house, she sat in the car for another thirty minutes and finished her conversation. She was humming when she went into the house. That turned into singing when she was in the shower, and sweet dreams of dancing with Hunter after she had fallen to sleep.

———

She tried on at least a dozen outfits before she finally chose one on Saturday night. Jeans—since it was a ranch party— boots, and the lacy shirt she had bought at one of the Western-wear stores in Ardmore. Butterflies flittered around in her stomach as she followed the GPS directions from Marietta to the address that Hunter had given her.

"Turn right," the woman's voice said. "You have arrived."

But she hadn't. The tree-lined lane she had turned into went on for a quarter of a mile before she saw the house. The sun was a big orange ball sitting on top of the place like a halo of sorts. She parked in between two pickup trucks and was about to open the door when it flew open, and Hunter offered her his hand.

"You look lovely tonight. I'll have to stake my claim early, or all the local cowboys will be infringing upon my territory."

She put her hand in his and swung her long legs out. He dropped her hand, put his arm around her waist, and guided her toward the porch.

"Thank you," she said, "but, Hunter, I'm not anyone's territory."

"Apologies." He grinned. "I just meant that I didn't want to have to share you."

"Then why did you invite me to a ranch party where, judging by the number of cars and trucks in this pasture, there are a hundred people?" she asked as they stepped up onto the porch, where a dozen people were already having drinks.

"Because I wanted to see you this weekend, and this party has been on the calendar for months. Before we go out to the barn where the party is really going on, I want you to meet my Uncle Jake."

"Is this his ranch?" she asked.

"Not really, and he's not actually my uncle." Hunter escorted her up onto the porch.

"Just a good friend, then?" She thought of a couple of really close friends of her dad's she had called her uncles since she was a little girl.

"Jake was Dad's foreman all the years I was growing up, and when Dad died a couple of years ago, he stayed on until I could pick up the reins." Hunter ushered her into the house and across the foyer.

"Well, hello." A man almost as tall as Hunter stepped away from the refrigerator with a beer in his left hand. He held out his right one toward Mercy. "You must be Mercy. I'm Jake Thomas. Hunter has told me about how y'all met. Quite a story."

"Yes, it is, but I thought he owned the bar." Mercy shook with him.

"I hope he doesn't decide to move. I'm too old to run this place by myself, and I would like to retire someday." Jake chuckled. "You two younguns better get on out to the barn and enjoy the party. You do dance, don't you?"

"Yes, sir, I do," Mercy answered.

"It's best to ask ahead of time to save embarrassment in case you might frown on drinkin' and dancin'."

"I don't frown on either one," Mercy said.

"Well, then it's right nice to meet you. I got to admit, you're every bit as pretty as Hunter told me you were."

"Thank you, Jake, and I'm glad to meet you too. Shall I save you a dance?" Mercy asked.

"Not on your life." Jake chuckled again. "All of the dances with you belong to Hunter tonight. He already set us all straight about that. Get on out of here and enjoy yourself. Barn dances are for the young folks. These old bones danced their last jig a long time ago, but if I were forty years younger, I might make Hunter work a little harder at keeping you."

"If you were forty years younger, Hunter Wilson wouldn't have a chance." Mercy gave him a brilliant smile.

The band was playing a slow waltz when she and Hunter appeared at the barn door, and he took her in his arms as if they had danced together every weekend for months. She wrapped her arms around his neck and enjoyed the feeling of dancing with a tall man who was smooth on his feet.

"You dance well, Sister Mercy," he murmured into her blond hair.

"I love Jesus, but I also love to dance, and I drink a little," she whispered.

"I saw a T-shirt that said something like that." He drew her even closer to his chest.

"Yep, I was going to buy one of those, but I figured Jenny would burn it," she said with a giggle. Lord, it felt good to just be herself again, and not worry about what Jenny would say or think.

"No doubt about that," Hunter agreed. The music changed to something faster, and he swung her out, then brought her back to "Here for the Party" by Gretchen Wilson.

Mercy had loved the song when it first came out around the time when she and Jenny had first moved into the house. Jenny hated the song so badly that Mercy listened to it with earplugs. To hear the lead singer on the stage belting it out was literally music to her ears.

"Cut in, partner?" A tall, dark, handsome cowboy tapped Hunter on the shoulder and smiled brightly at Mercy.

"Sorry." Hunter shook his head. "Not tonight, Grady."

The corners of Mercy's mouth turned up just slightly. Grady might have taken Mercy's breath away a couple of weeks ago. If he'd appeared in the dentist office, she would have had trouble keeping her eyes off him. But that was before Hunter Wilson came into her life.

"Do you find it amusing that I really don't intend to share your time tonight?" Hunter asked.

Mercy shook her head. "No, I'm flattered, but can we stop after this song, and get a beer?" she asked. "And if we're going to dance all night, I could use some of that barbecue over there to keep my strength up."

Hunter stopped in the middle of the dance, took her by

the hand, and led her toward tables laden with food. "We'll load up our plates, and then I'll go over to the bar and get us a couple of beers. We've got wine and hard liquor too."

"A cold beer in a bottle would be great," she answered.

"Coming up." Hunter pulled out a chair from a table for six for her. "Ease those aching feet, madam, because I intend to dance until daybreak, or until the soles of your boots are gone, whichever comes first." He kissed her on the cheek.

"Whew," Mercy exhaled when he was out of earshot. *If it is a dream, then please, God, don't ever let me wake up,* she thought. *And if it's the real thing—the kind of love that only comes along once in a lifetime—don't let it pass me by.*

"Hello." A blond-haired woman pulled out a chair and sat down beside her. "I'm Gloria," she introduced herself. "You must be Mercy. Hunter said he was bringing a new girlfriend tonight."

"Pleased to meet you," Mercy said. "I don't know if I'd be considered a girlfriend, but I *am* Mercy."

"Oh, no, here come the troublemakers." Gloria rolled her eyes toward the rafters in the huge barn.

Mercy glanced over and saw two hard-looking women marching toward their table. One was at least six inches taller than the other, but they were both dressed identically in skintight jeans, halter tops, white boots, and Stetson hats to match—and they both had platinum hair with just enough dark roots showing to testify that they weren't naturally blond.

"Hello." One of them pulled out a chair and sat down beside Mercy. "I'm Kim, and this is Tonya. We weren't expecting Hunter to have a date tonight, but"— she leaned in closer—"we can fill you in on all the details about Hunter. The ones he won't tell you. We know some things that will make your blond hair turn black, don't we, Tonya?"

The smell of bourbon on the woman's breath wafted across the short distance, and Mercy's nose curled at the stench.

"Mercy, I see you've met Kim and Tonya." Hunter handed her a longneck bottle of Coors.

Kim stood up and fell into Hunter's chest. "Dance with me, darlin'. I know you just brought this woman to make me jealous, and it worked."

"Sorry, sweetheart." Mercy took a sip of her beer, then set it on the table. "Hunter has promised this one to me. This is our song." She took his hand and led him out to the dance floor and wrapped her arms around his neck.

"I didn't know we had a song." His eyes were warming back up, but his voice still had an edge.

"If you aren't sharing me tonight, then I don't have to share you either," she said. "And this song will do until we find one that we like better. At least it kept that woman from making you drunk on the fumes from her breath."

Hunter threw back his head and laughed.

"They've left our table, and Gloria is probably tired of protecting my food," Mercy said when the song ended. "You never know about a spurned woman. Kim might have put arsenic in my baked beans after I foiled her attempts to plaster her skinny body to yours."

"I wouldn't put anything past those two," Hunter said.

"Let's sit this one out, and you can tell me all about Tonya and Kim. Are they twins?" Mercy tucked her hand into his and they walked off the dance floor together.

"No, just cousins," Hunter said, "and they love trouble. They're here as plus-ones with a couple of cowboys who work on the ranch. I see that they've moved on to another table, and that Gloria and her husband, Jeremy, are on the dance floor."

"That means we'd better get back to our food for sure," Mercy said. "I need to make a run through the ladies' room. I'll only be a minute."

"I'll hold down our places at the table," Hunter said.

She wondered what kind of stories Kim and Tonya could

tell as she crossed the barn and opened the door labeled for "cowgirls." She went into the first stall, finished her business, and was about to walk out when two women came inside. She recognized Tonya's gravelly voice and Kim's high-pitched slurred words, so she put the toilet lid down and took a seat.

"God, I'm so mad at Hunter that I could strangle him. I don't know why I let you talk me into coming to this damn party, Tonya," Kim growled.

"You dragged your heels, darlin'." Tonya raised her voice. "You shouldn't have given him time to recuperate after Raylene left him."

Mercy peeked through the crack in the door to see Kim slap a hand over her mouth and head for a stall. She covered her ears with her hands, but that didn't wipe out all the sound of upchucking.

"You need me to hold your hair?" Tonya called out.

"I'm good," Kim answered.

The toilet flushed, and Mercy peeked out the crack between the stall door and wall to see her go to the sink, cup her hands under the running water, and get a drink.

"The third is the charm, and I was supposed to get a chance at him and all those beautiful Wilson millions, but you're right, I should have moved in sooner," Kim fumed.

"Honey, you are not his type, so stop dreaming." Tonya leaned on the vanity, checked her makeup, and picked a bit of barbecue from between her teeth. "I told you not to drink bourbon after you'd been guzzling beer all afternoon. Not even a night in Hunter Wilson's bed is worth the way you're feelin' right now, is it?"

"Shut up," Kim whipped around and shook her finger at Tonya. "Betcha that big blond gal don't know about Carla. Or Raylene. Or—"

"Make a list." Tonya laughed. "If you can pry her away from his arms, you can tell her all about Hunter's scandalous past. And if she dumps him, then you'll have your chance at all those beautiful dollars, which I damn well expect you to share with me."

Kim pulled a hairbrush from her purse and worked on her hair. "And if she don't dump him?"

"Then all's fair in love and war, darlin'. I'd bet my money that you probably know a little more about the love business than that giant of a woman does," Tonya said.

"We'd better do it soon. Hunter seems to be all up in those big blue eyes of hers. Pretty soon it'll all be over except a three-tiered cake and I do's." Kim sighed.

"Well, then, let's get to it." Tonya took her by the arm and led her out into the barn.

Mercy sat still for a little while longer. Who were Carla and Raylene, and why did Kim talk about the third being the charm? Suddenly, she realized that she actually knew very little about Hunter Wilson.

Mercy finally stood up, walked out of the stall, and checked her reflection in the mirror. When she pushed open the ladies' room door, she saw that Kim and Tonya had cornered Hunter—again—not far from the table where he was supposed to be waiting for her.

His dark eyebrows drew down, and his mouth had set in a firm line. Tonya pointed toward Mercy, and Hunter shook his head.

"Maybe I've seen enough to know that I don't want to get tangled up in all this," Mercy muttered.

Kim laid a hand on Hunter's chest and stood on tiptoes to kiss him on the cheek. Then Tonya said something to Kim, and they both turned around and headed across the barn. Jake said something to Hunter, and the two of them disappeared toward the door leading outside.

Mercy crossed the room in long strides and sat back down at the table where her food and most of a beer still waited. Hunter waved and started that way.

"The two witches are headed this way again." Gloria slid

into the chair across the table from Mercy. "Don't let them get under your skin. They like to stir up trouble."

"My mama says that whoever stirs in a fresh cow patty has to lick the spoon," Mercy said.

Gloria laughed so hard that tears rolled down her cheeks. "Thank goodness I used waterproof mascara this morning," she finally got out. "Where you from, Mercy? Did you and Hunter meet at your ranch?"

"I'm from Marietta, Oklahoma, and I work for a dentist in Ardmore. Hunter and I met earlier this summer. The only property I've got is a rented two-bedroom house, and one old orange tomcat who begs scraps from me when he's not courting the tabby next door is my only claim to livestock." She smiled. "How 'bout you, Gloria? You from around here?"

"Next ranch over." She nodded to the west. "My husband Jeremy and I take care of the place for his parents since they're semiretired. Jeremy has been Hunter's best friend since they were too young to even remember."

"Why are Kim and Tonya pestering us?" Mercy wondered out loud.

"Maybe it would be a good time for you and Hunter to dance some more," Gloria suggested.

"I'm not running from them," Mercy said. "They can take

their dyed hair and white hats back to whatever beauty shop broom closet they live in."

Gloria giggled. "You certainly have a way with words. Y'all should join me and Jeremy for dinner one evening next week."

"Sounds like fun," Mercy said.

Kim slid into a chair on one side of Mercy and Tonya took the one in front of Hunter's dinner plate.

"I believe you are sitting in Hunter's place," Mercy said, "and he will be back soon."

"We won't be here but a little while," Tonya said. "We thought we'd fill you in on all the good stuff about Hunter."

"What stuff, ladies?" Hunter stepped up behind Mercy and laid a hand on her shoulder.

"I really think it's time for both of you to leave. I was talking to the guys who were supposed to have invited you, and they're telling me that they did no such thing."

"I'll go home," Kim growled. "I don't stay where I'm not wanted. But remember this, Hunter, I don't get angry. I get even. Come on Tonya. I don't stay where I'm not welcome."

They stormed across the floor and out of the barn.

"I should turn Jenny loose on those two," Mercy declared. "She'd have them saved, sanctified, and dehorned before she set them free."

Hunter chuckled and nodded in agreement. "I don't doubt that."

"Here comes Jeremy," Gloria said.

The short, red-haired guy wearing glasses would have been the last guy that Mercy would have picked for Gloria's husband. With her blond hair, big brown eyes, hourglass figure, and gorgeous smile, she looked like she would belong to one of the tall, dark, and handsome cowboys.

"See y'all later." Gloria stood up and met him halfway.

"I guess I'd better tell you a little about my past before you hear it from—" Hunter said.

Mercy butted in before he could finish. "We all have a past, Hunter. Let's not spoil this lovely barn dance with all that tonight."

Yes, she had questions, but tonight she felt like a bird that had been let out of a cage. She just wanted to have a good time.

Chapter 6

A BRIGHT ORANGE BALL PEEKED OVER THE EASTERN HORI-
zon, breaking the darkness, giving shape to the trees and
fence posts as Mercy drove home early Saturday morning.
The band had packed up and gone home at two o'clock, and
Gloria had insisted that the four of them go into town for
breakfast. She was singing along to a song on her playlist,
"I Feel Lucky," when she crossed the Red River bridge into
Oklahoma.

It hadn't been such a far drive to Hunter's spread near
Denton, and it hadn't taken her long to realize he owned a lot
more than an acre of sweet potatoes. The main house was so
big she figured she'd need Rollerblades to get from one end to
the other if she was in a hurry. The barn where the dance had
been held was enormous, and Gloria said the whole county

used it for a sale barn at one time or other through the year. A bunkhouse, stables, and other structures were also scattered around Hunter's Thunder Ridge Ranch. Mercy could see where a gold digger like Kim would get all dewy-eyed just thinking about the money she could wrangle out of Hunter if she was his wife.

When she finally reached her house, she got out of her car, wiggled the kinks out of her neck, and headed into the house with the orange tomcat right at her heels. Once inside the house, she threw her purse on the kitchen cabinet and opened a can of smelly cat food and carried it to the back porch.

"Now hush. And go find a big, fat sassy mouse for dessert," she said with a yawn. "I'm sleepy and I'm not going to open my eyes until noon. Jesus knows I love him, and he wouldn't want me to snore in church."

The cat purred, but Mercy didn't know if it was in sympathy for her or just his way of saying thank you for the food. She picked up her purse from the cabinet top, and started across the living room when she noticed the corner of a white envelope sticking out of the side pocket. Strange, she didn't remember putting anything like that there before she left last night. And she didn't remember seeing it when she freshened her makeup in the bathroom at the restaurant where they had breakfast.

Mercy pulled off her boots and threw clothing toward the dirty clothes hamper. She took the envelope from her purse and padded barefoot to the bathroom, where she ran a tub of hot water. She eased her body into the water and pulled her long hair up, then leaned back and let it dangle over the edge of the claw-footed tub. Then she reached for the white envelope and really looked at it. There wasn't a name on the outside, and the flap wasn't sealed but folded down inside the letter. She pulled out a single sheet of paper sporting the same cheap chain motel logo as on the envelope and read.

Mercy,

You ought to know that Hunter has been married twice already. He killed his first wife, Carla, and beat his second one, Raylene. So, do you want to be number three? If you don't believe me, ask his best friend, Jeremy. He and Gloria know the whole story. But if you've got a lick of sense, you'll get out while the getting is good.

Tonya

She read the lines again. Surely this was a sick joke. It sounded like a soap opera. She threw the paper on the floor and grabbed the supersize towel on the vanity. She was still dripping wet when she called Gloria—glad that they had exchanged numbers before they said goodbye not an hour before.

"Mercy, is everything all right?" Gloria asked.

"Tonya left me a letter in my purse, and I just found it. It says that Hunter has been married twice. Is that true?"

"You know that Tonya and Kim are…"

"Just answer me," Mercy butted in.

"Yes, Hunter has been married before," Gloria answered, "but you've got to talk to him, Mercy. This is his story to tell, not mine."

"Where's his first wife?" Mercy asked. Somewhere deep down inside she prayed for a remnant of hope to hang on to.

"Carla's been dead for six years," Gloria answered.

"And Raylene?" Mercy asked.

"Raylene's been out of the picture for three years. Mercy, please talk to Hunter, and let him give you his side of the story," Gloria said.

"I don't think I want to be wife number three no matter what story he tells me. Give him a message for me. Tell him that…"

"Is this the girl who stood up to Kim and Tonya?" Gloria snapped. "If you want to tell him something, you're going to have to do it yourself."

Mercy hung up the phone without another word. If she was going to talk to Hunter, she needed time to think before she did. She put on a pair of pajama pants and a faded T-shirt and fell into bed. She awoke sometime later to her phone ringing, but it wasn't the phone at all. The sound was someone ringing the doorbell.

She padded barefoot into the living room, and slung the door open just as Hunter pushed the doorbell again. Without a word, she stood back and motioned him into the house.

Hunter removed his cowboy hat and raked his fingers through his hair. "Jeremy just called me and said that Tonya put a letter in your purse. I guess we're going to talk about the past after all, right?"

"Did you really kill your first wife, Carla, and beat your second one?" she asked.

"After being out with me and getting to know me, you'd trust what they said before you even gave me a chance to explain?"

"Why didn't you tell me right away that you had an ex-wife or two? Were you going to explain after we fell into bed together?" she asked.

"I don't need this," he said. "Believe whatever you want. I thought there was something special between us, but evidently you aren't the woman I thought you were."

"Evidently you aren't the man I thought you were," Mercy whispered.

"Well, then, I should be going," Hunter said.

"That would be best," Mercy agreed, locked the door behind him, and went back to her bedroom. But this time when her head hit her pillow, she couldn't sleep for wondering if she'd just made the biggest mistake of her life.

———

The week dragged by like it had nowhere to go and eons to get there. Mercy was so out of sorts that on Friday, Dr. Nelson asked if she was ill. She assured him she was just dealing with some personal issues.

On Saturday night she drove to Madill for Jenny's wedding.

Mercy signed her name to the guest book and got a sickening little smirk from Lisa Payton.

She chose a seat among the folding chairs lined up perfectly in rows under the shade trees in the backyard of Jenny's folks' house and gave thanks that it was a lovely evening for a wedding. Big white clouds floated in the pretty blue sky and reminded her of the Sunday when she and Hunter had enjoyed the child's game of "name that cloud." A nice breeze flowed through the trees and she thought about how the wind had moved the delicate, drooping limbs of the willow tree.

She was thinking about how shocked her mother had been when she told her about the argument with Hunter. Deana had told Mercy not to be so judgmental. Then Brent slid into the chair next to her. She smelled his wintergreen gum and cologne before she even turned to look at him.

"I thought maybe you wouldn't even show up. I'm glad you did though." His gaze dropped down to the low neck of her dress.

"Eyes up here." She pointed to her face. "Lisa will string you up if she sees you talking to me or sneaking a peek down my dress."

He moved to another chair without another word.

The traditional bridal music began to play, and Jenny made her way down the grassy aisle on her father's arm. She wore a white satin tea-length dress and a shoulder-length veil caught up at the top of her French twist with a few real roses attached to an antique comb.

For Mercy, it was a bittersweet moment. Jenny had been

her closest friend for years, and now they were barely even speaking to each other.

After the ceremony and the wedding kiss, the newlyweds were walking back to the house where the reception would be held, when Jenny locked eyes with Mercy and flashed a smile toward her. Mercy decided to take it as a gesture of goodwill rather than smugness, and she blew Jenny a kiss.

How can you forgive her for being so nasty, and yet you can't forgive Hunter for whatever happened in his past? the voice in her head asked in a scolding tone.

I just don't want to be number three, she argued.

Chapter 7

THE TREES LOOKED AS IF A MAGIC FAIRY HAD WAVED HER color wand over them, creating a spectacular show of lemon yellow, burnt orange, and deep burgundy for everyone that fall. Hunter didn't notice them or the dark storm clouds banking up in the southwest. All he saw was the ribbon of highway in front of his truck and all he felt was a hollowness in his chest.

Mercy had weeks now to call him or to return one of the many messages he had left on her voicemail. At first he had been angry that she wouldn't even let him explain, and he had stormed out in anger. Then that very night the dreams started. Every night he could see her just out of his reach. He awoke every morning in a sweat, reaching for her and touching nothing but an empty pillow. He thought about finding another woman to put in bed next to him in hopes of erasing the hurt, but that wouldn't be fair—not even to someone like Kim, who'd let him know that she would be more than willing to take his mind off Mercy.

That gorgeous fall morning, he awoke and realized that until they had a discussion—whether it started a war or not—he wasn't getting any rest or peace. So, he dressed for church and went to the place he knew she'd be on Sunday morning. It might not be the right place to have an argument as big as he figured this one would be, but the fight had to be where she was…and church was it.

He parked his truck in the lot in the front of the church, and remembered the day when he had bought her basket and they lounged on a blanket under a big tree in the backyard. He should have told her about Carla and Raylene even then, but he hadn't wanted to spoil a wonderful afternoon by going over ancient history.

He shook the legs of his jeans down over perfectly polished boot tops and laid his cowboy hat on the leather seat. He checked his hair in the mirror on the side of the truck, and then he went into the church through the back door and headed straight for the choir room where he and Mercy had laughed together that morning a hundred years before.

"Ohhhh." One of the older ladies put her hand over her mouth. "Look." She pointed to him, and the others turned to see what she was talking about. "Hello, Mercy's fellow," she said with a big smile. "Did you come to fix our collars? We don't have a mirror yet, as you can see."

"Oh, shush, Hattie." One of the others wiggled her finger at the woman. "He's not here to fix our collars. He's come to find Mercy."

They all gathered around him like a bunch of hens.

"Ain't that right, son?" she asked benevolently.

"Yes, ma'am," Hunter answered. "Is she singing in the choir this morning? Did she already go into the sanctuary? I need to talk with her."

"Mercy's not here," Hattie said. "About three weeks ago, Dr. Nelson—that's the dentist she works for—decided to retire early. So, she was without a job. Mercy moved to Texas to be near her folks. She told us that she might be working in a bank or for another dentist. She hadn't decided yet."

"Do you know where in Texas?" he asked.

"Never did say, did she, girls?" Hattie asked.

They all shook their heads.

"But…" he started.

"Did you two have a fight?" Iva Nell whispered. "We were making bets about when you might actually be walking down the aisle with her, and we were all even thinkin' about whether we could line up to kiss the groom, when suddenly it was all over."

"Mercy wandered around here for a few weeks looking all down in the mouth and sad," Hilda added.

"Sorry, son, but you are too late," Ola Fay said with a shrug.

"Did she leave an address to move her membership to another church?" Hunter asked.

"Nope. I heard her tell the preacher she'd let him know later." Hattie shook her head.

"How about the dentist she worked for?" he asked. "Think he might know?"

"Probably." Iva Nell nodded. "But he and his wife left for a month to tour Europe. They'll be back here in about three weeks. We could ask them and call you if you'd give us your phone number."

"I think I can find out before that, but," he pulled a business card from his wallet and handed it to her, "please call me if you find out anything."

"We sure will," Hattie and Hilda chorused at the same time.

———

"Okay, you've been down here long enough to get over that cowboy. You've had several job opportunities, and none of them have suited you," Mercy's mother said that Sunday morning. "You have dark circles under your eyes, and I heard you crying in your sleep last night. I'm calling Hunter. You two need to get this worked out so you can move on."

Mercy shook her head. "Please don't, Mama. It's over, and I just need time."

"The only thing that makes a woman act like you're acting is a broken heart, and you aren't going to find any peace until you see Hunter again and hash this out."

"Mama, just let it go," Mercy said.

Deana took Mercy by the shoulders and turned her around to look at her. "Look me in the eye and tell me you don't want to get this straightened out."

"I'll get over this, and things with Hunter were just the last straw. First there was the trip to Acala to do missionary work, then Jenny getting mad and moving out of our house, and then Dr. Nelson retiring earlier than he'd originally thought. I don't want to talk about it, to you or to Hunter. I only went out with him a couple of times, and he tried to tell me about his past. So, why do I feel like this?"

"Well, we're going to talk," Deana said. "Sit down here at the table with me. It's a while until your father wakes up for breakfast. Tell me exactly how you are feeling. Mothers are supposed to help daughters through tough times."

Mercy plopped down in a chair and sat shoulder to shoulder with her mother. Deana was as tall as Mercy, but her hair, once black, had wide swaths of silver mixed in with the dark these days.

"I'm mad at myself more than I am at him," Mercy admitted.

"Did you talk with him about it? Did you hear his side?" Deana asked.

"Nope. I'll have to just get over him. Only trouble is, I know I'm measuring every other man by Hunter. I've had guys ask me out, but I keep seeing Hunter—the way he walked, the way he smiled…"

Her mother patted her hand. "I think you were wrong in not letting him explain, Mercy. Who told you about his two marriages, anyway? You didn't tell me the whole story."

"Couple of hard cases that were at the barn dance. One of them had a crush on him, or maybe she just had dollar signs in her eyes." Mercy remembered the way Kim had looked at him—and at her.

"And you listened to them without letting *him* have a turn?" Deana said. "That wasn't very smart."

"Hey, you're supposed to be on my side," Mercy snapped.

"When I gave birth to you, I didn't sign any papers saying that I had to agree with you even when you are stubborn as your father. I'm not so sure I would want you to be number three in any man's life, but you weren't in the right either. So, if you want to leave things as they are and wonder forever what his story is, then that's your business. But if you want to make a phone call and say, 'I'm wrong. Let's talk,' then that's your decision too. But, either way you better do something, because it's about to ruin the rest of your life."

"I'll think about it," Mercy said.

Chapter 8

"DAMMIT!" MERCY SWORE WHEN SHE SAW THE CHURCH youth director's vehicle in the driveway. Cody was at the house again. She had no intention of going out with him again. He was a sweet guy, but there was no zing—not like she'd had with Hunter. Her folks had invited him to Sunday dinner the week before, and it was evident that they'd be happy if she would give him a chance. After all, he was a "good guy," the youth director at their church, and had never been married. He didn't chew wintergreen gum or smell like he'd fallen into a vat of cheap aftershave. He was attractive, but his actions reminded her way too much of Brent.

Cody had called on Monday to ask her out, but she made an excuse. On Thursday, he had shown up at the house to play dominoes with her folks, and of course they needed a fourth hand. The sly looks and smiles, meant to melt her heart, just made her more stubborn, and she didn't even offer to walk him to the door at the end of the evening. And now it was Friday, and he was waiting in her parents' porch swing, when all she wanted was to unwind in a long, hot bath. She hopped out of the car, grabbed her purse, and didn't even bother to tug down her bright blue tight miniskirt.

"Hello, Mercy." Cody waved. "I thought I'd kidnap you for a hamburger and a movie."

"I don't think so," a familiar voice said behind her. "Mercy's already spoken for this evening."

"Hunter?" She turned abruptly. Her heart was suddenly in her chest, and her knees went weak. She almost took a couple of steps forward and wrapped her arms around him. "No, I am not going out with you, Cody, but I'm not going anywhere with you, either, Hunter." Her pulse raced so fast that she could hear her heartbeat in her ears. "What are you doing in Floresville?"

Hunter nodded toward Cody. "Do we have to discuss it in front of him?"

"We have nothing to talk about," she said. "I'm going inside. If you want to sit on this porch until you starve to death, then that's your business. But I hope you'll both be gone when I look out tomorrow at noon, which is when I intend to wake up." She slammed the front door as she disappeared into the house.

She threw her clothes on the floor, ran a deep bath topped with frothy bubbles, pinned her hair up, and sank down until the water was up to her chin.

"It's good enough for both of them," she grumbled. "Hunter should have called, and Cody should have stayed away."

"Mercy?" Her mother knocked on the bathroom door, then opened it and came in. "You've got a couple of tomcats out on the front porch."

"I know," Mercy said.

"What are you going to do about them? They both look furious," her mother said.

"I'm not doing anything about them. They can kill each other for all I care. If one dies and one leaves, don't tell me which one is alive. I don't want to know." She closed her eyes, but a vision of Hunter popped into her head and they snapped open.

"You never could lie," her mother said. "But if you don't want to take care of your problem, then I will. Just remember you had a chance," Deana told her.

Mercy had really thought she could face Hunter and not even experience a little, bitty flutter in her heart, but she'd been dead wrong. When she had heard his deep voice behind her, she had come close to falling into his arms.

Mercy heard someone rumbling around in her bedroom, but she didn't care if her mother was putting away laundry or just waiting for her to come out of the bathroom. This was one problem she had to solve herself.

"Mercy!" Her mother knocked on the door for the second time and didn't wait to be asked in. "Your bubbles are going flat, and the water must be getting cold." She opened the vanity drawer and took out a makeup kit and Mercy's toothbrush.

"What are you doing?" Mercy sat up, not caring if her mother saw her naked from the waist up. "That's my toothbrush, and you've got your own makeup."

"Yep, I do." Deana nodded. "Where is that special stuff you use to clean your face?" She opened the medicine cabinet door and reached in. "Oh, here it is."

"Mother! What are you doing?" Mercy got out of the tub, wrapped a big towel around her dripping body, and followed her mother into the bedroom.

"I'm taking care of your problem, daughter! I'm tired of you moping around here, so you're going to settle this thing with Hunter once and for all. I want my daughter back, so kill him or kiss him." Deana threw the items into the suitcase she'd gathered up in the bathroom and snapped it shut. "Now get dressed. There is a point where a mother has to hand the reins to the daughter and tell her to ride the horse or fall on her face. That point has come. It's time for you to ride this horse or else sell it to the glue factory and forget it. Life's too short."

"What are you talking about?" Mercy grabbed a pair of blue jeans from her closet.

"Get dressed in a pair of jeans and a shirt and meet me on the porch." Deana picked up the suitcase and shut the bedroom door behind her.

———

Hunter sat down in a ladder-back chair and didn't intend to move until Mercy came out of the house. Cody shrugged and walked away after fifteen minutes, leaving him alone on the porch to wait. He looked up when the door opened, but it wasn't Mercy who opened the door. It was a tall woman who introduced herself as Mercy's mother.

"How did you find my daughter?" she asked. "Have you been stalking her?"

"No, ma'am," Hunter answered. "One of the little ladies at her church called me. She said that the preacher had her forwarding address, and they gave it to me. I really need to talk to her. I'm miserable with the way things were left between us."

"You drove all the way out here just to talk?" Deana asked.

"Yes, and then I'm on my way back to Acala for a few days to help out my friend in his cantina," Hunter answered honestly.

"I see." Deana smiled. "You stay right here. I see Mercy's dad coming home from his golf game. Talk to him while I get things arranged for you."

Hunter stood up and introduced himself when Bob Spenser got out of his truck and walked up onto the porch. "I'm waiting on Mercy to come outside and talk to me," he explained after they had shaken hands.

"Deana will fix things. She's good at that, and she's never been wrong before, so I trust her judgment. You just wait right here, and don't give up."

"Thank you," Hunter said. "I appreciate that."

"I've got her ready." Deana rolled the suitcase out the door. "If you make me sorry I played a part in this, Hunter Wilson, I will personally shoot you right between the eyes and then feed your sorry carcass to the buzzards. You had better not betray my trust, no matter what happens this weekend. I'm not used to giving my daughter to some stranger to carry off for three days."

"And that goes double for me," Bob declared as he followed his wife out on the porch.

"Yes, ma'am." Hunter nodded. "I give you my word. I'll keep Mercy safe."

Hunter felt the cold air of Mercy's anger when she came out on the porch. Her hair hung in wet strings around her face. Her red tennis shoes weren't tied, and her T-shirt clung to her still damp body. Hunter felt like the poor old coyote who had just found a way inside the henhouse, only to have to face off with the farmer's shotgun.

"What is going on?" She glanced down at her suitcase.

"I told you to take care of your problem or I would." Her mother's tone didn't leave room for argument. "You're going away with Hunter for the holiday weekend, and you will resolve this one way or the other. Either way, I expect you to be back to your old self when he brings you home to us."

"I've got a job interview—" she started.

"And Monday's a holiday, so it's not on that day," her mother reminded her.

"What if I would rather be with Cody?" Mercy asked.

"Then on Monday night, you can call Cody and tell him you're ready to see him," Deana answered. "He's quite taken with you, but no man wants to walk around in the shadow of an old love. Cody deserves better than that. But right now, you two have to work things out one way or the other."

"I'm not going anywhere with Hunter, and that's a fact." Mercy sat down on the swing. "I'm too old for you to make decisions for me and too old to be kidnapped. I'm staying right here."

"Scared?" Hunter asked.

"I'm not scared of the devil himself," she declared.

"I think you're scared of your feelings," Hunter said.

"Oh, yeah?" She jumped up and faced him. "I'll show you that I'm not scared, and by the time this weekend is over, you'll wish I'd never walked into Sancho's Cantina. You might even put me on an airplane and send me home rather than bringing me back yourself."

"I might." He picked up the suitcase and headed for his truck. "Nice meeting you folks, and thank you for trusting me."

Mercy might forgive her parents someday, but as she strapped her seat belt she vowed that she would never forget this. She refused to look at Hunter as he drove through town. But then she didn't need to look at him to know what he looked like. All she had to do was close her eyes, and the back of her eyelids became a television screen where every single memory involving Hunter Wilson played out.

"You turned the wrong way," she snapped when he veered off the highway to the south instead of north. She'd assumed that they were going back to the spread in Denton to take care of their differences. He probably had another big barn dance planned. Maybe she'd feed him to Kim a bite at a time, and then play up to another cowboy.

"Nope, we're going on a little three-day holiday. That's where all this started, so we'll settle it there. Tonight, we have reservations in a motel in Odessa. Tomorrow morning, we head for Acala and spend Saturday, Sunday, and Monday until noon at Sancho's Cantina. My friend Mickey and his wife wanted a few days off to fly to Boston. They've got exciting news for his folks. Maria, Mickey's wife, is pregnant, and it'll be his parents' first grandchild, so they wanted to tell his parents in person."

"Stop this truck right here. I'll hitchhike home. I'm not about to go back to that godforsaken place. I hated it there. And I'm not playing barmaid in a cantina, either, so stop or I'll jump." She grabbed the door handle.

He patted her shoulder. "Mercy, I promised your parents I'd bring you home safe and sound. I'd planned on taking you to dinner tonight and making you listen to me, but when I told your folks I was on my way to Acala, your mother said I should take you with me and we'd have time to resolve whatever our fight was about. It sounded like good advice to me. And your mother threatened to shoot me if I didn't do right by you. You've definitely got her temper."

Mercy folded her hands over her chest and stared straight ahead. At least her mother had offered to shoot him, but Deana would have to stand in line, because Mercy was claiming first dibs on that.

Chapter 9

MERCY SLAPPED HER SUITCASE DOWN ON THE BED CLOSEST to the bathroom. The least Hunter could have done was get separate rooms, but evidently he didn't intend to let her out of his sight. As if she needed any man to come charging out of nowhere and protect her honor. She could sleep in a motel room with Lucifer himself and not be coerced into doing something she didn't want to do. If Hunter Wilson thought he was even going to get a good-night smile, he'd better think again.

"Pizza for supper?" He picked up the order card from the top of the television set.

"Sure. Black olives, extra cheese, and mushrooms," she said. "I'm taking the first shower, and I'm using all the hot water in the state of Texas. Then I'm drinking all the cold water I can, because tomorrow we're going to be in Acala with no decent showers."

"Good idea." He nodded as he reached for the phone to place the order for pizza to be delivered to their room. "Except you only got out of the tub about three hours ago, and other than a few dirty words and thoughts, you haven't done anything to need another shower so quickly."

"I hate the desert, and I hate to sweat," she told him.

"Yes, ma'am." Hunter tipped an imaginary hat toward her and picked up the remote control.

Mercy rifled around in her suitcase searching for a night-shirt and could have killed her mother on the spot for packing only a long blue, silky gown with spaghetti straps—and no robe. Well, if her own mother wanted to throw her into the lion's den in that attire, then so be it.

When she came out of the bathroom with her hair wrapped in a white towel and the flowing electric blue gown leaving little to the imagination, she thought Hunter's eyes would pop right out of his head. Good enough for him and her mother, both, for putting her in such a situation.

"I'm starving." She threw back the covers on her bed with a flourish and fluffed up the pillows.

"Pizza should be here in"—he checked his watch—"three

minutes or else we get it for free according to the order card."

A hard knock on the door let them know they'd have to pay for the pizza after all. Hunter gave the boy a bill and told him to keep the change. Then he filled two plastic motel glasses with ice he'd gotten at the machine right outside their door while Mercy was in the shower and filled them with root beer from two cans. He crawled up in the middle of the bed and set the box with her pizza in front of her and then put the drink in her hands. "Sorry, it's not a beer, but the vending machine outside didn't have anything but soft drinks. However, supper is served, my lady. Can I eat at this table with you, or should I eat on my own bed?"

"It's your party, Hunter. Eat wherever you want to!" she said as she opened the box, removed a large slice, and took a huge bite from the end. She was surprised at how good it tasted, but then she ate when she was anxious, when she was hungry, or when she was happy—and she was two out of three right then.

"Then I'll eat with you." He walked back across the bed on his knees and got his own pizza and drink. "Besides, I want to talk while we eat. I've got something to get off my chest, and maybe if you've got food in your mouth you won't argue with me."

"Don't bet on it," she mumbled around a mouthful of hot cheesy pizza.

"I've thought about this all the way to south Texas, and I thought I had a condensed version ready to tell you, but you deserve the whole story, not a shortened form of it," he said.

"I *want* the whole story," she said with a brief nod.

"I'll admit I should've come clean about it in the beginning, but it was too much to lay on you when we were enjoying that peaceful lunch on the church house lawn, and then later, I just wanted to be with you, not burden you down with my baggage and my past. Before I begin, you got any skeletons in your closet you want to rattle? Any husbands?"

"Nope. And precious few boyfriends. Not many men like a woman who's nearly six feet tall and could beat them at arm wrestling. Seems to make them feel less masculine," she answered.

"Okay, then..." He raked his fingers through his hair— his tell when he was nervous. "I'll start at the beginning. I fell in love with Carla when we were in the fourth grade. She had big brown eyes and freckles and I felt like I needed to protect and defend her. I loved her all the way through high school, and we married when we were juniors in college. I saw my life laid out before me in one straight, happy line. Carla was going to be a music teacher, and I was studying agribusiness. We graduated and came back to the ranch. My mother died when I was just a little kid, so she never knew Carla, but Daddy loved Carla. We went out one Saturday night. Dancing." His voice went flat, and he stared straight ahead at the blank television screen.

"Eat." Mercy pointed at the slice of pizza in his hand.

"Later." He laid the slice back in the box. "Carla never could hold her liquor, but she sure loved to go out dancing. She was a funny drunk." He almost smiled.

"What do you mean, 'a funny drunk'?" Mercy asked.

"She liked to tease me, especially when she'd had one tequila too many," Hunter answered. "That night we drove her car instead of my truck, and she got mad when I told her she was too drunk to get behind the wheel. I took the keys from her, but she had one hidden up under the wheel well because she was always misplacing her keys. I thought I had things under control, but she beat me to the car, got in, and locked the doors. She rolled down the window enough to tell me if I didn't trust her judgment to find my own way home. Said I could walk or talk one of those women who'd been flirting with me all evening into bringing me home." He paused and shook his head.

"We had a hellacious argument through the window, with me begging her to open the door, and her telling me that she was just buzzed. She pulled out onto the highway in front of a semitruck, not three blocks from the club where we were dancing. Five minutes after she'd told me she was just buzzed, she was dead. I saw the ambulance going past when I was calling my dad to come and get me. My whole world crumbled around me. I blamed myself for her death, because I should have remembered that she was always losing her keys and had that hidden spare. I got through the funeral and wished I could crawl in the six-foot hole with her and let them cover me up. I'd never known life without Carla. She was the only girl I'd ever kissed. We made love when we were sophomores in college, and I'd never had another woman. Her temper kept me on my toes. Her love made me whole, and I was as good as dead!"

"Good Lord," Mercy murmured. She saw the scene vividly as he described it and felt like he'd never be able to love her or any other woman the way he'd loved Carla.

"After three years and too many women and drunken nights, I met Raylene. She was taller than Carla and not nearly as sassy, but a whole lot like her. We married in December and by February I knew I'd made a big, big mistake. Carla couldn't be replaced, and Raylene had married me for a free ride on my checkbook. She maxed out every credit card I had and wanted more. One morning we had a big argument, and I told her she couldn't charge anything more until we paid some bills. Then I stormed out of the house and headed for the airport. That day I was supposed to fly to Kansas to look at a bull my daddy and I were going to buy for the ranch, but then I realized I'd forgotten my wallet. I had only gone about two miles, so I had plenty of time to go back and get it. Besides, I had this weird feeling about leaving after an argument like that. The last time I'd seen Carla, we'd had words, and I guess I was scared that I was about to make another big mistake. I figured I'd slip inside the house, we'd make up, I'd grab my billfold, and maybe we'd figure out a way to save our marriage." Hunter stopped and downed half the glass of root beer.

Mercy had a feeling he was going to say that when he got home Raylene had shot herself, or else run out of the house and gotten killed somehow, just like Carla. Mercy put the piece of pizza back in the box and pulled the covers up over her bare arms.

"I eased into the house and heard the noise before it dawned on me what I was hearing." He put the glass on the bedside table beside the phone. "I went to the bedroom to find her, and there she was tangled up with one of my hired hands in the middle of the sheets I'd just crawled out of. He jumped up and started muttering about how sorry he was until I grabbed him by the arm and dragged him through the house and slung him out the front door. Then I went back to the bedroom to find Raylene sitting up in the bed filing her nails, with a smug look on her face. She said, 'I won't cheat on you again if you give back the credit cards and never ask me about them again.' I grabbed her by the hair and dragged her down the hall and pitched her out the door. She landed in the same spot her lover did, but when she got up, she started cussing me, telling me she was taking me to the cleaners. I pitched her car keys out the door while she ranted and raved out there as naked as a jaybird and I told her to get out of my life forever. So, I guess if that's wife abuse, I'm guilty. And if I murdered Carla by not wrestling her to the ground and taking her keys, then I'm guilty there too."

Mercy felt like a fool for not letting him explain his side of the story when he came to her house in Marietta, but who knew, even yet, where a relationship with Hunter could lead? He'd had two bad experiences, so how in the world could he trust any woman again?

"I'm sorry," she said honestly. "What happened then?"

"Divorce happened. I had a good lawyer, or Raylene might have ended up with half the ranch. That plus Jeremy found out about a couple of other hired hands over on his ranch that she'd been having affairs with. So, she settled for a few thousand dollars out of court, but I had to pay all the credit card bills. It was an expensive lesson, like Daddy said. But it taught me to be careful where women were concerned."

"No one should have to endure all that," she finally said after several long moments of silence.

"If you've got any more questions, ask them now, please. I'll answer anything and everything. I don't want another letter to find its way into your hands." Hunter picked up a piece of pizza and took a bite.

"What about all those other women and drunken nights?" she asked.

"I got tested when I woke up from my stupidity," he told her. "I'm clean of any diseases. You have nothing to worry about there."

"Then I have no more questions, except can I have a piece of your pepperoni pizza?" She pointed toward his food without taking her gaze from his eyes.

———

Mercy lay awake until well after midnight and stared at the ceiling. He said he'd been with lots of women. She'd only had the short-lived romance as a freshman in college and then a couple of other fairly long relationships after that. Would he compare her with women who were more bedroom savvy than she was?

At dawn her eyes snapped open, and she still didn't have an answer to the question that had been on her mind when she finally went to sleep.

"Mornin'," he said. "You always wake up this early?"

"Nope, and I'm not a morning person," Mercy answered without turning her head to look at him.

"Then I guess we'd better get on the road and find some coffee," Hunter said.

"I'd like something more than just coffee. I'm a big breakfast person." Mercy rolled out of bed, gathered up some clothing and went to the bathroom.

"Then we'll stop at a little diner on the way that makes a wonderful breakfast." He raised his voice. "It's only about ten minutes from here."

Mercy managed a smile. "I want bacon, eggs, gravy and biscuits, maybe a side order of pancakes, and an extra-large milk to start with."

Chapter 10

Two hours after they had breakfast that morning, Hunter pulled into the small border town of Acala. It wasn't as hot as she remembered, but nothing else had changed. Same dusty streets. Same cantina. Same church right next door.

Mercy thought about Jenny and Kyle helping with church services the next day and considered surprising Jenny by attending. But if her old roommate found out she was here for three days with Hunter Wilson without a chaperone, she'd climb up on her soapbox and start preaching at Mercy. If she even found out that Mercy had spent last night with him in the same motel room, it wouldn't matter if they were as innocent as newborn baby lambs, Jenny would never believe they hadn't shared the same bed.

"Here we are." Hunter drove his truck around to the back of the cantina, and Mercy was surprised to see a sweet little white frame house with a deep front porch. She had never thought about where Mickey and his new wife might live, but there it was, with a lovely flower bed facing the street on the opposite side of the cantina.

"Mickey and Maria left this morning and won't be back until Monday morning. I've got a key, so I'll get us in and come back for our luggage," Hunter said.

"It's a far cry from the place where I stayed last time I was here," she said as she walked up onto the porch.

Hunter opened the door, stood to one side, and let her go inside. "I'll be right back."

"Air-conditioning," she said when a blast of cold air from a ceiling vent came down on her.

"Surprised?" Hunter asked. "Mickey loves this part of the world, but he likes his luxuries too." He brought in her suitcase first, and then his bags.

"This is lovely," she admitted. "Does Mickey make enough on that cantina to live this well? I didn't even know air-conditioning existed in this town."

"Mickey doesn't have to worry about money. He could live anywhere in the world and do whatever he wants. He just likes the laid-back life down here. When the electricity fails, the A/C is powered by a big generator that takes care of the house and the cantina. Maria says you're to have the master bedroom since it has a private bathroom. She also says if I don't treat you right, I'll answer to her." He opened a door and carried her things into that room. "My room is right next door."

A king-sized bed took up very little of the huge room. Double doors opened out onto a deck. Bright colored flowers were planted in pots and hanging from baskets.

She opened the doors and inhaled deeply to take in the aroma of roses, gardenias, and azaleas, and then saw a movement in her peripheral vision. She whipped around to find Hunter standing in the doorway with his arms crossed over his chest.

"The door was open," he said with a shrug.

"Yes, it was, and this is lovely," she replied.

"So, this will be okay with you for you for a couple of days while we help Mickey and Maria out with the cantina?"

"You mean this is a working vacation? No one told me that!" She threw up her palms and sat down on the stool in front of a vanity. "What's my job supposed to be? Do I get to put my ear to the wall and turn up the jukebox when the gospel music gets too loud next door at the church?"

"I thought you'd put on a sexy little costume and dance on the tabletops for the men. We could put a hat on the floor, and you could keep all the coins they throw in it!" Hunter teased.

"And what time am I supposed to have my hat dance regalia ready?" she asked.

"We open the cantina today at five o'clock. I do the short-order cooking and bartending. All you have to do is stay behind the bar and smile. That should be enough to bring in more customers than old Mickey gets in a whole month. Wait until the menfolk around here learn there's a blond angel at the cantina. They'll flock in by the droves," he smiled.

"Flattery will get you nowhere," she told him. "It's thirty minutes until we open up the cantina. I would like a shower before then. You said grill, right? Does that mean tacos? I eat when I'm angry, when I'm nervous, or when I'm happy."

"Which one are you today?" Hunter asked.

"Nervous and maybe a little happy," she answered.

"That's a good beginning," Hunter said. "Take as long as you want. I'll be in the cantina getting things ready when you finish."

He disappeared, and she heard the front door close. The two-bedroom house was a lot bigger than it looked on the outside. Did Jenny and Kyle have a place similar to this? Did the mission provide a parsonage that had a generator? Or maybe even a few swamp coolers?

She fished her cell phone out of her purse to call Jenny, but she couldn't talk to her when she was about to go help in the cantina. She didn't have time for a long lecture, and their relationship was fragile these days. The two times that Mercy had called her, Jenny had sounded frazzled and in a hurry to get off the phone. Evidently, missionary work was a lot more involved than just having Bible school for a week in the summertime. With a sigh, she slipped the phone back in her purse and headed to the bathroom to take a shower.

"Tomorrow, I'll go see Jenny. I'll just surprise her with a visit," she promised as she dropped her clothing on the rocking chair next to the vanity and padded naked and barefoot into the bathroom.

She adjusted the water, then stepped inside and closed the glass door. Standing under the warm water, she remembered the makeshift shower in the adobe hut where she and Jenny had stayed at the beginning of the summer. Was that really just at the beginning of the summer? So much had happened that it felt like years and years.

Looking back, Mercy could see that it wasn't being in Acala

or even the incident at the cantina that had changed her. Those things were merely the straws that broke the camel's back. What had finally brought things between her and Jenny to a head was the fact that Mercy had reached the end of tolerating Jenny's control. She might not have handled it as well as she should have, but the end results had been the same. She had stood up to Jenny, and that caused a split in their friendship.

"I miss her, though," Mercy muttered as she stepped out of the shower and wrapped a towel around her body. "I miss sharing recipes and going shopping together and talking through our problems over a quart of ice cream."

While she flipped her hair up on top of her head and secured the ponytail with a rubber band, then pulled a bandanna from her pocket and tied a loose bow around it, her thoughts went to Hunter's story about his two wives. Why would he ever want to get involved with another woman—especially a tall blond who spoke her mind?

She tugged a white eyelet lace camisole down over the waistband of a pair of flattering skinny jeans. She would have brought different clothes if she'd been doing the choosing, but at least her mother hadn't packed silk business suits or after-five party dresses. She checked her reflection in the free-standing full-length mirror in the corner and smiled. Maybe her outfit would make him eat those teasing words he'd said about her dancing on the bar.

She slipped on a pair of sandals and locked the door behind her as she left the house. There were no dust tornadoes or spiders crossing the lawn when she made her way around the house and swung open the doors of the cantina. The place was already half full, and the jukebox was blasting away in a lively tune. Men were bellied up to the bar and sitting around the mismatched tables.

Several of the customers whistled when she walked across the floor. One of them called out, "Can I buy you a shot of tequila?"

"No, you may not," Hunter yelled from behind the bar. "She's with me this weekend."

"Hey, isn't that the señorita who came in here demanding we turn down the jukebox?" another one asked.

"That's right, I am, but this weekend, I'm here to help Hunter, not to have Bible school," she answered.

The guy held up his beer in a toast. "You chose the better side."

Mercy rounded the end of the bar, took an apron from a hook, and wrapped it around her waist. "I can draw beer and serve up bottles."

"Only if you want to," Hunter told her.

"My job is to help you, and like you said, figure out what we're going to do about us. Mama always says the best way to get to know a person is to work beside them for a few days," she told him.

"Hey pretty lady, could I get a pint of beer down here?" someone called from the other end of the bar.

"You got it." She located the pint jars and drew it up.

In a couple of hours, Mercy and Hunter were working together as a team. They had little time for talking, but she felt like she had found out all kinds of things about him. He was kind, and more than once he'd chipped in to help pay for a customer's beer. He worked hard, which told her that he would do anything for a friend in need, and the few times that something didn't go right, he took it in stride, and didn't lose his temper.

The last one surprised Mercy after the Raylene story, but then she might not have handled things as well as he did. If a person she loved treated her so horribly, she would have done more than just tossing them out naked in the yard.

At the end of the evening, Hunter locked up, and Mercy picked up a towel from a stack under the counter and wiped down the top of the bar.

"So, what have you learned about me from working beside me?" Hunter sat down and propped his boots up on a table.

Mercy drew up two jars of beer and carried them to the table. She set them down and then followed Hunter's lead. Feet on the table, beer in hand, she let out a long sigh. "Ahhh, it feels good to sit down."

"Thanks for the beer," he said and took a long drink. "Are you going to answer my question?"

"I learned that you're kindhearted and a hard worker," she answered, "and that you look pretty good in a Hawaiian shirt."

"Well, I learned that you are gorgeous no matter what you're wearing or how you fix your hair, and that I like working beside you. I know that comparing people is often like comparing apples and oranges, but neither Carla nor Raylene liked to get their hands dirty. A couple of times during the time I was with each of them, I came out here to help Mickey, and they refused to come with me," he said.

"I can't fault them," Mercy said. "I might not be here either if my mother hadn't packed me up and sent me with you. Did they help you on the ranch?"

"Nope," he said and took another drink of his beer. "Carla hated anything to do with the ranch. She worked in a local bank as a teller just so she wouldn't have to be stranded, as she called it, on the ranch. Raylene didn't do anything except shop, spend money, and cheat on me. But I don't want to talk about them."

"What do you want to talk about?" Mercy asked.

"You," he answered. "Why did you major in business?"

That seemed like a silly question to start off the conversation, but Mercy answered it. "Because I didn't know what I wanted to do with my life, and it seemed like a broad enough field." She tipped up her beer and took a long drink.

"Want a job?" Hunter asked.

"Are you asking me to tally up the cash register?" she asked.

"We'll do that together, and put the money in Mickey's safe," Hunter said. "I need an office manager at the ranch. I've got a staff that takes care of the oil business in town, but I need someone to take care of the ranchin' business. I hate spending time in front of a computer. I want to be outside with the hired hands, not sitting at a desk inputting data or doing payroll. Jake's been on me for months to hire someone. Interested?"

"Can I think about it?" Mercy asked.

All kinds of scenarios played through her mind at warp

speed. If she and Hunter did get into a serious relationship, what would happen to her job if everything went south? Would she live on the ranch or in an apartment in town? What would the job and benefit package look like?

"It's a lot to think about, so yes, you've got time. Can you give me an answer in ten minutes?" He wiggled his dark eyebrows.

She air slapped his arm. "Don't push your luck."

"I have been lucky," Hunter said. "I've been beating around the bush, not knowing where to start this conversation." He paused, took a deep breath, and then went on. "I never thought I'd feel anything again, but there's chemistry between us, and I'm not running from it."

"Me, either, but neither of us should be going too fast. We need to take things slow, and be sure that..."

Hunter butted in. "You sound like Jake, but I agree with you. We don't have to rush into anything."

Mercy covered a yawn with her hand. "Not bad company, just a tired body."

"Then let's go on to the house and finish straightening up the cantina tomorrow. We could both use a good night's sleep." Hunter set his feet on the floor, stood up, and offered his hand to Mercy.

She wasn't surprised at the chemistry between them when she put her hand in his. If their relationship did get off the ground and fly, would she always feel this way?

———

Mercy couldn't believe it when she woke up and looked at the clock and saw that it was already after noon. The aroma of freshly brewed coffee and bacon wafted under her door. Her stomach reminded her that it had been a long time since she'd eaten a cantina hamburger on the run the evening before. She crawled out of bed, brushed her teeth, and headed for the kitchen in an oversized T-shirt that barely covered her underpants. Her mother had no doubt packed it for her to wear with jeans, but it had become a nightshirt when she went looking for something to sleep in other than the fancy blue gown.

"Good morning," Hunter said. "Did you sleep well?"

"A heck of a lot better than the night before," she admitted as she filled a mug with coffee. "Something smells good."

"Bacon is done. Biscuits will come out of the oven in ten minutes, and I'm about to scramble some eggs and make some pancakes," Hunter told her.

"That sounds great." Mercy set her coffee on the counter

and opened two doors before she found plates behind the third one. She set the table for two and brought out butter and two kinds of jelly from the refrigerator.

Hunter whipped up pancake batter. "Did Mickey leave us any orange juice?"

"Yep, right here." She took a bottle from the fridge and took two glasses from the cabinet. "We're all set, except for syrup. Where would I find that?"

"Pantry." Hunter used an egg turner to point in the direction of a door on the other side of the room. "We seem to make a pretty good team in the kitchen as well as the cantina."

"Yes, we do," she agreed. "You didn't tell me that you could cook—other than in the cantina, that is."

"Dad didn't know anything about running a kitchen, so he hired a housekeeper and cook. She had this thing she called the goose and gander law, which was basically just saying that boys should learn to do what was usually girls' work, and girls needed to know how to do what was dubbed boys' jobs," he explained. "I'm glad she taught me the basics. I'm not a gourmet, but I know enough to keep body and soul together. How about you?"

When the timer went off, Mercy removed the pan of biscuits from the oven and set them on the counter. "I like to cook. Jenny and I used to spend hours looking over new recipes to try."

"So, you had good times with her as well as bad ones?" Hunter asked.

"Seems that way." Mercy busied herself by putting the hot biscuits onto a plate and taking them to the table. "How about you? Were there good times?"

"More with Carla than with Raylene," he answered. "Have you thought about my job offer? If working together helps us get to know each other, then that might be a good thing, right?"

"Might be," she agreed, "but I'll need a week or two to think about it. You are a very sexy man, Hunter Wilson, and it would be easy to say yes right now. But let's see if we still even like each other when there's three hundred miles between where I live and your ranch."

"You looked up the distance, didn't you?" Hunter grinned.

"Yes, I did, but that doesn't mean..."

He cut her off by holding up a palm. "You like me, don't you?"

"Yes, but I didn't want to be kidnapped," she smarted off at him. "But liking and loving and getting along every day in a work situation are different than an attraction."

"Want to hear about what goes with the job?" He brought the rest of the food to the table and sat down across from her. "You saw how big the house is, so you can live there if you want to. You'll get the full medical package with the job, and two weeks' vacation after you've been there a year."

"To come out here and work in a cantina, I suppose." She picked up a piece of bacon with her fingers and took a bite.

Hunter chuckled. "Well, now, if that's what you want to do on your vacation, I'm sure Mickey would be glad for the help."

Mercy was stunned at what he had just offered, but there was no way she could live with him in his house. That would be testing temptation entirely too far. On the other hand, she would have her own office, and only be responsible to Hunter. That would definitely go over on the plus side of the list when she made it.

"Give us both a week to mull over this," she said as she began to fill her plate. "What have we got planned for this afternoon?"

"We have to put the cantina to rights, count the money and get the cash register ready for tomorrow, and restock the bar..." He paused.

"I can do the cleanup if you'll restock the bar," she said.

He slathered butter on two biscuits. "You've got a deal, but I'll help with the sweeping and mopping after I get the cash register ready. You don't have to do all that alone."

"I'd like to visit Jenny for a little while tomorrow," Mercy said.

"I'll need to update Mickey tomorrow, so feel free to do anything you want before we open," Hunter said. "I'd forgotten that Jenny lived here."

"She'll probably fuss at me for what I'm doing, and for not attending church services tomorrow, but…" She shrugged.

Hunter laid his fork to the side, reached across the table, and covered her hand with his. "She's lucky that you are even going to see her."

===

Mercy was sweating by the time they had the cantina ready to open. She made a mad dash through the bathroom, washed her face, redid her ponytail, and applied a little lipstick. She had just rounded the end of the bar when the doors swung open and a dozen men crowded into the place, along with four or five women.

They all found their way to the bar, ordered, and then took their drinks to tables. Hunter busied himself making burger baskets and tacos, while Mercy drew up drinks. She was paying very little attention to the customers right up until the whole place went so quiet that she could hear the gospel hymns being sung in Jenny and Kyle's church next door.

At first, she thought that the jukebox had simply run out of songs, but when she turned around, she saw what all the folks were staring at. A woman had pushed her way through the doors and was now standing just inside the cantina. She had a mop of bright red hair that had to be natural because a bottle could never produce that color. Freckles danced across her nose and colored contacts made her eyes Crayola green. She wore a pair of skintight black pants, a low-cut black top that left half her breasts exposed, a black cowboy hat, and boots with a turquoise phoenix inlaid on the tops. For a full two minutes she just stood there like a statue, or maybe a model. No, that wasn't it—like a woman who was picking out a man to follow around behind her like a puppy dog and help her take those boots off when she was ready.

Even Hunter had a smile plastered on his face like a little boy who'd found a whole stack of *Playboy* magazines in the trash can. Then a dozen men came into the cantina and all of them went slack-jawed at the sight of her.

"What are you smiling at?" Mercy asked him.

"Same thing all the rest of the men in here are grinning at," he said. "It's not often we get a second woman in here as beautiful as you."

"So, you think she's beautiful, do you?" Mercy whispered.

"Hello, señorita," one of the guys said. "Can I buy you a drink?"

"No, I've picked out the man who will buy me a drink." She pointed straight at Hunter and made a beeline for the bar.

A man who'd been sitting on a barstool for a while got up and used his clean red bandanna to dust off the seat. "I hope you were pointing at me, ma'am," he said.

"Thanks for the stool, but I was pointing at the sexy bartender," she said.

"Sorry, it's against company rules for the bartender to buy drinks for customers," Mercy told her.

"Are you jealous?" Hunter whispered.

"I'm not the jealous type," she told him.

"Then I will have a beer and a double shot of tequila," the lady told Mercy, but she winked at Hunter.

"Any particular kind?" Mercy asked.

"I don't care what kind as long as it's cold. I need something to cool me down while I look at the hot bartender." The woman dropped her eyes from Hunter's face to just below his belt buckle.

Mercy set a long-necked bottle and a double shot of tequila on the bar in front of the woman. "Are you from around these parts? We haven't seen you before."

"I come to this cantina for a little fun every few weeks. Haven't seen you or your brother in here before. What happened to the chubby little fellow and his wife?" she asked, but her eyes stayed on Hunter like she could have him for breakfast, lunch, and dinner.

"She's not his sister," the guy that had given up his seat said.

"I see. Are you his wife?" The woman grinned.

"No, I'm not his wife," Mercy answered.

"Then let's dance, sweetheart." The woman stood up and held out her hand to Hunter. "If she's not your sister or your wife, you're a free man, and I like what I see."

"Anything to please the customer." Hunter tossed his towel at Mercy. "And since you aren't jealous."

Mercy glared at the two of them while the woman plugged money into the jukebox, wrapped her arms around Hunter's neck, and plastered her body so close to his that light couldn't find a way to get between them. Mercy watched the woman tangle her fingers in Hunter's hair.

Enough was enough. *Anything worth having is worth fighting for*. Her mother's old saying popped into her head, and she tossed the tea towel on the bar and made her way out to the dance floor.

"Go get 'er," one older man said. "She ain't got no right to your man."

"And then make him sleep on the couch tonight," another one said.

The entire cantina went quiet for a second time that evening. Even the music on the jukebox seemed to fade when Mercy walked out into the middle of the floor. "Excuse me." She tapped the woman on the shoulder. "This is our song, and I don't let my man dance with a strange woman when our song is playing."

"But he said you aren't his wife or his sister," the woman said.

"He doesn't know what I am, but you do, honey." Mercy edged between the woman and Hunter. "You knew when you walked in here that he wasn't running the range. He's got a brand, and if you are thinking about doing any rustling, you should know what happens to women who try to steal what belongs to me."

"What is it that happens?" She stopped dancing and propped her hands on her hips.

"They go home bald, because I will snatch all that red hair out of your head, and then try to claw out your fake green eyes," Mercy told her.

"What I want, I take." The woman looked up at Mercy. "I'm not afraid of you, darlin'."

"Well, you better want something outside this cantina, and you'd do well to be afraid of me, because I will fight for what I want." Mercy wrapped her arms around Hunter's neck and led him back to the bar in a fast two-step.

"I thought that other song was our song," Hunter said as the song finished. "And what's this about me having a brand and fighting for what you want?"

"I don't share well with others." She picked up the tea towel and drew up another beer for a customer. "And according to what happened at the ranch party, neither do you."

"You are so right. What's mine is mine." Hunter grinned.

Chapter 11

MERCY AWOKE EARLY ON MONDAY MORNING AND SLIPPED out of the house. Hunter had told her that the parsonage was located right behind the church, so she meandered down the block until she reached a small adobe house with a sign beside the door that she recognized. It had hung in the living room of their house when she and Jenny lived together, and the lettering read: THEN SINGS MY SOUL.

She knocked on the door and held her breath, hoping for at least a semi-warm reception.

"Mercy!" Jenny squealed. She grabbed Mercy and pulled her through the door as if Mercy were an apparition that could disappear in a sudden cloud of vapor if she didn't hold on. "What are you doing here? Come in, come in. I'll make tea." Jenny led her through the tiny living room. Colorful mismatched rugs were thrown here and there on the bare wood floor, and the sofa was the same one she'd taken out of their house in Marietta.

"It's a long story," Mercy said as she followed Jenny to a kitchen so small that the table and chairs from their old house filled half the area. "Can I help you make tea?" She pulled out a chair and sat down.

"No, just sit there and let me look at you," Jenny said. "I don't really care what brought you here. I'm sure God has answered my prayers. I've been begging for Him to send me help, and you have to be it."

Mercy sure didn't feel like an answer to anyone's prayers, but with such a warm reception from Jenny, she didn't argue. "What do you need help with, Jenny?"

"I hate this place." With tears streaming down her cheeks, she turned to face Mercy.

"What?" Mercy could hardly believe her ears. "You were so happy to be coming back here. What happened?"

"I hate it, and it's not Christian to hate anything or anyone, but I do, and I hate marriage more than living in this place." Jenny sat down across the table from her friend and placed her trembling hands over Mercy's. "I need someone to talk to."

"Then quit being a missionary right now," Mercy said. "Hey, everybody is not cut out for this kind of work. Just admit you made a mistake and go home. And why do you hate marriage? Is Kyle mean to you?"

"It's not just missionary work," Jenny said. "It's this marriage thing. I can't talk to anyone about it. I wrote to my mother, and she said most women feel this way at first and that after children come along, I won't hate it so bad. She says the first year of marriage isn't ever what you think it is. Mercy, listen to me." Jenny sounded desperate. "Don't ever get married. Be an old maid and forget about men."

"What?" Mercy asked for the second time. Who had stolen her friend Jenny? Who was this woman in her body?

"I'm sorry to spring all this on you, but I mean it. It's awful." Jenny shook her head. "The real world of marriage is awful. Don't do it."

"What are you talking about?" Mercy might have been at cross horns with Jenny, but she would fight for her if Kyle was abusing her.

"Kyle tries to be a kind husband. And we have good times together, except"—she drew in a deep breath—"in bed. I hate sex."

"But why?" Mercy asked.

"It's messy. It's smelly, and it's so degrading." Jenny blushed and laid her head on the table.

"Oh my." Mercy had forgotten about Jenny's vow of celibacy until after marriage, but she remembered it right then, and didn't have a clue what to do. "Let me make a pot of tea and you just sit here. Where's the sugar bowl?"

"In the cabinet above the stove there—if the roaches haven't eaten it. I hate bugs, and I hate dirt, and I have to battle both all day and then dread bedtime and sex at night. Married life is awful," Jenny said just above a whisper.

Mercy prepared the tea and set a cup in front of her friend. "Okay, Jenny. Let's talk. I mean really talk. Have you ever read anything about how to please a man, or has Kyle read anything about pleasing you? Have you ever even read a good, sexy romance novel?"

"I don't read trash," Jenny whispered.

There was at least a faint glimmer of her old friend— enough to put a smile on Mercy's face.

"Well, I'd suggest you read a little trash if you want to stay out of the divorce courts," Mercy said. "Did you bring your laptop with you?"

"Yes, but what has that got to do with my problem? Are you changing the subject? Please don't. I'm serious"—Jenny wrung her hands—"and I need help. I know you had that experience with Liam, and you've been in serious relationships. Do you know anything about sex?"

"There are books you can read, and yes, I've had sex," Mercy told her. "Get out your laptop, and let's get busy."

"And just what would the people think if they found out their missionary's wife had read such garbage?" Jenny looked like the only bunny rabbit at a coyote convention.

"There are some things you don't have to advertise, Jenny. And what goes on in your private bedroom after you shut the door at night isn't anyone's business but yours," Mercy told her. "And you can delete it after you read it on the internet. It's not porn. As a matter of fact, some of it's even written for Christian women."

"How do *you* know so much?" Jenny took a sip of her tea.

"I am not a virgin and haven't been in a long time." Mercy sipped the hot tea and wished for a good cold beer instead. "I have read books about love between men and women—which includes lovemaking. I was curious, and that's only natural. Besides, a woman shouldn't get married without knowing something about sex—which is evidently exactly what you did. What did you expect, Jenny?"

"I expected..." she stammered and covered her scarlet

face with her hands. "I don't know what I expected. Something wonderful, I guess, like fireworks going off in the room and a beautiful glow afterward. All I experienced the first time was fear and pain and since then it's just been a duty."

"Hey, girl, it's been a long time since a wife just did her duty. Guess what? We are actually allowed to enjoy our husband's bodies as much as they enjoy ours. That's what makes a marriage last," Mercy told her.

"I'll never enjoy it." Jenny shook her head.

"Will you read the books I have in mind if I buy them for you?" Mercy asked.

"Are you sure no one will ever know?" Jenny asked.

"I'm positive. We'll hide them in a file that even Kyle won't find." Mercy smiled. "And you'll let me know if they help?"

Jenny took her hands away from her face, but it was still red. "Can we get at least one today?"

"Yes, we can, and in a few days, you should be feeling better. And don't forget, Kyle is probably just as bewildered as you are," Mercy said. "Now, tell me about what else is going on down here."

"Nothing. I dread the nights so bad, I can't stand the days," Jenny said. "What are you doing in Acala? You said last summer you'd never set fohere again." Jenny seemed to relax a little.

"You remember Hunter Wilson?" Mercy asked.

"Yes, I do. You didn't bring him to my wedding, so I figured you'd come to your senses," Jenny answered.

"That's the one," Mercy said. "Well, we dated a couple of times and then I got really mad at him, and we had this big argument, but I couldn't get over him, so my mama sent me with him to either kiss him or kill him. That means either make up or else get over him, not really kill him."

"You argued with him?" Jenny asked. "You never raise your voice."

"Yep, and I was so miserable I didn't know what to do about any of it. The dentist's office shut down earlier than I'd planned, so I moved in with my folks. Mama, bless her heart, let him kidnap me and bring me out here to work at Mickey's for the weekend. We're supposed to be settling our differences. When I go home, I'm either supposed to be over him or madly in love with him."

"Which is it going to be?" Jenny asked.

"I'm not sure, yet, but I don't want to be over him." Mercy went on to tell Jenny about the red-haired woman who'd come into the cantina the night before. "There I was fighting for Hunter, and you were right next door singing hymns. We've both come a long way since we were down here at the beginning of summer, haven't we?"

"I wish I could go back to that time." Jenny sighed. "I'll get my laptop hooked up, but the internet is slow down here. You really think this might help?"

"I do, and I've got a couple of hours," Mercy said. "Where is Kyle?"

"At the mission. I'm so miserable that I know I'm horrible to live with, so he stays over there most of the day," Jenny said as she brought her computer from the living room. "I keep up with my folks and my old church friends on Facebook when I can get it."

Luck was with them that day and the internet came right up. "It's an omen," Mercy told her. "Jenny, I want you to be happy, and that means having a healthy sex life with your husband, so go into this with that attitude."

"I promise I will," Jenny said.

Mercy chose the two books that had helped her, and then added a really sexy, but not quite erotic, romance book. "When you finish these, then I'll send you some more, but these three are going to turn your life around. You may not like this place, but you'll be looking forward to getting into bed, or the shower, or the sofa or even this kitchen table, with Kyle by next week."

"Oh. My. Goodness!" Jenny clamped a hand over her mouth. "Do you really do that anywhere but bed?"

"Oh, darlin' friend." Mercy chuckled. "The shower is the best because you're all wet and slippery. Y'all haven't taken a shower together yet?"

"Of course not!" Jenny gasped.

"That's number one on the list, then, but washcloths are forbidden. You use your hands and soap, and, honey, I promise you'll be ready for sex so fast, you won't wait to dry off and make it to the bed," Mercy told her.

Jenny's face was so red that Mercy thought she could probably fry eggs on it, but she continued. "If you want your marriage to work, then you have to work at it."

Mercy wondered if she was talking to Jenny or to herself about her relationship with Hunter as she found the books, ordered them, and then hooked Jenny up with the app to read them on her computer.

"I can't believe I'm going to do this," Jenny said, "but I prayed, and God sent you to me, so I'm going to count that as His will. The Bible says to be careful because we might entertain angels unaware."

"I never thought of myself as an angel, especially when I've been working in a cantina," Mercy said with half a giggle.

"They come in all forms, and, Mercy, I'm sorry for all the times when I was hateful to you. I was so jealous of you, and that wasn't Christian either," she said.

Mercy's phone rang and she pulled it out of her hip pocket. "Hello, Hunter. Is breakfast ready?"

"No, but Mickey called to ask if we could stay over another day. There's fog in Boston, and his flight is delayed. What do you think?" he asked.

"Of course," she said.

"Good, then breakfast will be ready when you get here," Hunter told her.

"I'm so sorry," Jenny said, "I should have offered you something to eat."

"No problem. Hunter is an amazing cook," Mercy said. "I should be getting on back, though. You've got some reading to do, and if you want my advice, start with taking a shower together tonight."

"I'll try, but"—Jenny blushed again—"I usually get undressed and into my gown in the dark."

"It's time to come out of that shell." Mercy stood up. "I'll expect a phone call from you in a few days."

"Okay," Jenny said as she walked Mercy to the door. "I hope it works."

"Have a little faith." Mercy bent and hugged her.

Chapter 12

MERCY SLIPPED BETWEEN THE COOL SHEETS FOR THE LAST night of their stay. She laced her hands behind her neck and considered the events of the past few days. The bewildered expression on Jenny's face when she admitted that she hated the marriage bed kept haunting her.

Whoa, the voice in her head pulled tight on the reins. *Hunter is not going out again on a limb that broke both times he trusted it to hold his weight before. So, if you play this game on the impulse you're having right now, you can expect to come out with a heart so broken it will never be the same.*

"Well, I'm a good sturdy limb," Mercy said as she crawled out of bed and looked out the window at the stars. Jenny, bless her heart, might be looking at those same stars with a different attitude if she had taken a shower with Kyle that evening. If Hunter was still awake, he could be looking at them too. Did he really want her to come to the ranch, live with him, and manage his ranch office? She was beginning to like that idea more and more.

She wrapped her arms tightly around her body, and paced the floor, back and forth, from the bed to the door, and back again, several times.

Finally, she eased the door open, half expecting to find Hunter still reading on the sofa. She could see the light under the door of the guest room, which meant he was still awake. She should not go into his room. She should go back to bed and count sheep or recite Psalm 23 frontward and then backward until she fell asleep. If that didn't work, she could do multiplication tables all the way through the thirties. She would feel like a complete idiot to open his door and make the first move, then have him tell her that he was serious about taking things slow.

Follow your heart, the voice in her head said.

She went out into the living room. He wasn't there, and she turned around to go back to her own room, but the voice she had heard earlier repeated the message. She whipped around before she lost her courage and went into his room. He was standing at the doors leading out to the deck, staring out at the stars like she had been doing just minutes before.

"Mercy?" He looked around. "Is something wrong?"

"Nothing is wrong. I was staring at the same stars a little while ago," she said as she crossed the room, slipped her arms around him, and laid her cheek against his broad back.

"They're almost as beautiful tonight as you are," he said.

"I wanted to look at them with you," she said.

"I like sharing simple things with you, Mercy." He turned around and took her in his arms. "Working in the cantina. Having breakfast together. Even looking at the stars. Money can't buy times like this."

"Money is just dirty paper with pictures of dead presidents on it," she whispered as she listened to the steady beat of Hunter's heart. "I've never been real interested in that stuff."

"I can tell." Hunter kissed her on the forehead. "You are here. Does that mean you think our relationship might work out?"

"I do, and I figure this could be our third date," she whispered.

"What has the third date got to..." He grinned. "Oh, now I know what you're asking, but darlin', this is our fourth or fifth date, so we're kind of behind on what the books say we should have already done."

They were curled up together, arms and legs entwined, when Mercy awoke the next morning. She didn't move a muscle but just stared her fill of Hunter. This was right. It didn't matter that he had been married twice or played the field. It didn't matter that she'd been a good Christian woman. What did matter was that they were compatible—in and out of the bedroom.

He opened his eyes slowly and then kissed her on the cheek. "Good morning, Sister Mercy."

"Good morning to you, and honey, after last night, maybe you shouldn't ever call me that again," she whispered. "I believe that I will take that job you offered me, Hunter, and I'd like to live in the house with you."

"House or bedroom?" he asked.

"House to begin with," she said.

"When can you be ready to move in?" he asked.

"Give me a couple of weeks to get my things in order," she told him.

"I might be able to wait that long." His grin widened.

"Good, but I can't wait that long to..."

"Oh, honey, I'd love to spend the whole day in bed with you, but if you'll look at the clock, you'll see we've slept away the morning. Mickey and Maria are probably not even a half an hour from here right now. But I wouldn't turn down an offer for a quick shower together."

She jumped out of bed and headed toward the shower. By the time he arrived, she was already naked and wet. He grabbed a bar of soap and lathered up his hands. She did the same and hoped that Jenny and Kyle had as much fun the night before as she and Hunter were having.

━━━━━━━

Mercy's hair was still slightly damp, but her suitcase was sitting by the door when Mickey and Maria arrived. She was glad they couldn't see inside it because it was a tumbled mess, but she had no regrets about spending the time with Hunter rather than folding and organizing her things.

"We are home!" Maria said. "But only for a little while. Hello, Mercy, I'm Maria, and this handsome fellow is Mickey, my husband."

"I'm pleased to meet you," Mercy said with a nod.

Mickey barely came up to Hunter's shoulder, and Maria was even shorter, but they made such a cute couple. Her black hair, dark brown eyes, and curvy figure would make any man take a second look. Mickey was a handsome blond with clear blue eyes and a smile that would draw women like a moth to a flame.

Mickey crossed the room, shook hands with Hunter and then pulled him in for a hug. "I've got big news that I wanted to share with you in person and not on the phone. I'm giving the cantina to Maria's brother, and Maria says that we will give the house to the church for a parsonage."

Mercy could hardly believe her ears. Jenny was going to have a nice house, but why?

"I can see the questions in your eyes." Maria smiled at Mercy. "I came here to visit my brother a few months ago. He lives on a little melon farm just outside of town. On Sunday night, he went to the cantina, and I went to the mission to church. Afterward, I went to the cantina for tacos and a beer and met Mickey. I fell in love with him, and the rest is history."

"Sound familiar?" Mickey patted Hunter on the back.

"Little bit, but if you'd gone to the cantina instead of the church that night, you might have still met Mickey," Hunter said.

"I prayed that night that God would send me a good man," Maria said. "If I hadn't been in church, I might not have asked for that, so we owe the church."

"Jenny is going to be over the moon with happiness to get a nice house like this, but where will your brother live?" Mercy wanted to call Jenny right then, but it was Maria's surprise, and she wouldn't spoil it. Still, she couldn't wait to get Jenny's call when her friend found out the good news.

"He'll live where he always has. It's only two miles away," Maria answered. "I see Jenny sitting on the front pew at church on Sunday morning. She seems sad. I hope the house makes her smile."

"I'm sure it will," she said.

"Why are you giving away your cantina and house?" Hunter asked.

Mickey slipped his arm around Maria. "I've fought the tie and suit for a long time now," Mickey said, "but the folks are getting older now, and it's time for me to grow up and step into my place in the business. I've got a good woman—and a baby on the way who should be raised somewhere other than in a cantina. Instead of coming over here to run the cantina for me, you can fly to Boston and spend some time with me and Maria and get to know your godson."

"We'd love that, wouldn't we, Mercy?" Hunter asked.

She nodded. "Maybe it will be a goddaughter?"

"No, it's a boy," Mickey declared with a twinkle in his eyes. "I will have a boy, and in a couple of years Hunter will have a daughter. That way we can bind our families together by marriage when our children are older."

"In your dreams," Maria said. "Our child will make his or her own decisions."

"And I've got a feeling that mine will too," Hunter said.

Maria kissed Mickey on the cheek. "But it is a good dream. If we could marry our child off to Hunter and Mercy's, we might get grandchildren who are tall."

Mercy blushed, and Hunter chuckled.

Chapter 13

THE SIGN THAT SAID ACALA, TEXAS, DISAPPEARED BEHIND Mercy that afternoon, but more desert spread out ahead of the truck. Before long, Hunter would drop her off at her folks' house, and she had a lot of things to take care of in the next two weeks. Her older sister was not going to like the idea of her living in the same house as Hunter, no matter how good the job was.

As if on cue, her phone rang, and she regretted even thinking about Rachel. "Speak of the devil and he, or in this case, she, shall appear," she muttered.

"What did you say?" Hunter asked.

"I'll tell you later." She answered the phone on the fifth ring.

"Hello, Rachel. How are things in Floresville?" she asked.

"Mama told me what she did, and I don't agree with her." Rachel's preachy tone reminded Mercy of Jenny's.

"Mama's decision to send me away with Hunter so we could work out our problems has helped, so it doesn't really matter if you agree or not," Mercy said.

Hunter jerked his head around to raise an eyebrow.

"My sister," Mercy mouthed.

"Didn't know you had one," Hunter said.

Rachel was on a tear, quoting scripture one minute and singing Cody's praises the next. Mercy didn't even try to interrupt, but just let her go on and on for a good five minutes. "Well, what have you got to say about that?"

"You want the truth?" Mercy asked.

"Of course, I want the truth, but what I want most is for you to come home with a better attitude, stop moping around and making mama feel sorry for you, go out with Cody who really likes you, and settle down." Icicles hung on Rachel's words.

"Okay, then you asked for it. I'm coming home with a new attitude. I will not be moping around, but I'm not going anywhere with Cody. I'm moving to Denton, to Hunter's ranch. He's offered me a job as his ranch office manager and a room in his house as part of the benefit package," Mercy told her sister.

A long, pregnant silence made Mercy look at the phone screen to see if the call had dropped or if Rachel had hung up on her.

"Does Mama know this?" Rachel finally asked.

"Not yet, but I suppose I'd better give her a call since you're going to be a tattletale," Mercy answered.

"Oh, no, I wouldn't drop this load on her and Daddy for anything. That's your job, but I think you're making a big mistake," Rachel said.

"It's my mistake to make if I am," Mercy told her.

"You're right, but I'd hoped you would give Cody a chance. Would you at least go out with him one time before you finalize this decision?" Rachel had put on her big-sister whining tone.

"That ship sailed last Friday," Mercy answered. "Go find another woman for him. He's a good guy, and I know he's your friend, and that you and David have helped him with the youth group at church ever since you got married, but I'm not interested in him."

"Why do you have to fall for bad boys?" Rachel moaned.

"I have no idea, but I can't wait for you to meet Hunter. You and David should bring the boys over to the ranch"—she glanced over at Hunter, who was nodding—"for a weekend. I'm sure they'd love getting out of the city."

"We'll see," Rachel said. "We'll talk more later. Goodbye."

"Do you think that went well?" Hunter asked.

"I do," Mercy answered. "Rachel is ten years older than me. She's married to David, who helps out with preaching when he's needed at the church my family attends. They have two teenage boys, Matthew and Luke."

"I hear an 'and' or maybe a 'but,'" Hunter said.

"She's my sister, but she's kind of like Jenny. She wants to tell me what to do, who to date, and…" She paused and collected her thoughts. "Maybe that's why it was so easy to let Jenny boss me around. Rachel had already conditioned me for that."

"I won't ever boss you around," Hunter said.

"Not even as my boss in an office setting?" she asked.

"Nope, if you can run a dentist business, you won't have any trouble with the ranch. I wouldn't be surprised if we aren't using the same software program," he answered. "I like you just the way you are right now. I wouldn't change a thing about you."

"Thank you for that." Mercy sucked in a lungful of air and let it out slowly. "On another issue, what usually happens the day after some woman comes and sneaks into your bed? Do you call her or forget you ever knew her?"

"There's nothing usual about what happened between us,

Mercy. But I can tell you this, I have never had feelings like this for any other woman. I think about you all the time. I was miserable when I couldn't find you, and then when you moved away," Hunter answered. "And darlin', I've never offered another woman a job."

"Can you put the past behind you? I'm not Carla, and I can never be a replacement for her. I don't want to be. And I'm *sure* not Raylene. I'm just me, and this relationship isn't going to be about anyone else but the two of us. I want you to be sure that..." She paused when he laid a hand on her shoulder.

"This weekend has shown me how to put the past where it belongs, but Mercy, I don't want to wait two whole weeks before I see you again. Will you come to the ranch this weekend?" he asked. "I could show you the office, and you could tell me what you want changed, and we could maybe have dinner one evening with Gloria and Jeremy."

"I'll be there on Friday afternoon, and maybe I can make dinner at home for Gloria and Jeremy?" she replied.

Home.

She'd just said home, and that one word put a smile on Hunter's face.

"Well?" she asked when he didn't answer right away.

"I would really like that. Can you make it a long weekend and not leave until Monday or even Tuesday?"

"How about I just move in on Friday?" she asked.

"Darlin', you have made me a very happy man," he said.

"But I still want my own room. I'm not moving in with you into your bedroom until we've both had time to figure everything out," she said.

"We'll go as slow or as fast as you want." Hunter stopped the truck on the side of the road, got out, jogged around, and opened her door. He wrapped her up in his arms and hugged her tightly, and then kissed her so long and passionately that they were both breathless.

Chapter 14

MERCY SETTLED INTO THE BIG RANCH HOUSE AND INTO HER office without any problems. She'd been there a week, and every night she fought against knocking on Hunter's bedroom door. She saw him very little during the day, but she dreamed about him every night. A week after she arrived, Gloria and Jeremy invited them to go to a bar east of town for burgers, beers, and dancing.

When they were all four in Jeremy's truck, since he had volunteered to be the designated driver that evening, and buckled in, Gloria reached across the back seat and whispered, "Why are you so jittery this evening?"

"Does it show that much?" Mercy asked.

Gloria nodded. "Are you and Hunter..."

Mercy cut her off by shaking her head. "Is this bar different from the cantina?"

"It's just bigger, I would imagine," Gloria answered. "I've never been to a cantina."

The antsy feeling in Mercy's heart settled down. She had handled the cantina, so she could do this without embarrassing Hunter.

"I love to dance, but I'm a sleepy drunk so I only have one beer," Gloria said. "Jeremy has one shot of tequila when we first get there to loosen him up for dancing. By the time we leave that's out of his system. You and Hunter can drink or not drink tonight. That's up to y'all."

"Thank you." Mercy finally felt like smiling.

The Long Horn wasn't much bigger than the cantina, but the parking lot was huge and almost full when they arrived that evening. Hunter got out of the passenger seat and opened the back truck door for Mercy. When her feet were on the ground, he draped an arm around her shoulders.

"Have I told you that you are beautiful?" he asked.

"Only about a dozen times," she answered, "but thirteen is my lucky number so…"

"My darlin', you are gorgeous," he told her as he paid the man the cover charge and led her inside.

Jeremy and Gloria headed for the bar, got their drinks, and then claimed a small table for four in the corner.

"You want to drink or dance first?" Hunter asked.

"Dance," Mercy answered.

He took her hand in his and led her out to the middle of the dance floor. Mercy recognized "Millionaire" by Chris Stapleton the moment the band began to play the prelude.

"This is really our song," Hunter said. "Like the lyrics say, love is more precious than anything else."

"It sure can't be bought with money or sold for any amount, can it?" she asked.

"Amen, darlin'. I believe this song was written just for us," Hunter whispered.

The warmth of his breath on the tender part of her neck caused shivers to dance up and down her spine.

"Can I cut in?" A cowboy tapped him on the shoulder.

"Not this time." Hunter didn't miss a step. "This is our song."

The cowboy stepped away, and Hunter said, "Every song they play tonight is our song,"

"We take a request every hour,"—the lead female singer stepped up to the microphone—"and the one for this hour is 'Got My Name Changed Back' by Pistol Annies. Must be someone out there who's recently gotten a divorce. Whoever you are, this song is for you."

"Could we sit this one out and have a beer?" Mercy asked. "I need to visit the ladies' room, and I am getting thirsty."

"Sure thing," Hunter said. "I see Gloria headed that way, so just follow her."

She and Gloria had just shut the doors to two of the stalls in the women's bathroom when she heard two familiar voices.

"Dammit!" she whispered.

"Crap!" Gloria's voice came from the stall beside her.

"Do you think Hunter will put Mercy packing when we tell him my news?" Kim asked.

Mercy leaned over to peek out the crack between the door and the frame. Kim and Tonya had both dyed their hair the straw color that Mercy's was naturally.

"He won't have a choice once you are in the house. You can fire her if he doesn't." Tonya giggled. Kim laughed with her and leaned into the mirror to apply more bright red lipstick.

Mercy thought about the lipstick color that she'd worn the night of the ranch party, and wondered why Kim was imitating her.

"You know it ain't easy for a man to think he's been

forced into marriage because he was too stupid to use birth control," Kim said.

"He's one of those good guys. He'll step up and do the right thing," Tonya assured her friend with a sideways hug.

"He's either going to pay for an abortion or marry me and give the baby a name." Kim slurred a couple of words.

Mercy wondered why the woman was still drinking if she was pregnant, and if this baby could possibly be Hunter's— her breath caught in her chest for just a moment, and then steel stiffened her backbone. She trusted Hunter, and he had not told her anything about sleeping with Kim.

"He won't give you money for an abortion. You know how he feels about that. Raylene had to sell off one of her diamonds that time she got pregnant by one of the hired hands. She didn't dare tell Hunter since it wasn't his kid, and she didn't want children anyway. What are you going to do if he says it ain't his?" Tonya asked.

"I'm going to remind him of that night when he came home after tearing up to Oklahoma to talk with Mercy about that little note we slipped in her purse, how that he got so drunk that he probably don't remember sleeping with me," Kim answered.

"You better get your story down straight and not forget details," Tonya told her.

Kim's expression changed to sadness and a lonely tear found its way down her cheek. "Darlin' Hunter, you were drunk out of your mind, but you came to our trailer, and we spent the night together. Now we've got a baby on the way, and I don't want to ruin your life, but I can't raise a child on my own." Kim dabbed the tear away with a paper towel. "Is that good enough?"

"It should work just fine. I bet Mercy has her bags packed and is on the way back to whatever town she came from last week before dawn," Tonya answered.

Mercy clapped her hand over her mouth. She was trying to decide what to do—have the catfight in the bathroom or drag Kim and Tonya outside for it when something fluttered in her peripheral vision.

She took the piece of toilet paper from Gloria and read: *Don't believe a word. Hunter got drunk all right, but he spent the night with us when he got back from Oklahoma.*

Mercy stepped out of the stall and said, "I just overheard you saying that you are pregnant, Kim. Is that right?" she asked.

Kim stepped close to her. "You did, and I am, and it's Hunter's baby."

Tonya took a step forward to stand beside her friend.

"He'll marry her, because he's always wanted children, so you are out of the picture as of tonight."

"You want the story? He needed someone to take care of him that night you were so hateful to him about his wives. He came out to our trailer, and we got to drinking, and you know what that can lead to."

"No, I don't," Mercy asked. "Tell me, Kim, what *does* drinking lead to?"

"Oh, don't play stupid," Kim snapped. "You might be naive, but surely you know a few things about sex, honey. When Hunter drinks, he likes company. I mean in bed. He likes little women so he can feel all powerful. He says a big woman like you makes him feel like he's a lot less a man."

"Oh? What else did he tell you?" Mercy asked.

"Just that you weren't even his type, and he didn't know what in the hell he made the trip up to Oklahoma for anyway," Kim growled. "I can't believe you'd come back to the ranch, even just to work for him. I even let him call me Carla when we was in the middle of sex."

"Oh really?" Mercy asked.

Kim nodded. "He showed up at my trailer door on Friday night and we spent the whole weekend together. You're just the hired help, and you won't even be that for long."

"And I'm her witness that this all happened," Tonya declared.

"I see." Mercy hoped that Gloria was getting all this loud and clear. "And now you're pregnant. How far along are you?"

"It wasn't then that Hunter made me pregnant. It was that time when you tossed him out in Oklahoma and wouldn't let him explain all about his other two wives. You know, they don't matter to me at all. I'd do anything to be his number three." Kim headed toward the bathroom door.

"Kim, your imagination is only exceeded by your reputation." Mercy blocked her way. "You tell a good story, but it's all a big lie, and you know it as well as I do."

"Are you calling both of us liars?" Tonya popped her hands on her waist. "Don't forget there's two of us and only one of you. It's time to pick up your pretty little purse and go home to whatever boulder you crawled out from under. God only knows, you're too big to have crawled out from under a little rock."

Mercy drew herself up to her full five feet eleven inches and looked down on Tonya as if the other woman were no bigger than a buzzing housefly. "I'm not leaving. And I heard the whole conversation when I was in the bathroom, even the little rehearsal with the trained tear. It's time for y'all to get out of here while you've still got a smidgen of your drunk dignity left."

"You can't tell us what to do," Kim snarled. "We've got dates, and we're here by invitation."

"And you're leaving by demand, with or without your dates," Mercy said.

"You don't have to believe me." Kim touched her stomach. "Let's just go tell Hunter about this here baby and we'll see which one of us he chooses. Come on, we'll go right this minute."

"Deal." Mercy stepped to the side. "Let's just do that. You must have been a lot drunker than usual when he was in bed with you and calling you Carla that weekend you're talking about. I hope you weren't moaning in ecstasy and calling him Hunter, since you couldn't have been in bed with Hunter Wilson those nights. Because he was in bed with me, and when he's in bed with me the only name I hear is Mercy."

"You bitch!" Kim's hand knotted into a fist, and she raised it toward Mercy. "Come on, Tonya. Let's get out of this place. It's not big enough for me and her both. If I stay, I'll have to mop up the floor with her blond hair, and I'm not in the mood to get my hands dirty tonight."

Gloria came out of the stall, and said, "I'll tie one hand behind her back to make it a fair fight, and then stand back while she whips both of you."

"You!" Tonya hissed. "I could tell you a few things…"

"Let's don't go there, or I might not stand back," Gloria said.

Both women stormed out of the bathroom.

Gloria giggled so hard that she had to dab her eyes with a paper towel. When she got control, she said, "I started to come out sooner, but it sounded like you were handling it fine without my help, so I just listened."

"Think they'll come back?" Mercy asked, suddenly feeling drained when the adrenaline rush left her body.

"No, fate has stepped in for you again by putting us in the ladies' room when they came in," Gloria answered. "You did a fine job there, girl. I'm proud of you."

"Thanks," Mercy said. "I got to admit, it felt good, but I'm glad you didn't have to tie one hand behind my back. I bet they've been in a lot more fights than I have."

"Honey, it's not the size of the opponent, it's the fire in your heart," Gloria said. "Let's go on back to our table and get in some more dancing."

━━━━━━

Hunter and Jeremy brought the drinks back to the table and waited…and waited…and waited. "Do you think those two women are all right in there?" Hunter finally asked Jeremy.

"They're probably just gossiping, or…" Jeremy pointed toward the bathroom door.

"Dammit!" Hunter said. "How did they know we'd be here?"

"Well, I sure didn't tell them," Jeremy said, "but don't worry, it could be me that they're bad-mouthing tonight. Tonya has tried to put a wedge between me and Gloria for months. Don't underestimate Mercy. She can take care of herself."

"Maybe you're right." Hunter hoped his friend was right. Things were going so well, both on the ranch and in his and Mercy's relationship, that he sure didn't want any more trouble.

"They're leaving, so that's a good thing." Jeremy motioned toward the two women who were storming out of the bar. "Here come Gloria and Mercy now."

Hunter got up and pulled out Mercy's chair. "I got you a bottled beer. It's good and cold."

Mercy picked up the bottle and took a long gulp.

"She needs to cool off after what happened in the bathroom," Gloria said.

"We said no secrets when I decided to move here, so here goes." Mercy told him what had happened.

"Looks like you've got my back," Hunter said.

"All the time." Mercy leaned over and kissed him.

Chapter 15

HUNTER AND MERCY WATCHED THE FALL SUN APPEAR ON the horizon the next morning from the porch swing. She was snuggled down into his shoulder, wondering why she wasn't sleepy after dancing the night away and then driving into town for breakfast with Jeremy and Gloria.

"We've done it all," he said. "Danced, ate, and watched the sun come up. Think maybe now we'd better sleep a while before we give the hired hands their paychecks at noon?" he asked.

"Darlin', we haven't quite done it all just yet." Mercy pushed away from him and took his hand in hers. "You want to make love on this porch swing? Chains look a little weak to hold both of us up, and it would take an acrobat to keep from falling out of it, but we can give it a try if you're too tired to lead me to your bedroom, or mine since it's closer."

"You're always full of good ideas." He laughed.

"How about taking a shower together like we did in Acala before we fall into the bed?" she asked.

"I'll show you how tired I am," he said as he swept her up like a bride and carried her all the way to his bedroom and kicked the door shut with the heel of his cowboy boot.

Mercy was grateful for the alarm clock that sounded loudly at eleven o'clock. They had to be up and dressed, and Hunter still had to sign the payroll checks by noon.

"I may start taking Saturday morning off every week," he said as he got out of bed.

"No, you will not," Mercy disagreed. "You need to set an example for the people who work on this ranch."

Hunter pulled on his pants. "Speaking of that example business, I believe we should go to church tomorrow. Jake still attends the small one where my family went. I'd like to go there, and I think you'd be comfortable in it."

"Church?" She could hardly believe her ears.

"Sure, church." He nodded. "You think that halo-wearing altar boy your parents fixed you up with is the only man in the world who goes to church? I haven't been since the ordeal with Raylene, but I'm ready to go now—with you by my side. I'm sure they'd love to have us singing in the choir. So, what do you say? Will you sit beside me in the choir loft and sing in that pretty soprano voice of yours?"

"Yes, Hunter, I will," she answered. "You said Jake goes to that church, right?"

"Yes, he does, and nearly everyone who works here goes to church on Sunday. Mama encouraged folks to go wherever they felt most comfortable."

"Okay," she said. "Wait until I tell Jenny you made me crawl out of bed with you and go to church. She'll think I'm lyin' for sure."

———————

The next morning, Hunter couldn't keep his mind on the sermon, but kept wondering why he hadn't said those three important words—"I love you"—to Mercy yet.

"Do you like her?" he remembered his father asking when he'd announced his engagement to Raylene.

"Like her? I love her with my whole heart." He remembered his reply very well.

"Love ain't exactly what I'm talking about," his father had said. "I loved your mother with my whole heart and when she died, she took my heart on to heaven with her, and I'll get it back someday. But I liked your mother as well as loved her. She was my best friend. So do you *like* this woman, son?"

"Yes, Dad." Hunter muttered the answer he'd given under his breath and remembered the sting of the lie he'd told his father.

"Who you talkin' to?" Mercy asked.

"Daddy," Hunter whispered. "Just a conversation with a friendly spirit."

"That's good," Mercy said. "I'm glad you can still feel him around. I talk to my grandmother sometimes."

Do you like Mercy? His dad was back.

I like her, and I love her. It's real. Like what you said about you and my mother, he told his father.

═══════

After Sunday dinner at a local restaurant, Hunter drove to a pond on the back side of the ranch.

"What are we doing here?" she asked.

"I just wanted to…" Hunter couldn't say the words.

"Do you still have a blanket behind the back seats?" Mercy asked.

"Yes, I do," he said.

"Then let's go stretch out under that weeping willow

tree over there"—she pointed—"and either take a nap or figure out what shapes those big old white clouds look like again."

"You never cease to amaze me," Hunter said.

"Good." Mercy unfastened her seat belt and got out of the truck. "I wouldn't want you to ever get bored with me. Besides, I loved that day when we sat under the willow tree beside Lake Murray."

Hunter slid out of the driver's side, pulled the blanket out, and together they straightened it on the grassy knoll of the farm pond. "You've been here a while, so…" He left the sentence hanging and stretched out on his back on the blanket.

"Yes, I have, and I love it," she finished the sentence for him, and laid down beside him. "I love my job. I love everything about ranch living. It's laid-back, and I don't even have to commute to work, or get dressed up or wear scrubs."

"What do you hear from your sister and your mother?" he asked.

"Mama says she hears happiness in my voice when we talk. Someday when I have kids, I hope that I can hear the emotion in their voices. Mama has always been able to do that with me and Rachel both," she answered. "Rachel is coming around, but it's not easy giving up the older sister control."

"*When* you have children?" he asked.

She remembered what Kim and Tonya had said about Hunter always wanting children.

"Maybe I should have said if I have kids," she answered. "I love children and even thought about going into early childhood development in college."

"What changed your mind?" he asked.

"Jenny did." She scooted over closer to him and laid her head on his chest. "She was training to be a dental hygienist, and we had this dream of working together. I would hold down the office, and she'd help the dentist. We were lucky enough to get jobs like that."

"Do you want kids?" Hunter asked.

"I would love to have a whole yard full of them." She wondered where he was going with this. "Do you want a family?"

"Yes, I do—with you," he said.

Mercy's breath caught in her chest. She didn't know if she was ready for that or not, so she didn't say anything for a long while. "Are you proposing to me, Hunter? Because I might live with you, but I'm not going to be a single mother."

He flipped over on his side. "What would you say if I was? Do you like me?"

"Yes, I do like you. I didn't realize until recently when I really thought about what makes my parents' marriage work so well. They love each other, but they're friends, and that's what I want. I don't know what my answer would be until you ask me properly, but I know that I like you and that I love you."

"I think I've loved you since that night you busted into the cantina. Ever since then you've been on my mind. I've had trouble saying I love you because of my past."

"The past is just that. We can't change one bit of it, but we can live for today, and do everything we can to make each other continue to love each other the next day," she said.

"Okay." Hunter stood up and then dropped down on one knee. "I don't have a ring, but I love you, Mercy. Will you marry me?"

"Yes, I will. In four weeks," she said.

"Why four weeks?" Hunter asked, and kissed her—long and passionately.

"I need to call Mama." She was out of breath when the string of kisses ended. "I hope you always affect me like that."

"I'll do my best to see that I do," Hunter said. "Call your folks, darlin'. I'm just glad that we are five hours away from them."

She pulled her phone from the pocket of her flowy

skirt and called her mother's cell phone. When her mother answered, she blurted out, "Mama, can you put together a simple wedding in four weeks?"

"Of course I can," Deana said. "I'm putting you on speaker with your dad and Rachel. She and David came here for Sunday dinner. Are you planning to get married at our church here?"

"Nope, in Acala," Mercy said. "In the cantina."

Hunter raised an eyebrow and mouthed, "For real?"

"Over my dead body," her father raised his voice. "No daughter of mine is getting married in a beer joint! Respectable people say their vows in a church, and you will too."

"Bob Spenser, if Mercy wants to get married in a cantina, I'll make it look just like a church, and you can pretend," Deana said.

"Put it on speaker," Hunter said, "please."

Mercy did what he asked.

"Mr. Spenser, would it make you feel better if we had the ceremony in the church where Jenny and Kyle are serving as missionaries, and then our reception in the cantina? Mickey and Maria are getting things arranged to move to Boston, and I would love for Mickey to be my best man."

"I can live with that," Bob agreed.

"Kyle can perform the ceremony for us, and…"

"And afterward we'll come back to the ranch for our honeymoon," Mercy finished for him.

"Oh, really?" Hunter cocked his head to one side. "I thought I'd take you to Paris or maybe the Bahamas for a honeymoon."

"Nope, I want to be married to you, and start our lives right here on Thunder Ridge," she said.

"You two work out those details," Rachel said, "and congratulations."

"Thank you," Mercy said. "We can talk later about the details, right?"

"Yes, probably daily," Deana said.

Mercy ended the call and cupped Hunter's face in her hands. "I love you, Hunter Wilson, and I can't wait to start our family."

"Nobody said we had to wait." He grinned.

Chapter 16

HUNTER DRESSED IN THE GUEST BEDROOM AT MICKEY AND Maria's house. He pushed his legs into stiffly starched black jeans and tucked in a white shirt with pearl snaps. He slipped a black leather bolo tie over his neck and slid the sterling silver steer horns up to a comfortable place, then put on his freshly shined black cowboy boots. He feathered back his freshly styled hair and wished that just once, when something important was about to happen in his life, his hands wouldn't be clammy.

"Hey, man, don't you look sharp." Mickey poked his head in the door just as Hunter was slipping on his Western-cut tux jacket. "Maria thinks it's funny that I have to dress up to see you get hitched. I wore a bright floral shirt to my own wedding."

"You look like a penguin," Hunter said. "Maria cooks too well for you."

"You think so?" Mickey frowned. "Hey, we'll see what you look like in a couple of years. Bet you won't be wearing those tight jeans!"

"Mercy, whatever are you thinking about? You look like you are a million miles away. Have you been reading the material you sent to me?" Jenny blushed.

"What material?" Gloria asked.

"Self-help books," Jenny said seriously, but slid a sly wink over at Mercy. "Without them I wouldn't still be married to Kyle. She really ought to think about being a counselor."

"All Mercy is going to counsel is cows," Gloria said.

"Are you ready for ranch life, Mercy?" Rachel fastened the buttons up the back of her dress.

"I've been ready for a month," Mercy said, "and Jenny, I don't read that material. I live it."

"I'm glad," Jenny said. "Every woman should enjoy…" she stammered.

"Life," Mercy finished the sentence for her.

"That's right," Jenny agreed.

"Are you ready?" Bob poked his head in the door.

"Ready as I'll ever be," Mercy declared. "With Hunter beside me, I can handle anything. Hurry up, Rachel. I refuse to be late to my own wedding."

———

Hunter's heart stopped beating for just a second when he saw his beautiful bride coming down the aisle of the old church.

Her ivory brocade dress left her shoulders bare, and she wore the single strand of pearls he'd given her the night before. The same ones his mother wore the day she married his father. The journey from the back of the church was short, so in just shy of a minute, Mercy was beside him.

"Who gives this woman to be married to this man?" Kyle asked.

"Her family and I do." Mercy handed Jenny her bouquet, and then Bob put Mercy's hands in Hunter's. "Promise you will be good to her, treat her with respect, and love her with your whole heart."

"I promise," Hunter said.

Bob kissed Mercy on the cheek and patted Hunter on the back, then took his place beside Deana.

"Dearly beloved," Kyle said, "we are gathered here today

to finish a fight that began many months ago next door in the cantina. Mercy didn't like the noise from the jukebox interfering with her gospel singing in this church, and she stormed into the cantina to argue with Hunter. And that's how they found each other and fell in love. I'm honored to be asked to perform this ceremony. The couple has asked me to keep this short and sweet, so I'll ask Mercy to repeat her vows at this time."

Mercy's hand trembled slightly, and Hunter squeezed it gently. "Hunter. I love you. I've loved you forever, but I didn't know you until recently. I promise to share my dreams with you, my hopes with you, and give you my heart and my love for the rest of this life, and through eternity. We are two souls made to love, honor, and respect each other here on earth. When this life is over, we will begin another in eternity, but we'll still be in love and still one complete soul. I give you my promise to be your wife until and even on the other side of this life," she said and slipped the plain gold band on his finger.

"Hunter Wilson, do you accept this pledge from Mercy Spenser?" Kyle's voice quavered.

"I do, sir." Hunter couldn't take his eyes from Mercy's face. He heard the preacher, and he had heard a sniffle from

Deana when Mercy said her vows, but in his heart he and Mercy were the only two people floating on this cloud.

"Do you have a ring as a token of your love for Mercy?" Kyle asked.

"Yes, sir." Hunter slipped a gold band that matched his on Mercy's finger. "Mercy, I promise to help you through times of pain and sorrow and to be with you in times of joy and happiness. I promise to share my dreams with you, my hopes with you, and give you my heart and my love for the rest of this life, and through eternity. We really were two lost souls until we found each other in the cantina. And I, uh," Hunter stammered. "Every time I look into your eyes, I'm speechless. Words can't begin to tell you how much I love you. I had more ready say, but right now all I can think of is how lucky I am."

"Amen," the preacher said softly. "By the authority vested in me, I now pronounce Hunter Wilson and Mercy Spenser husband and wife. Hunter, you may kiss your bride."

He bent her over in a true Hollywood kiss, then took her hand in his. "And now Mickey and Maria have prepared a little private reception in the cantina for our friends and family. It's right next door."

Jenny was first in line to hug Mercy when they got to the

cantina. "I owe you too much for words to express. I have a lovely home, a king-sized bed that's getting lots of use, air-conditioning, and it's just around the corner from the church. Kyle and I are so happy, and it's all because of you."

"No, my friend, it's because you were willing to set aside your notions and do a little research," Mercy told her.

Hunter touched her on the shoulder. "I hate to tear you away, but it's time for our first dance as a married couple."

She put her hand in his. "What is our song tonight?"

"Whatever you choose that's on the jukebox." He handed her a fistful of change.

He led her across the floor, and she fed the money into the slot and pushed the button to play Shania Twain's song, "From This Moment On."

"Don't you think this one fits us perfectly?" She smiled at him.

"Yes, and I'm going to love every moment I spend with you, Mrs. Wilson," he answered as the prelude of music started.

"I love you," Mercy said.

"There's only two words to describe what we have, darlin', and those are always and forever." Hunter dipped her and then brought her up for a kiss to seal their vows.

Enjoy this complete novella from
beloved bestselling author Carolyn Brown.

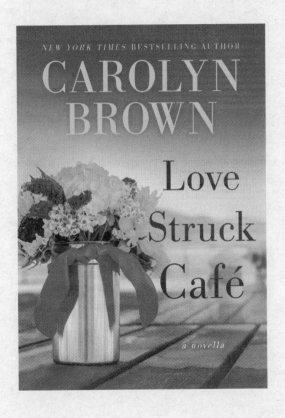

Chapter 1

FLINT WALKER HAD BEEN DRIVING SINCE DAYBREAK, AND HIS plan was to stop at the casino right in Terral, Oklahoma, for a bite of lunch. The signs along the road had advertised the best barbecue sandwiches in the state at the River Star Casino, and Flint loved barbecue—almost as much as he loved chicken-fried steaks.

He passed a sign that welcomed him to Ringgold, Texas, and from what he could see on his phone GPS, he was just five miles from deciding if the advertisement about the best barbecue sandwich in Oklahoma could pass a lie-detector test. He glanced over to his left and saw a two-story house with a wide front porch. When he shifted his eyes back to the road, a big yellow dog was sitting right in the middle of it. He honked but the animal just looked at him like he had rocks for brains and didn't move an inch.

Flint braked hard, swerved to the left, slid across the gravel parking lot in front of the house, and finally brought his pickup truck to a stop just inches from the porch. He hopped out of his vehicle to make sure he hadn't grazed the dog, only to see the animal wagging its tail and coming toward him at a snail's pace.

"What the hell!" A brunette stepped out onto the porch and let the old wooden screen door slam behind her. "Did you have a blowout?"

Flint shook his head and pointed. "No, ma'am. That dog right there was in the middle of the road."

The lady clapped her hands. "Go home, Max, and go through the pastures, not on the road."

As if the old dog could understand every word she said, he dropped his head and started out around the end of the porch toward the backyard.

"He's old and gets confused," the woman said. "Sorry that he scared you."

"No problem," Flint said. "I'm just glad I didn't hurt him."

He started to turn around and get back into his truck but noticed something stenciled on the window of the house: CHICKEN FRIED.

"What's that?" He pointed at the sign.

"This is the Chicken Fried Café. We make the best chicken-fried steaks in the state," she answered.

"Are you open for business?" Flint asked.

"Barely." She wiped a tear away from her cheek with the back of her hand.

"Is that a yes or a no?" he asked.

"Yes, I'm open," she answered.

He left his truck, and in a few long strides, he had climbed the four steps up to the porch. "Then I'll see just how good your chicken-fried steak is."

"All right then, but I'm doing it all today, so it might take a little while." She opened the door and went on inside.

That's when he noticed the red and white HELP WANTED sign thumbtacked to the wall next to the screen door frame. "Where's your staff?" he asked as he removed his cowboy hat and hung it on a rack with ten empty hooks just inside the door. Evidently, the place catered to a lot of cowboys to have places for coats and hats.

"I've been running this café for ten years now, and my biggest problem is keeping help," she answered as she headed for the kitchen. "Don't suppose you want to apply for a waitress job, do you?"

"No, ma'am." He removed his fleece-lined leather coat and hung it beside his hat. "I'm just passin' through on my way up north."

"How far up north?" She raised her voice to be heard.

"Don't know. Colorado, Wyoming, maybe even Montana." He sat down at the table nearest to the kitchen. Red-and-white-checkered oilcloths covered ten tables for four. A pint jar filled with sunflowers sat in the middle of each of the tables. Pictures and framed newspaper clippings of what he supposed was Ringgold both past and present hung on the walls. Shiny black-and-white tiles covered the floor in a checkerboard pattern.

Before the lady had finished making his steak, the door opened and two guys in overalls, cowboy boots, and mustard-yellow work coats entered the room. Like Flint, they hung their coats and hats on the rack and then sat down at a table in the middle of the café.

"Hey, Jasmine, me and Elvis want the Monday special. We both been hungry for meat loaf all week," one of the men called out.

"I'll get right on it, Amos. How are you and Elvis today?" Jasmine yelled through the window that had a ledge for passing food through.

"Old, and gettin' older every single day," Amos answered, then focused on Flint. "Ain't seen you around these parts. You got business around here?"

"No, sir," Flint answered. "I'm just passin' through on my way up north to find me a ranch to buy."

"Plenty of ranches here in Texas," Amos said. "One right out beside my place that just went on the market today. If I wasn't so damned old, I'd buy it and double the size of my place."

"You'd be crazy to do that," Elvis said and folded his arms over his chest. "Me and you both are goin' to die, and our kids is going to sell off everything we got. Kids today don't want to live in a place like this where it's twenty miles to a decent grocery store or a doctor."

"Ain't that the truth." Amos removed his glasses and cleaned them on a red bandanna that he pulled from his bib pocket, then squinted across the room at Flint. "What's your name, son?"

"Flint Walker," he answered.

"Well, if you change your mind by the time you get done eatin', that ranch is about two miles south of here on the west side of the road. Looks like crap right now because the old folks that lived there moved out after that big fire we had more'n a decade ago. Fire didn't hurt their house but burned up their stock, so they went to live close to their kids up around Amarillo. You could buy the place a helluva lot cheaper than what you'll likely have to give for a ranch up in Wyoming, and besides, you're going to freeze your butt off up there come winter," Amos said.

Elvis put in his two cents. "And winter lasts ten months out of the year up in them parts."

"Come on now," Flint said. "That's a bit of an exaggeration."

"Might be, but it'll seem like that long when you're ass-deep in snow and tryin' to bust ice off the waterin' troughs," Elvis said.

The old guys reminded Flint of his grandpa and his best friend. Flint had been put on the ranch payroll when he was ten years old. On Saturdays, Grandpa Zeb and his foreman, Sam, would take Flint with them to a diner in the little nearby town for lunch. Those two old guys would talk the ears off of whoever came into the café for lunch.

"I appreciate you tellin' me about the land." Flint smiled. "But I kinda got my heart set on going north."

"Order up!" Jasmine called out. "Crap! I don't know why I said that. I'm the one who'll be serving as cook, waitress, and cleanup girl until I can find some help."

"I'll get it." Flint pushed back his chair and went to the window.

"Thanks," Jasmine said. "I overhead you talking to Amos and Elvis. Glad to meet you, Flint Walker. I'm Jasmine Thurman."

"My pleasure." He picked up his platter of food and carried it to his table. "How would I go about getting a glass of sweet tea?"

Jasmine jogged around the wall separating the dining and kitchen areas and handed him a tall glass. "Fountain and ice are right there. Help yourself." She nodded toward the end of the room and hurried back to the kitchen.

Amos and Elvis went over to the fountain, and each of them poured themselves a cup of coffee. Amos added cream and sugar, but Elvis took his black. Instead of going back to their table, they took the one right beside Flint's. He sat down, cut into his chicken-fried steak, and took a bite. He had to admit that it was pretty damn good.

"Good, ain't it?" Amos asked. "Jasmine can cook like an angel, but she can't keep waitresses or dishwashers since we're so far from anywhere. Wait 'til you taste them mashed potatoes. I don't know what her secret is, but by golly, she can outdo my wife. Don't you never tell Hetty I said that, 'cause she's a right fine cook. If you was to stick around here, you could eat Jasmine's cookin' every day."

"Yep, and that sweet tea didn't come from no packaged mix, neither. She brews it up right here in the café from scratch," Elvis added.

It was beginning to look to Flint like he was going to have to agree to look at a scrubby old ranch just to be able to leave town. "It's really good food. Are you two the neighborhood recruiting team or something?"

"Nope, just tryin' to get young folks to move into Ringgold rather than move out from here," Amos said. "Since the fire, we ain't got but about a hundred people in town, and that's if we rake 'em up in a pile for about ten miles any which way you go. Where you comin' from anyway, Mr. Walker?"

Flint tasted the potatoes. The fellows were right about them being good. Then he took a bite of the fried okra and the hot yeast roll and determined that the whole dinner beat a barbecue sandwich. "I'm just Flint, not Mr. Walker," he said, "and I came from a little town just south of Stonewall, Louisiana, which is just down the road a piece from Shreveport. My granddad passed just before Christmas, and I wanted to keep the ranch left to me and my five cousins."

"But they wanted to sell out, right?" Elvis said. "Most young kids your age don't realize that God ain't makin' any more land, and keeping it in the family is important. I'm talkin' about my own kids and grandkids."

Flint wondered why in the world he was telling two complete strangers anything at all about his life. "Yep, the vote was five against one, and I couldn't afford to buy them out, so we had an auction and sold everything, but I'm not really a kid. I'm almost forty years old."

"To old codgers like us that's still trying to run ranches when we are eighty, you're a kid." Elvis finished off his coffee and took his mug across the room to refill it.

"And now you're lookin' to buy another ranch?" Amos asked. "Hey, are you any kin to Zeb Walker?"

"That would be my granddad who passed away," Flint answered. "You knew him?"

"Nope, but I sure knew *of* him. Zeb raised the best Angus cattle over that way. My breeder bull was sired by some of his stock. August is his name, because that's the month he was born. I'd be willin' to sell you a couple of his calves to get you started if you was to settle around here," Amos said.

"Thanks, but I've got my eye on a couple of places up north." Flint finished off his dinner and pushed his plate back.

"Goin' to freeze your ears and other vital things off up there." Elvis brought his coffee back to the table.

"You worked for your grandpa, did you?" Amos asked as he moved over and sat down at Flint's table. "He teach you everything you know?"

"Yes, sir, he did," Flint said. "I lived with him from the time I was born. My daddy wasn't in the picture, and Mama raised me on the ranch."

Elvis took his coffee over to the table with Amos and Flint. "We could use some young blood like you around here for sure, especially in the Texas and Southwestern Cattle Raisers Association. Around these parts, the youngest one of us is past seventy."

Flint was glad when the door opened and a burst of cold air seemed to push another elderly rancher into the café. He hung his hat on the rack but draped his coat over the back of the fourth chair when he sat down.

"Hey, Jasmine, I need a chicken-fried steak," he yelled.

"Sure thing, Clark." Her voice came through the window. "Order up!"

"I'll take care of it," Flint said as he pushed back his chair.

"Thanks," Jasmine said. "I appreciate it."

He carried his dirty dishes to the kitchen and picked up

the tray with two platters of food and a basket of fresh bread on it. He took it to the table and set it down. "Here you go, guys. Y'all have a nice day. Nice visitin' with you."

"If you ain't in a hurry, get another glass of tea and sit a spell longer," Elvis said. "This is Clark Gibson. He's a rancher like us, but he also runs a little real estate business on the side. He's the one that's got that ranch listed that I was telling you about. Clark, this here is Flint Walker. He's just traveling through on his way up north to look at a ranch."

"That truck with Louisiana plates out there belong to you? You wouldn't be related to Zeb Walker, would you? I knew him well from the National Cattlemen's Beef Association conferences."

Evidently, Flint's grandpa's reputation did not stop at the Louisiana border. "Yes, sir," Flint said. "That's my grandpa."

"Did you ranch with him? I am Clark Gibson." He stuck out his hand.

Flint shook with him. "Pleased to meet you, sir."

Clark had a full head of gray hair and a white mustache. His brown eyes had perked right up at the mention of someone looking to buy a ranch. "I got a steal a couple of miles south of town. Got two good ponds on it that are spring fed. It's not huge. Just six hundred and forty acres, and it's been let go so it needs some work, but the price is low. It's been on the market for a while now, and the folks sellin' it are gettin' antsy." He leaned forward and lowered his voice. "I'm not supposed to tell you, but I bet you could get it for a good price if you was to make an offer, and man alive, it would be good to have Zeb Walker's grandkid down here to work with us."

Flint wondered exactly why these old guys were so intent on him sticking around and looking at that particular ranch. Sure, they either knew or had heard of his grandfather, but that didn't mean the apple always fell right next to the tree. Was there some kind of conspiracy going on here? If he bought the ranch for a song, would he find out that the whole deal wasn't legal, and they were all three con artists? Maybe they had sold this same sorry old ranch a dozen times already, only to have the owners find out they had bought a place that wouldn't grow a bale of hay to a hundred acres.

He might just have to stick around and take a look at the place, but these guys weren't going to hoodwink him. He wasn't a wannabe rancher, and he knew good land when he saw it.

"Where's the nearest motel around here?" he asked.

Elvis grinned. "That would be Nocona, going east on Highway 82."

"Henrietta, going west, and Waurika has a small one if you're going north," Amos added.

Jasmine brought out a plate and set it in front of Clark. "Or you could work for me for a few days. I'll give you room and board, plus minimum wage. I only need someone for a week. My cousin is buying the cafe and will be coming to take over real soon.

"Oh, no!" Clark exclaimed. "What if she can't cook as good as you?"

"She's a great cook, and you'll love her. What do you say, Flint Walker? Want a job for a week where you don't have to pay for motel bills?" Jasmine asked. "You'll have to work from six in the morning until three in the afternoon, but you can go look at ranches after the day ends."

———————

Lord, have mercy! What have I done? Jasmine panicked as she waited for his answer, but she was desperate for help. Thank goodness there was a lock on her bedroom door upstairs.

"Sure, why not? Do I pay for my dinner or am I on the clock?" Flint asked. "You aren't going to ask me to wear an apron, are you?"

"Consider your meal as your sign-on bonus," Jasmine said, "and aprons are optional."

Four ladies came into the café and took a table in the back corner. Flint carried his dirty dishes to the kitchen and grabbed an order pad and a pen from a worktable. Jasmine had never had a male waitress (or should she call him a waiter?) but she'd bet that there would be an increase in business for the week with a sexy cowboy helping out.

She went back to the kitchen but stole glances at him through the serving window. When he stood up beside her, she had barely come to his shoulder, which would put him at over six feet tall. His dark-brown hair curled up on his shirt collar, and his mossy green eyes had little flecks of gold floating in them.

Now why would I notice that? Jasmine asked herself.

"Good afternoon, ladies," Flint said as he pulled the pad and pen from the hip pocket of his tight-fitting Wranglers. "What can I get y'all to drink?"

"You're Jasmine's new help?" one of the gray-haired ladies asked.

"Yes, ma'am, for the next week," he answered.

"We'll all have sweet tea, two with lemon, two without. I'm Hetty," she said. "This is my friend Lola, and these are my two cousins, Doris Anne and Mary Sue. They live down in Bowie. Those two old codgers over there belong to me and Lola, and don't you believe a word they say."

"They're tryin' to sell me a ranch south of town. They say it's a good piece of property," he said.

"That you can believe. They know ranchland a whole lot better than they know their wives." Lola giggled at her own joke. "You're not from around here, are you? Is that pickup out front with the Louisiana tags yours? You got a drawl that will make all the young women around these parts drool."

"That's my truck, and that's where I'm from." He smiled. "I'll get your drinks while you decide what you want." He pointed to the four menus stuck between the napkin holder and the ketchup and steak sauce bottles.

Jasmine's hands shook as she rinsed the dirty dishes that had accumulated on the worktable and put them in the dishwasher.

Desperate times call for desperate measures. Her best friend Pearl's voice popped into her head.

"Flint looks like a decent fellow," she whispered. "Amos and Elvis liked him well enough to want him to stick around, and they are pretty good at reading people."

Her cell phone rang. She dried her hands and pulled it out of her apron pocket. "Were your ears burning?" she answered when she saw that it was Pearl calling.

"No, but I got this sudden urge to call you this morning. Did you find a waitress? Is there any way you can talk Diana into coming over sooner?" Pearl asked.

"I found some help, but..." She went on to tell Pearl what she had done.

"That is so unlike you, but that voice you heard would surely be something either me or my granny would have said," Pearl told her. "Is he handsome?"

"Hold on a minute," Jasmine whispered as she put the phone on camera mode and took three discreet pictures of Flint and sent them to Pearl. "Take a look for yourself."

"Oh. My. God!" Pearl gasped. "He looks like a model from the covers of those Western romance books we've been hooked on for years. Those green eyes are downright mesmerizing."

"I know," Jasmine groaned, "but I can keep the bedroom door locked."

Pearl giggled. "Maybe you'd better put a lock on the outside of the door as well."

"Why would I do that?" Jasmine asked.

"For his protection," Pearl answered, "but then you are looking forty in the eye, girlfriend. If you want to have a family, you're runnin' out of time."

"I'm not forty yet," Jasmine protested. "I've still got time to have a couple of kids. Do you think I've done a stupid thing here, Pearl?"

"Hell no! Maybe he'll even settle down over in that area, and honey, I'll be in to have dinner one day this week. I want to meet this guy," Pearl told her. "Right now, the kids are getting off the school bus. See you later."

The call ended, and Jasmine went back to work, but the way Hetty, Lola, and their friends were whispering behind their menus, she figured the rumors would be flying by the time they got home.

Chapter 2

By two o'clock that afternoon, Jasmine had run out of everything and could only offer hamburgers and fries to the customers. At closing time, the café was still full, and she hadn't even had enough time to stop for a cup of coffee since Flint Walker had arrived at noon.

She left the kitchen long enough to flip the Open sign to Closed at three o'clock and lock the door. "Flint, would you be the doorman and unlock the door as the folks leave?"

"Yes, ma'am." He nodded. "And I suppose I should lock it back every time, even if there's people sitting on the porch waiting to get in?"

"That's right," she told him.

He didn't let the last of the customers out until almost four that afternoon. By then, dark clouds had begun to float in from the southwest. Flint hadn't believed in signs and omens before, but now he was beginning to wonder if he'd been wrong. First it was the dog, and now dark clouds shifting up toward Ringgold. That usually meant a storm, and he immediately wondered if it could mean he'd made the wrong decision about sticking around in a town so small that if you blinked when you drove through it, you would miss it.

Or run over a dog if you shut your eyes for a second, the aggravating voice in his head said.

Flint shook the silly superstitions out of his head. "Would you have a garage, a storage shed, or somewhere I can unload my things?"

"There are four rooms and a bathroom upstairs. Three bedrooms and a sitting room. You can take your pick of either of the spare bedrooms," she answered.

"That would be for my clothes and such," Flint said. "I've got a saddle and some things…"

"The garage out back. I keep extra supplies out there, but there's lots of room for whatever you need to store there, and thanks for all the help this afternoon. I would have had a tough go of it without you," she said. "The key to the garage is hanging beside the back door."

"Thanks." Flint nodded. "Looks like I just might get it all

out of the weather in time. Those clouds are bringing rain. I could smell it when I let the last customer out."

"You go on and get your things unloaded. I'll start the cleanup, and then we'll call it a day," Jasmine said.

"Won't take fifteen minutes, and then I'll help you," Flint threw over his shoulder as he grabbed the key, his coat and hat, and headed out the front door.

Jasmine had just finished taking the last load of dishes to the kitchen when he came in the back door. "Got my truck parked by the garage. All right if I bring in my suitcases by this way?"

"That's fine," she answered. "Take them right on upstairs and pick out either room on the right side of the hallway."

He brought in a couple of suitcases but was only gone a few minutes before he came back down to the kitchen. "So, when you bought this place, did you have to remodel the downstairs part of the house and put in two restrooms?"

"No, the previous owner did that," Jasmine answered. "I just did some cosmetic touches. Some fresh paint and new tablecloths, mainly."

Flint rolled his shirtsleeves up to his elbows and said, "I'll be glad to rinse the dishes and put them in the dishwasher if you'll unload that second one. I don't know where things go, so we can get done faster if we're organized. Or I can put the chairs on the tables and sweep and mop the dining room floor if you'd rather I do that."

Wait until Pearl hears that he knows his way around the kitchen and how to mop, Jasmine thought.

"I thought you were a rancher," she said.

"I am a rancher, but my mama died about ten years ago. Grandpa and I had to learn to do a lot of things when we lost her, so I know how to clean house, how to cook a little, and how to do laundry," he answered.

"I'm sorry," Jasmine said. Even though her mother drove her crazy at times, she couldn't imagine life without her.

"Thanks," he said with a brief nod. "Now, dishes or mop?"

"Mop, please. The disinfectant spray is in the broom closet…"

"I also know how to clean tables." He grinned as he opened the door at the end of the cabinets. "But I like ranchin' a whole lot better than cleaning or dirty laundry."

"I like cooking better than cleaning," Jasmine said, "but one goes hand in hand with the other. Are you really going to look at the old Buford ranch?"

"Doesn't hurt to look, but I doubt that I'll buy it," Flint answered. "I'm mad at my cousins for selling the family ranch, and I want to get farther away from them than just one state over."

"Why didn't you buy your cousins out?" she asked.

"Money." He shrugged. "I didn't have enough by any means, and the bank said no. My cousins didn't want to split the yearly profits six ways, and besides I don't think I could have survived paying out that much money that needed to go back into the ranch. So we sold it and split the profit six ways. Do you always give your help free room and board?"

Jasmine nodded. "If they need it, but this is the first time I've ever hired a cowboy."

Flint grinned. "I'm not a bad person. Never even had a parking ticket in my life. I just don't have to be in a hurry to go north, and my grandpa taught me not to close the door on an opportunity."

He systematically cleaned each table, set the chairs up, and then swept the floor before he brought out the mop. By the time she had the kitchen ready for the morning rush, he was done. Jasmine glanced up at the clock to see that it was only five thirty. These past few days she hadn't finished the cleanup until sometime around six, and that was with getting all the customers out by three.

"So, what now?" Flint dumped the dirty mop water and used bleach to take care of the mop.

"Now we leave this behind us and go upstairs to relax. I'm used to having leftovers for supper. I haven't eaten all day, but I'm almost too tired to chew. I'll probably just grab a toaster pastry," she said.

"I've got a better idea." Flint went to the dining room, brought two chairs into the kitchen, and set them beside the worktable. "You sit down right here, and I'll make you my famous omelet."

"Are you serious?" Jasmine's eyes grew wide.

"Yep," Flint said as he filled a glass with ice and sweet tea and put it on the table. "I've worked up an appetite this afternoon too. I haven't taken time to draw a good breath since noon, and you've been at it since six this morning. My biscuits could be used for hockey pucks, so we'll have toast." He took eggs, onions, peppers, cheese, and bacon from the refrigerator.

Jasmine sank down into one of the chairs and kicked her shoes off under the table. She wasn't sure if she was the luckiest woman on earth or right the opposite. Flint had been a great help all afternoon, and now he was making supper for them. Most of her waitresses left as soon as they flipped the

OPEN sign on the door over to CLOSED. But the downside of having really good help was that it made her wish she was keeping the café.

The grill had cooled down. Rather than fire it up again, he set a cast-iron skillet on the stove, and with the ease of someone who knew his way around a kitchen, he fried the bacon first, then used the grease to make the omelet. When it was done, he sprinkled cheese on top, added crumbled bacon and a handful of diced tomatoes, then put the lid on it and set it at the back of the stove. While the cheese melted, he made them each two pieces of toast.

"You're pretty good at that," she said.

"I do a good job on this, chili, and bologna sandwiches. Grandpa did a lot of the cooking, and just so you know, I can make thwock biscuits in a pinch." He grinned.

"What kind of biscuits is that?" she asked.

"The kind you buy in round tubes, peel off a bit of the paper on the outside, and then thwock them on the edge of the cabinet." He chuckled. "But even then, I burn them if I'm not real careful."

Jasmine laughed with him. "Then I'll take care of the biscuits for the breakfast run in the morning."

When the toast was done, he buttered it, put in two more

slices, and carried the skillet to the table. "Just sit still. I'll get plates and silverware for us. Do you want jelly or picante?"

"Grape jelly for my toast. Picante for the omelet." She hadn't been waited on in forever. The last time she had even had a blind date, the guy had taken her to an all-you-can-eat buffet, and that had been six months ago.

The aroma of bacon, slightly warmed tomatoes, and onions wafted across the kitchen when he removed the skillet lid. She inhaled deeply, enjoying the mere smell of food that she didn't have to cook.

"Supper is served. Pass your plate, madam," Flint said.

He cleans. He cooks. He even serves, she thought. *Why is he not married?*

"Do you do this for your girlfriend?" Jasmine asked.

"No girlfriend in the picture. No marriage in the past. Grandpa kept telling me I was letting all the good ones get past me," he answered as he slid half the huge omelet onto her plate.

She took a bite and decided it tasted too good to cover with picante. "Very good," she muttered.

"Thank you," he said. "How about you? How it is that a woman who can cook like you do and who is as gorgeous as you are isn't married?"

"Haven't had time to put into a serious relationship," she admitted. "My friend Pearl reminds me daily that my biological clock is ticking."

"Guess we've got that in common," he said. "I was too busy running a ranch, one that my cousins didn't do jack squat to build up and yet got their portion of the inheritance."

"Didn't your grandpa have a will?" Jasmine asked.

"He just never got around to making one," Flint answered. "He always swore he was going to live to be a hundred, and he kept talking about consulting with the lawyer, but..." He shrugged.

"How many kids did he have?" Jasmine could have listened to him talk all night. That deep Louisiana drawl was every bit as sexy as he was.

"Four," Flint answered. "My mama was the oldest, and then three boys who couldn't wait to get off the ranch. Two of them went to the army. One of those died in the Gulf War, the other in a friendly-fire accident. The third one passed away with cancer just before Grandpa did. How about you? Brothers, sisters?"

"One sister," Jasmine answered. "We can stand each other at holidays for maybe two or three hours. She got furious with me for leaving a good corporate job and buying this café out in the middle of nowhere. She's a high-powered lawyer in Sherman."

What if this guy is a con artist? What if his name isn't even Flint Walker? You never did have a lick of sense. Her sister Kathleen's voice was so clear in her head that Jasmine looked up to see if she'd come through the back door.

You should listen to your sister. This time it was her mama talking. *She's always had a good head on her shoulders, and just look at how far she's gone with her life.*

Hush, Wynona, her deceased father whispered in Jasmine's head.

"Thanks, Daddy," she muttered.

"Did you say something?" Flint asked.

"I was just talking to myself," Jasmine answered. "If I'm going to put you on payroll, even for a week, you need to fill out a simple form for me, and I'll need to copy your driver's license and Social Security card," Jasmine said.

"Sure thing." He pulled out his wallet and laid both cards on the table.

See there, she thought, *I'm not so stupid after all. I've run this café for ten years. I can read people pretty damn good.*

She wasn't about to admit that she'd had misgivings about

him at first, not with her mother and sister both taking up residence in her head.

When they'd finished supper, Flint offered to do the cleanup, but she protested. "You've cooked. I'll help with the dishes. Both dishwashers are running, so we'll have to do them by hand."

"I'll wash," he said as he ran a sink full of water. "What do you normally do at this time of day?"

"I watch some television or read, or catch up on my laundry, or do some upstairs cleaning," Jasmine answered. "All those things that most folks do at the end of a day." She dried the dishes and put them away, then removed her apron and got out the papers for him to sign for tax purposes.

He picked up his driver's license and Social Security card and slipped them back into his wallet, filled out the papers, and gave them back to her. "I haven't put my signature on one of those forms in thirty years."

"How's that?" she asked.

"Grandpa put me on the part-time payroll when I was ten years old, and I've never worked anywhere else but on that ranch."

"Well, Mr. Flint Walker, you do a fine job of being a waiter. I'd never have guessed that you didn't have experience working in a café somewhere." She filed the forms in the file cabinet over in the corner.

"That comes from helping out at the ranch sale every year. Mingle, serve, and be nice to the buyers." He grinned. "So, it's time to call it a day?"

"Yep, make yourself at home," she answered. "There's a small refrigerator in the sitting room that's got beer and bottles of sweet tea in it. If you get hungry, there's always snack food here in the kitchen. And thanks again for agreeing to work for me for a week and for delaying your trip up north."

"No problem. I could use a week to get over having to leave my home. Hopefully then I'll be able to go on north with a fresh mind and not try to buy the first thing that I see." Flint followed her up the stairs. "Besides, look at it like this. I wouldn't have even stopped here if it hadn't been for that big yellow dog in the middle of the road. Maybe Fate is talking to me. That critter looked almost just like our ranch dog back in Louisiana. His name is Gator."

"Did the new owners keep him with the ranch?" Jasmine asked.

"No, our foreman, Sam, took him home with him," Flint answered.

Jasmine was very aware of him behind her. Even above

the smell of food that permeated his shirt and hair, she caught an occasional whiff of his shaving lotion—something woodsy with a hint of vanilla.

She sent up a silent prayer. *Lord, please don't make me have to admit to my mama and sister that I was wrong about him.*

"You going to take the first shower or am I?" he asked when they reached the hallway.

"You can have it," she said. "I need to make a couple of phone calls."

"Thanks." He nodded and headed toward the bedroom that was right across the hallway from hers.

She closed the door to her room, sat down in an old wooden rocking chair beside the window, and watched the sunset. The bare trees became silhouettes as the sun disappeared on the horizon, leaving streaks of purple, yellow, and orange in between the dark clouds that hovered overhead.

"Are those clouds an omen?" she muttered as she pulled up her contact list and punched in Pearl's name.

"Hey, how did your cowboy work out?" Pearl answered. "Did he make it all day, or did he decide after an hour to get his sexy self on across the Red River and head north?"

"He's still here, and..." She went on to tell Pearl more about him.

"If you get tired of him, kick him over here. Wil can use him on the ranch, and I'll let him cook and clean all he wants." Pearl chuckled.

"You do know what Mama and Kathleen would say, don't you?" Jasmine asked.

"Is this the woman who defied her family and bought Chicken Fried Café ten years ago? Where is that sassy broad?" Pearl asked.

Jasmine inhaled deeply and let it out slowly. "That headstrong woman is tired tonight and second-guessing herself. Flint seems like a good person, and we had a full house from noon until closing. I think a lot of people were coming just to take a peek at my new cowboy waiter."

"Hard worker. Good for business," Pearl said. "It don't get no better than that. Too bad he's only committed to work for a week. You and Diana could use a good worker to help while the cafe changes hands.

"Amen." Jasmine sighed.

"Think you'll continue to have a full house while he's there?" Pearl asked.

"If the rumors keep spreading, I just might," Jasmine answered. "Hetty and Lola came in for lunch with two of their cousins from Bowie."

"What about Amos and Elvis?" Pearl asked.

"They were the first ones here after Flint arrived. Then Clark came in and sat with them," Jasmine told her.

"That's a real fine start to feed the gossip vine. I'm surprised y'all didn't have another fire over there." Pearl giggled again.

"You think he's that hot?" Jasmine asked.

"Any woman with good eyes would think he's hot!" Pearl answered. "But I wasn't talking about Flint. I was talking about all that gossip setting the cell phone towers on fire. I'm just glad the wind isn't blowing toward Henrietta or we might get the aftershocks of it all the way over here."

"Oh, hush!" Jasmine laughed out loud. She could always, always depend on Pearl to make her laugh, and to encourage her to see the positive side in anything. But then Pearl had left a good-paying job to run a fifties-style motel about eleven years ago. Even though the motel burned down, that's where she had met Wil, who had become the love of her life. So as far as Pearl was concerned, everything worked out just fine.

"You go enjoy your evening with Tall, Dark, and Handsome. I've got supper ready to serve to Wil and the kids," Pearl said. "We'll talk more tomorrow, and I'll drop in as soon as I can make time and meet this knight in shining apron."

"He doesn't wear an apron. He carries his order pad in his hip pocket," Jasmine protested.

"I bet that sets the old ladies to fanning with the menu." Pearl giggled. "You might want to put those little white pills that cures hot flashes on the menu."

Jasmine laughed even harder. "Give my godchildren kisses for me."

"Will do," Pearl said and ended the call.

———

Flint stood under the hot water a little longer than usual, letting it beat on his back. The work he'd done that day wasn't anywhere near as hard as what he'd done on the ranch, but every muscle in his body was so tight that hours of massage wouldn't work out the knots.

"I shouldn't have let leaving the ranch irritate me so much," he muttered. "But dammit! The cousins could have worked with me." Just thinking about it tensed up his face as well as his back. Finally, he turned off the water, stepped out and dried himself off, and then dressed in a pair of pajama pants and a tank top. He hung his towel on a hook on the back of the door and headed to the bedroom. He used the trash can for a dirty clothes hamper and then went to the sitting room, picked up the remote, and turned on the television.

He sat down on the end of the love seat, leaned his head back, and had barely closed his eyes when his phone rang. He fished it out of his pants pocket, grinned when he saw who was calling, and answered. "Hello, Sam, how did you enjoy your first day of retirement?"

"I didn't," the old ranch foreman answered. "I was bored out of my mind. I've got to get me a few chickens, maybe some rabbits or a goat or two, so at least I'll have some livestock. I'm glad I've got ten acres. If I'm not dead of boredom by the time another spring rolls around, I might put in a garden. How far did you get today?"

"Well, that's a long story." Flint chuckled. "It all started with a big yellow dog, not a lot different from old Gator. I'm so glad you took him home with you, Sam. His old bones wouldn't have taken the cold up north."

"Me and him has been buddies for more'n ten years, and he's the only livestock I got right now. No way would I leave him for the new ranch owners," Sam declared. "Now tell me about the yellow dog."

When Flint finished his story, he could imagine Sam shaking his head and could hear him chuckling.

"Boy, I told you that getting away from here so you wouldn't have to look at the ranch you couldn't keep would be the best thing for you. I want you to look at that run-down place there in Texas. Building something back up might be just what you need to get over losing your home," Sam told him. "That yellow dog might've been an angel sent straight from heaven to guide you to the right ranch. Now tell me more about your new boss lady."

"I knew you'd ask about that, so I took a couple of pictures of her, and I'm sending them right now, but Sam, this town only has a café and a church, and I don't even know if they have services in the church. It doesn't even have a school. From what I gathered from customers today, the kids go to Stoneburg, which is south of here. Give me one good reason I should even think about putting my money into a ranch here," Flint said.

"Number one: A big yellow dog made you stop. Two: They make good chicken-fried steaks. Three: If you go to Montana or Wyoming or even Colorado, I'll bet you dollars to cow patties that any kids you might have will ride a bus farther than that school is from Ringgold," Sam said. "And four: Damn, that's a pretty woman you got for your new boss lady."

Jasmine came into the room and sat down on the other end of the sofa. She reached around and pushed a button, and a footrest came slowly up. "This is a double recliner. If you want to really relax, use the buttons on the end."

"And she's got a sweet Texas twang to boot. Get off here and talk to her, Flint. You can talk to a disgruntled, retired old ranch foreman any old time. Goodbye now," Sam said and ended the call.

Flint found the buttons and was reclining with his feet up in no time. "This is pretty fancy," he said.

"I figure I deserve a little extra after working hard all day. What are we watching? I should tell you that I don't have cable. We get two stations that play reruns for the most part. I do have a DVD player and lots of movies behind those center doors," she said.

He handed her the remote. "You choose. I'll probably sleep through whatever we're watching."

"If you snore, I'll throw things at you," she warned.

"I don't snore," he said, "but in case I snort a little, you can throw anything but snakes at me. I'd have a heart attack if I woke up to a snake crawling around on me."

"Big old cowboy like you is afraid of snakes?" she teased.

"In this cowboy's way of thinking, there's only two kinds

of snakes in the world—cobras and rattlesnakes. And there ain't no wrong way to kill either one. A .22 rifle or pistol works fine. A garden hoe will do, and if you ain't got either one of those, then a big rock will take care of the job," he said.

"I keep a .38 pistol in my nightstand and a sawed-off shotgun under the cabinet in the kitchen, so I'll protect you from snakes if you will protect me from mice or rats. I hate those wicked, evil critters," she said.

"You do know that sawed-off shotguns are not legal, don't you?" Flint asked.

"Only if the barrel is sawed off to be shorter than eighteen inches. Mine is one half an inch over that length, so it's legal. Now, about those rats?" She raised an eyebrow.

He stretched out his hand. "Deal, but if I see a really big rat can I use the shotgun?"

She put her small hand in his. "Honey, you can use anything you can find."

The sparks that jumped around when their hands touched lit up the room like the Fourth of July.

He dropped her hand, but the heat was still there. Reruns of *Law & Order* were on television; the episode playing was about a man who'd had his wife murdered for cheating.

"I can kind of relate to that guy," Flint muttered, "but I'd never go that far."

Jasmine nodded. "Me too."

"I sort of lied to you about relationships," he admitted. "I was in a very serious one for a couple of years, and then the woman cheated on me with one of my cousins."

Jasmine hit the mute button and jerked her head around to face Flint. "The same cousin that was one of those that sold the ranch out from under you?"

"Yep," Flint said. "It all happened about four years ago. They're married now and have a little boy."

"No wonder you want to get as far away from that area as possible," she said. "That's what put me in Ringgold. My boyfriend was cheating on me, and I wanted to get away from Sherman."

"Have you gotten over it?" he asked.

"Yeah." She nodded. "But that guy didn't steal my inheritance."

"How'd you get closure, as they call it?" he asked.

"Closure is just something that therapists promise. It's not a real thing." She smiled. "You just put it away in the past. Kind of like putting a box in a storage unit and never going back there to open it again. Pretty soon you forget what's in the box, and you don't even care if the mice or rats have destroyed it."

Flint didn't even realize he was holding his breath until it came out in a whoosh. "She laughed in my face when the whole group of cousins and their spouses heard my proposal. I wouldn't mind sinking that box in a river full of gators."

"Then do it, and then move on," Jasmine told him. "Until you do, that woman and all those cousins have power over you."

"How'd you get to be so smart?" he asked.

"By deciding that no one—not my mama or sister or my ex-boyfriend or anyone else—was going to have power over me. Every now and then, something has to remind me to take my control back, but for the most part, I'm a fairly peaceful woman," she told him.

Flint had talked to his grandfather about his ex and to Sam about his frustrations with the ranch, but both older men had told him that life wasn't perfect, so just move on. Basically, that's what Jasmine had said, but the way she had put it made more sense to him.

"Pearl's aunt told us that when one door closes, another one opens, and usually what's behind door number two is a helluva lot better anyway." She pushed a button on the remote and found that the credits were rolling. "Let's do a movie. Got a preference—action, chick flick, humor?"

"Something funny," he said.

"*Home Alone* it is, even if Christmas is over." She got up, found the movie and put it in the player, then sat back down. "I always watch this one when I need a good laugh."

"I don't think I've ever seen it before. Grandpa liked his old Westerns, so that's what I grew up on." Flint couldn't believe that he had been so open with Jasmine or even with Amos and Elvis. Maybe this café had special healing powers, and Sam was right about that yellow dog being dropped down from the Pearly Gates.

Chapter 3

THE CAFÉ STARTED OUT BUSIER ON TUESDAY THAN IT HAD been on Monday. Half a dozen ranchers were waiting on the porch when Jasmine opened the door. Clark was the first one into the café and chose the table where he'd sat with Amos and Elvis the day before.

"You given any thought to lookin' at the ranch I told you about yesterday?" he asked as he pulled out a chair and sat down.

"Yes, sir, and now that I've slept on the idea, I reckon I would like to look at it," Flint answered. "What can I get you to drink?"

"A cup of coffee and a big glass of cold milk, and tell Jasmine I want the big country breakfast with a chicken-fried steak, eggs over easy, and biscuits and gravy," he said.

"I'll just have coffee." Amos chuckled, taking a seat at the same table. "My mama weaned me years ago."

"Mine did, too, but my doctor says that old men need calcium," Clark argued.

"While they're fussin' about this like it was something political, I'll have a glass of orange juice, a cup of coffee, and what Clark ordered," Elvis said, making himself comfortable in a third chair. "It's cold out there this mornin', and I used up a lot of my energy getting the chores done. Same for Amos. Put it all on one ticket. I'm buying today."

"Yes, sir."

Flint ripped the ticket from his pad and laid it on the shelf. "Looks like we're going to be hoppin' this morning," he said to Jasmine.

"Sounds like it, and I hear tires on the gravel driveway out front, so there's more on the way." Jasmine grabbed the ticket and picked up three cube steaks, dropped them in an egg-and-milk mixture, and then dipped them in flour.

Six tickets were on the shelf when Jasmine yelled "Order up" for Clark, Amos, and Elvis's breakfasts. Flint gathered up three platters, served them to the guys, then made sure their glasses and coffee mugs were refilled.

"So, you want to go see the ranch today?" Clark asked.

"We've got bad weather coming in tomorrow morning. Rain for sure, and maybe even some ice, if the weatherman is right, but then he's been wrong before."

Flint had never done anything on impulse in his life, and yet he could almost feel his grandpa and Sam both behind him, pushing at his shoulders. "Sure," he said. "If everyone gets out of here by three, I could go right after that."

"Sounds good," Clark said. "I'll be waiting out front for you."

"Mind if I bring Jasmine with me?" he asked.

"Not a bit," Clark answered. "Sometimes a woman sees things us guys miss."

Flint nodded in agreement and hurried off to wait on another table where two couples had just sat down. When he got their order, he laid it on the shelf, and rounded the end of the wall. "Hey, do you reckon we could go look at this land that Clark and the guys are pestering me about and then do cleanup afterward? If we do it first, it'll be dark before we can get out there."

"What's this 'we' business? You got a mouse in your pocket?" Jasmine asked.

"I'm asking you if you'll go with me," Flint said. "Have you ever been out to that ranch?"

"Nope, but I knew those old folks that lived there. They

used to come back this way to visit Amos and Hetty, and they always came in for a meal while they were here." Jasmine set a platter of food on the shelf and yelled, "Order up."

Flint picked it up and raised an eyebrow.

"Yes, I'll go with you, and we can clean up after we get back." She grabbed another order ticket and went to work.

"Thanks." Flint grinned.

═══════════

By closing time, Jasmine's feet hurt worse than usual. Her shoulders ached, and for the second day in a row, the café had made more money than she often did in a whole week. She should tell Diana to either bring a good-lookin' cowboy with her, or rustle one up when she arrived next week. That shouldn't be too difficult. Jasmine could kick any mesquite bush between Ringgold and Sherman and at least a dozen cowboys would come out looking to two-step with her.

"You ready?" Flint asked.

"Yep." She removed her apron and hung it on a hook. "Give me a minute to make a trip through the ladies' room, and I'll be right out."

She made sure the front door was locked and the sign turned over, then picked up her purse and left by the back door. Cold wind hit her in the face and almost took her breath away, and she dashed back inside. She ran up the stairs, got a heavy coat from her closet, and then hurried back outside. She had her foot on the bottom step of the back porch when she remembered that she had not locked the kitchen door.

"I'm so sorry," she yelled.

"No problem." Flint held the door of his truck open for her. "It's not dark yet, and I'm not expecting this to take more than fifteen minutes. I'm just doing this to make the guys happy."

She climbed into the passenger seat of his truck, fastened her seat belt, and watched him round the front of the truck. His swagger said he was used to walking in boots and was comfortable in his skin. That foolish woman who'd let him slip through her fingers must have had rocks for brains.

"Do you really have no intentions of even considering this ranch?" Jasmine asked when Flint had settled behind the steering wheel.

"Never say never." He grinned. "I shouldn't, for sure. I had no intentions of stopping here in Ringgold. I had my heart set on a barbecue sandwich at that casino just over the Red River. Chicken-fried steak is my favorite food ever, but barbecue comes in a close second. If it hadn't been for that dog, I wouldn't have even noticed your café. Did you ever consider advertising out on the road?" He started the engine and pulled around to the front of the café where Clark was waiting.

"Yep, and then I realized how much it would cost, and that ended that idea," she answered.

"Expensive, is it?" he asked as he followed Clark out onto the road and turned right.

"Too rich for my blood, and word of mouth is working just fine for me," Jasmine answered.

Five minutes down Highway 81, Clark turned off the road to the west, crossed under a ranch sign that was dangling in the wind by a couple of rusty chains that looked like they would break if someone sneezed on them, and drove down the long lane to a little white frame house.

He parked outside a yard fence that was made of two-inch pipe and had been white at one time but now was rusted and in bad need of paint. Flint pulled in beside him and climbed out of his truck.

Clark rolled down the window and handed Flint a key ring. "One is to the house. One to the barn, and one to lock up the front gate. You don't need me to check things out. I'll pick up the keys tomorrow at Chicken Fried."

"Thanks," Flint said. "I'm glad you aren't going to pressure me."

"Either you love it or hate it. There's not much I can do to sway a real rancher like you. I've got a meeting down in Bowie in half an hour. I'll see you kids tomorrow." Clark rolled up the window and backed around so he could drive back down the lane.

"I don't know jack squat about ranches," Jasmine said as she got out of the truck, "so I probably won't be much help."

"You'll be more than you think." Flint opened the yard gate for her and stood to one side. "Take this key and we'll go into the house. We'll walk through it, but don't say anything until we're finished."

"Why?" Jasmine asked.

"I want to know how it makes you feel, not whether you like the looks," he explained.

Jasmine had done that very thing when she checked out the café, so she understood what he was looking for. She opened the door and walked into the empty living room. Oak hardwood had been used for the trim and the flooring. A few scuff marks here and there said the house had been lived in. When she walked across the room, there weren't any squeaks or soft spots, and there were no watermarks on the ceiling. A nice little nook that had built-in cabinets was set off to one side of the huge country kitchen with more cabinets and a walk-in pantry. A two-car garage opened off the side door, and the hall led into two guest rooms, a bathroom, and a sweet master bedroom with a private bath.

A pretty nice little ranch house, but then she was supposed to be getting a "feel" for the place, according to Flint.

Flint was right behind her. When they'd checked out all the empty closets, and discovered a sunroom off the utility room, he sat down on a porch swing and patted the space beside him. "Now, tell me what you think."

"Peace," she answered. "I feel that this is a peaceful house, but a ranch isn't just a house. It's land and fences and barns and hard work. What do you feel?"

"Peace," he echoed. "I can make a ranch produce, and I know how to repair fences that are down and build new ones. I can work cattle and run a ranch, but when I come home in the evenings, I want to feel what I did at home. I want to be comfortable and feel contentment."

"Do you feel like that here?" she asked.

"Yes, I do, and I came out here with the thought that I would hate this place," he answered.

Jasmine's pulse jacked up a notch, and her heart threw in an extra beat. Flint probably wouldn't work for her after the week was up, but she had really enjoyed the past couple of days working with him and also the time they'd spent the night before talking about the past.

He stood up and offered her his hand. "Let's go look at the barn."

She put her hand in his, and the exact same sparks danced around the sunporch that she'd felt when they shook hands the night before. Jasmine had thought Pearl was just lovesick when she had told her she'd had that kind of reaction to Wil Marshall back when she had first met him.

And that was during bad weather too, she remembered. Was history about to repeat itself?

What can you be thinking? Her sister's voice was in her head again. *You've known this guy two days and you're hearing wedding bells?*

Jasmine stiffened her back and set her mouth in a firm line. *I've run my own life for more than ten years with no help or support from you. If I want to marry Flint tomorrow, it's my business, but rest assured I'm not thinking that far ahead.*

"What happened there?" Flint dropped her hand and headed out to a barn. It had been red at one time and had a big Texas star painted on the side, but the star was dirty, and the paint had faded to somewhere between pink and red.

"What do you mean?" Jasmine asked.

"I could see that you were enjoying sitting there with me, even if it was cold, but then your expression changed. Tell me the truth. Did something come to mind that changed your feelings about this place?" Flint asked.

"I was doing some mental battling with my sister," she answered. "It had nothing to do with this ranch. It was about her always trying to boss me around."

Flint chuckled and slowed his stride to match hers. "Kind of like my cousins."

"Probably, but let's give all that to the rats and alligators." She smiled. "All it does is ruin our evening. What do you look for in a barn, anyway?"

"The roof, the size," he answered as he bent down and picked up a handful of dirt and let it sift through his hands. "This feels like a good mixture to grow alfalfa and make a cash crop of soybeans."

"Why do you think the bank here would finance a ranch when the one over in Louisiana wouldn't?" Jasmine asked as they went into the barn.

"I was asking for a loan to buy a place ten or fifteen times this size. I have enough from the sale of Grandpa's place and what I've saved over the years to put half down on a place like this and still have some working capital to get me through until the ranch begins to support itself." He looked up at the ceiling. "No leaks. Good metal roof. It would keep hay nice and dry, and there's four stalls over there"—he pointed—"that I can use if I need to help a young heifer birth a calf. I wonder if that old tractor and the work truck are part of the deal."

Flint wandered to the tack room and opened the door. They were met with a musty, unused odor that said no one had been in the place in several years. Tools were arranged neatly on a wall covered with pegboard. Power tools sat on shelves, and Jasmine could see a half bath beyond a door on the other side of the room. Four chairs were pushed up to a table with a box of dominoes on its top. She could imagine the previous ranch owner and his buddies playing games and talking about cows, hay, and fences on cold days.

"We've got a little while before dark. You mind if we drive around the fence line?" he asked.

"You are really interested in this place, aren't you?" she asked.

"I'd have liked to have something bigger, but this is a perfect size for a one-man operation through the winter. I might be able to hire some teenagers in the summer for part-time help, and by next fall, I'll be ready to put some cows on the place," he answered. "But I'm not an impulsive guy, so I'll have to sleep on it. If I do decide to buy, do you reckon I could work for you another few days until I can get the paperwork all done and the utilities turned on?"

"You've got a job at the café as long as I'm around. Diana will be here on Sunday night and will start to work Monday morning. We've already signed everything, and she asked if I would stick around until I find a place to live," Jasmine answered. "I promised her a week. She's hired a couple of waitresses and a dishwasher, so after Saturday, we shouldn't be as rushed as we have been."

"If you don't need me to work, I'll be glad to pay room and board until I can get moved in—that's assuming that the bank okays a loan and I can get everything I need to move out here," he said.

She smiled up at him. "Flint Walker, I expect that we'll find something for you to do while you wait on the ranch to be yours, if you decide to make a bid on it."

Jasmine had been telling the truth when she said she knew nothing about ranching, but suddenly, she had the overwhelming desire to learn.

Chapter 4

FLINT SLEPT POORLY THAT NIGHT. HE KEPT THINKING ABOUT the sign hanging above the cattle guard on the way to the ranch: PROMISED LAND RANCH. The name seemed to be an omen. Maybe he had found his own personal promised land west of the Louisiana-Texas border. If he bought the place, he would want it in writing that he was buying the brand as well as the land.

Clark was the first one in the café the next morning. "What did you think of the place?" he asked as he hung up his coat and hat.

Flint carried a cup of coffee to Clark's regular table. "I'd like to think about it one more day. Mind if I keep the key and go out there again tonight?"

"Not a bit," Clark answered. "You got any questions?"

"Do the tractor, work truck, and the tools in the tack room stay with the ranch?" Flint asked.

"I can find out, but I reckon they would. The folks that left the ranch are in a nursing home now, and their oldest son is selling the place. I don't think he'd have a bit of use for what's in that barn or anywhere else on the place," Clark said. "The asking price is"—he quoted a price—"but I think you could offer fifty thousand less and they'd jump on the chance to sell."

Flint couldn't believe his ears. "Are you serious?"

"It's been on the market for a long time. Not many people want to settle here, and since it's right between Amos and Elvis's land, it doesn't have a lot of room for expansion," Clark explained.

Flint's radar shot up. "Why didn't one of them pick up the land? Seems like a really good deal."

"They're both up in years, just like me, and we haven't got a single kid interested in ranching. Why buy something that they'll just sell off?" Clark asked.

"Will the owners let me keep the ranch name and brand?" Flint took out his order pad about the same time that Amos and Elvis pushed through the door.

Clark waved his friends over to the table. "I don't think

keeping the name or the brand will be a problem, and it's my turn to buy breakfast. Tell Jasmine to put it on my tab."

"Colder'n a witch's tit out there," Amos said and then laughed at his own joke. "I want a big bowl of oatmeal with raisins and brown sugar, biscuits and gravy, and a side order of pancakes."

"I'll have the same." Elvis shivered as he sank down into a chair. "It's started to drizzle, and the temperature is down around freezing. The weatherman is callin' for slick roads. Folks will be stickin' close to home."

"Make that three orders of the same," Clark said.

Flint took the order back to the kitchen instead of laying it on the shelf. "I have enough money to buy that ranch without going to the bank for a loan and still have working capital for a year," he told Jasmine. "I never thought I could just buy one outright. I figured I'd have to put part of it on a mortgage."

She looked at the order and went right to work. "Does that make up your mind about buying it?"

"Maybe," he said. "There's no one else in the dining room. I'll make the pancakes."

"Tell me the pros," she said.

"I like the place. I like the name, and I can probably keep the brand. If what's in the barn goes with the property, it will

save me a bunch of money. I might have to work on the tractor and the truck, but I'll have the tools to do that. It's not far
from the best chicken-fried steaks in the state, and I already
have a friend here," he said.

"Now tell me the cons." She dipped up three bowls of oatmeal and added a fistful of raisins and a couple of spoonfuls
of brown sugar on the top.

"It's not as far north as I'd hoped," he said as he poured
six pancakes onto the grill. "It needs work…" He paused. "I
can't think of any more. Is this too good to be true, Jasmine?
Is there something wrong with that place?"

"Not that I know of," she answered, "and I'm glad you
consider me a friend."

"I asked if we could go back and look at it one more time
tonight," he said. "Will you go with me?"

"Be glad to," she said as she put food on a tray. "And if
your working capital runs low, you can always pick up extra
money right here in the café."

"That's good to know." Flint couldn't have wiped the grin
off his face if he sucked on a lemon.

Friend, my ass! He could hear Sam chuckling as if the old
guy was right there in the room with him.

Flint never blushed, but he could feel heat traveling from

his neck to his face. He picked up the tray and hurried out of the kitchen so Jasmine didn't notice his red cheeks. He'd only known her for three days, and he damn sure didn't believe in love at first sight. He'd known his ex for a year before he asked her to marry him, and look what that got him—a broken heart.

He set the food on the table, and Clark motioned to the fourth chair. "Ain't nobody else in here, so you might as well sit down and visit with us."

"Hey, Jasmine, bring yourself a cup of coffee and join us," Amos called out.

"Give me two minutes," she said from the kitchen, "to get this second pan of biscuits out of the oven."

"Clark was telling us that you like the Promised Land." Amos stirred milk into his oatmeal. "And that you're going to keep the name and brand if you buy it."

"I'm going back to look at it again before I make up my mind," Flint said.

"We wouldn't mind havin' you for a neighbor," Elvis told him, "and if you need anything we got, we don't mind sharing."

"There's an old tractor and work truck in the barn. Do they run, or were they parked there for parts?" Flint asked.

"Last time Delman fired them up, they were running," Amos answered, "but that's been a few years. They might need an oil change or radiator checked. He probably drained the water out of both of them when he put them away. He and Ginger left at the beginning of winter."

Jasmine brought out a fresh basket of hot biscuits and set them on the table. "What are you boys up to this morning?"

"We was talkin' about the Promised Land," Amos said. "I never did understand why Delman and Ginger named the place that."

"Ginger told me that it was the land of milk and honey, just like in the Bible," Clark said. "She said that one section of ground had been good for her and Delman for the better part of their married life, but when he got Alzheimer's, she couldn't run it by herself."

"If it was all that good, then why hasn't it been snatched up?" Flint asked.

"Not big enough for some folks. Too big for others," Amos said. "Did you drive around?"

"We checked out the fence lines, but it had started getting dark, so we didn't see much else," Flint answered.

"Tonight, you follow them ruts from the barn to right smack in the middle of the property. You'll find a nice spring-fed pond that never goes dry and a little cabin sitting up on a slight rise not far from it. That's where Delman's only permanent hired help lived. Thomas died the year before Ginger made the decision to move, but it wouldn't be a bad place if you was to hire someone to help out," Amos said.

Flint immediately thought of Sam and the fact that he was bored with nothing to do. "Why is the cabin even there?"

"That's where Ginger and Delman lived until they got the house built. The old recluse who lived there before them put that cabin up with wood he cut off the ranch when he was clearing land," Elvis answered.

"Anything else y'all know about the place? Has it got a curse on it or some bad mojo?" Flint asked.

"Not even a witch would dare put anything like that on a place called Promised Land." Clark chuckled. "I'll be by for lunch tomorrow. You can either give me the key or keep it at that time. I'm willin' to go to the bank with you if you decide to buy the place."

"I won't need to go to the bank," Flint said, "but thanks for the offer."

"Won't take but a week to close the deal if we're working in cash," Clark said. "Taxes and insurance is up to date, but you'll have to do some transfer work on the brand and then take care of a little paperwork on insurance."

Flint heard what he was saying, but it was hard to keep it all straight when Jasmine was sitting so close to him that her knee was pressed against his. He found himself stealing glances at her full lips and wondering what it would be like to kiss her.

Thank God the door opened, and several customers came into the café. "We'll talk more tomorrow. If I was to buy it, how soon could I plan on moving in?"

"Anytime that you want to," Clark said. "I've been left in charge of things. You could put up ten percent in an escrow account and move in tomorrow if you wanted to."

"You might want to get the utilities turned on first," Elvis advised. "It's about to get cold."

"The cabin has a fireplace, though," Amos reminded him.

———————————

Jasmine went back to the kitchen when Flint went to wait on the new customers. Her mind was all awhirl with an idea of asking him if she could rent the cabin, but until Flint made up his mind about buying the place, she couldn't say a word.

She had promised herself a whole month of rest before

she even looked for another job after she turned the café over to Diana. If Flint would rent the little cabin to her, she could have some time to finish the two cookbooks she'd been working on for a couple of years.

"First things first," she told herself as she picked up a biscuit from the pan and stuffed it full of crispy bacon. "Mercy! Life can sure turn around on a dime sometimes."

"What was that?" Flint asked.

"I said that life sure has its twists and turns," she answered.

"Oh, yeah," he said. "The ladies just want pancakes, sausage, and coffee. I thought I'd help you get them ready. Sure has been slow today compared to yesterday."

Depends on whether you're talkin' business or the way my pulse jacks up every time you walk into a room, she thought. *Pearl has teased me for years about finding a cowboy like she did her husband, Wil. The way you affect me, I'm wondering if I just might be on the right path, but holy smokin' hell, I've only known you two days.*

"I like a slow and steady day every now and then." Her voice sounded a bit breathless in her own ears. She flipped several sausage links onto the grill and turned them slowly so they would brown evenly.

Flint was close enough to her that she could feel his warm

breath on her neck. She hadn't had shivers chasing up and down her spine in ages—had actually forgotten what it was like to be that attracted to a man.

"I'm going to talk to Sam after we see the cabin tonight," he said.

"Who's Sam?" Jasmine asked.

"He was our foreman and stayed on after Grandpa died to help me until everything was settled, and he's stood beside me through all this business of getting the ranch stuff sorted out," Flint answered. "He's like an uncle to me, and he tells me he's bored already with retirement, and it's only been a few days. If I buy the place, I'm going to offer to let him live in the cabin and help me out on the ranch."

"Well, dammit!" she said, and then wondered if she'd really put those words out in the air.

"What?" Flint flipped the pancakes over.

Jasmine shrugged. "I've been working on a couple of cookbooks for a long time. I promised myself a few weeks of rest where I could work on them once I leave this place. I was thinking I might rent that cabin from you."

"There's three bedrooms in the house. You can have one of those rent-free and use the other one for your office if you'll cook for me and Sam." He grinned. "Me and Sam will be busy most of the time, so you'll have all the peace and quiet that you want to work on your cookbooks."

"You'd do that for me?" she asked.

"Hey, pretty lady, you did something similar for me," he reminded her with a nudge on her shoulder. "We might both find our promised land."

I'd be happy to just find a cowboy, she thought, but was very careful not to say it out loud.

———————

Jasmine bit back a groan that evening when they followed the path to the cabin, and then another one when she saw the view from the porch. The place was really too small for her to lay out all her book plans, but it was so cute that she would have made room somehow. The whole place was just one room, with a fireplace on one side and a kitchen area on the other. There would be room for a sofa or a recliner and a bed in between the two.

"It's perfect for Sam." Flint took several pictures of the inside and then stepped out onto the porch and took one of the sunset beyond the pond and sent them to Sam.

Within two minutes his phone rang, and to Jasmine's surprise, he put it on speaker and motioned for her to sit beside him on the porch step.

"What is this? You going to buy that ranch you told me about and live there?" Sam asked.

"Don't know just yet," Flint said. "I wanted to talk to you about it. I've got you on speaker with me and Jasmine. We came out here to look at the place one more time before I make up my mind. I can buy it with no bank loan, and still have some working capital to last about a year. What do you think?"

"I think that's about the prettiest little cabin I've ever seen. Is it big enough for two?" Sam's voice sounded downright wistful.

"Nope, but it would be big enough for a ranch foreman. The house is big enough for two guys to live in, but..." Flint let the sentence hang.

"Are you asking me to leave Louisiana and move to Texas? If so, how soon do you need me to get there? I can pack up and be ready to roll tomorrow if I can bring Gator with me." It didn't take a psychoanalyst to hear the excitement in his voice.

"We won't have cattle for a few months, but I guess he could chase rabbits and tree some squirrels." Flint sounded every bit as excited as Sam. "But what about that ten acres you've got rented?"

"It's just by the month, and to get to put my boots back

on a ranch, I'll lose the rest of this month's rent. When will you make up your mind, son? Don't you know it's not nice to tease an old cowboy?" Sam said. "What can you do to convince him, young lady?"

"That's something he'll have to decide for himself, but I..." Jasmine inhaled deeply and locked eyes with Flint. "I would love for him to buy it. He's offered to let me stay in the house and have the extra bedroom to work on some cookbooks I've been writing if I'll cook for you two."

"Well, hot damn!" Sam laughed out loud. "We get a ranch and a cook all in one fell swoop. And I have a cabin all to myself with a porch for Gator to sun his old bones on while he waits for the cattle to get there. This sounds like we've done gone to the promised land."

Flint laughed with him. "Jasmine, would you tell him what the name of the ranch and the brand is."

"It's called Promised Land Ranch. I don't know what the brand looks like," Jasmine said. "Do you think it's crazy for us to make plans like this when we've only known each other three days?"

"Oh, hell no!" Sam said. "I think Fate has worked in both y'all's favor."

"Then start packing, Sam," Flint said. "I'm going to tell

the Realtor tomorrow that I'll take the ranch. And by the way, we've got some mighty fine neighbors on both sides of us. You're going to like them."

"Son, I feel like I'm floatin' on clouds right now. Want me to get a mover to bring the stuff from the storage unit out there, or is it too soon? I can throw a sleeping bag on the floor and be happy," Sam said.

"Go ahead and get a mover lined up. With any luck we can get things out here by the first of the week and get to work on the ranch," Flint told him.

"But, Sam, I've got an extra bedroom you can use if your stuff isn't here for a couple of days," Jasmine offered.

"Thank you, Miz Jasmine," Sam said. "Now, take me off speaker, Flint. I've got a couple of things to say just to you."

Flint hit the button and put the phone to his ear. "What do you need to say?"

"That you best not let some other cowboy come in and steal that woman out from under you. I ain't even met her and I already like her, so put the past away—cousins, old girlfriend, and all of it—and look forward to a future with that girl. She's a keeper. I can hear it in her voice," Sam said.

"Three days," Flint reminded him.

"Three days. Three months. Three years. Fate has took you to the promised land, but you got to do a little for yourself. Put on your flirtin' britches and get busy. Now I'm off to start packin'," Sam said and ended the call.

Flint put the phone back in his pocket. "I guess I've made up my mind. I just hope Sam isn't disappointed when he sees this place."

"It sure looks beautiful from right here," Jasmine said. "I guess I'd better be doing some furniture shopping for my two rooms."

Flint shrugged. "No need to do that unless you just want to. I inherited everything in the house, even if I did lose the ranch, so there's lots of stuff coming this way. We'll probably have to store part of it out in the barn anyway."

"I'm surprised your cousins didn't fight you for the household goods," she said.

"It was all too countrified for their tastes," Flint said. "They're all city folks with different tastes than Grandpa had."

"All right, then." Jasmine stood up. "Do you think we might go through the house one more time? I'd like to see the two rooms I'll have again."

"You can use more than two rooms," Flint said. "If you

need to spread out your book work on the kitchen table or the living room floor, then just do it."

"Really?" Jasmine asked.

"Honey, as pretty as you are, me and Sam just might sit on the sofa and watch you work." He grinned.

"Is that a pickup line, Flint Walker?" She smiled back at him.

"It could be," he answered. "It's the best I've got today. Think it might work?"

"Not as a pickup line, but I do like a little flattery," she answered.

He glanced down at his jeans. *Are these good enough to be called flirtin' britches?*

Chapter 5

Stars danced around a quarter moon hanging in a black velvet sky that evening. Jasmine could see the whole show out the side window of Flint's truck. She wondered if she had just committed to something she would regret later. Flint had mentioned that he didn't do things on impulse. Jasmine couldn't really say that. She had quit her job in Sherman and bought a café on impulse. She had hired a total stranger to help her at Chicken Fried and then offered him free room and board. And now she had made up her mind to move into the same house with that stranger.

When they got back to Ringgold, Flint slowed as they got near the café parking lot. "I thought maybe we'd go up to that casino and have a barbecue sandwich, or whatever else you might want, to celebrate my decision to buy the ranch."

"Are you asking me on a date?" Jasmine asked.

"I guess I am. It can be anything you want it to be—a dinner between friends where we'll talk about your cookbooks and what we'll do at the ranch, or it can be a date," he answered. "You call the shots."

Jasmine was hardly dressed for a first date, but then, the past three days had taught her that this man behind the wheel was no ordinary cowboy. At least the jeans and shirt she'd worn all day didn't have stains on them. "A barbecue sandwich does sound good, but I usually clean up a little better than this for a date."

"You look great." He passed by the café and headed on north.

Cowboys, truck drivers, and folks just passing through stopped by the café all the time since it was right off Highway 81. Pretty often, guys flirted with her, but none of them ever sent her hormones into overdrive like Flint did by simply saying that she looked great.

"From what the sign said, it's only five miles from here to the casino. Terral must be pretty big to have a casino," he said.

"The town might have four hundred people, but it's doubtful," she told him. "You'll find lots of casinos in Oklahoma wherever there's a bridge across the Red River."

"Do you ever play the slots or the poker tables?" Flint asked.

"Not me." Jasmine shook her head. "I'm way too tight with my money to give it away like that. I don't buy lottery tickets either. I'm one of those 'Bird in the hand is worth more than two in the bush' people. Sometimes, it is kind of nice to sneak off over the bridge and grab one of their sandwiches, though. They really are good."

"Well said," Flint nodded in agreement. "I'm not a gambler, either, and yet here I am, taking a chance on a small ranch with neighbors I only met three days ago."

"Some things are gambles, others are just a matter of using common sense. There might be a fine line between them, but you're smart enough to know the difference," she said.

He crossed the Red River bridge, and only a few hundred yards ahead was the casino. He found a parking spot and nosed into it. "It's not as big as I thought it would be."

"It doesn't take a big building to take your money." Jasmine unfastened her seat belt.

Before she could sling the door open, Flint was there to open it for her. He held out his hand to help her.

Yep, this is a date, she thought. *I wonder if he'll want a good-night kiss.*

She stole a quick look at his lips and wished that she didn't have a rule about kissing on first dates. Kissing was a second-date thing, and sex was out there about the fifth or sixth date. The ex in her past that had broken her heart had been one of those smooth-talking guys and had gotten lucky on their second date. She'd buried her head in the sand for the next several years before she finally woke up and realized that she was his safety blanket. They were living together, and he was telling his other women that if he left her, she might do something drastic. Finally, she had taken her life back, kicked him out, left her job, and bought a café.

I guess he was right, Jasmine thought. *By his standards, I did act irrationally.*

The trouble was that she had never trusted guys again. She had gone out with a few over the years. Some got to the kiss-goodnight stage, a couple to the sex stage, but none of them lasted long because she simply couldn't—or wouldn't let herself—trust them.

"You're awfully quiet," Flint said as he opened the door into the casino for her.

"Letting ghosts from the past rise up when I shouldn't." She walked into a warm place with a hint of cigarette smoke blended with barbecue permeating the air.

"I do that sometimes, but tonight, we need to tell them to get lost. We're celebrating a change in our lives. I never dreamed when I said goodbye to the Walker Ranch that I'd find a home." He ushered her into the restaurant with his hand on the small of her back.

More of those little shivers ran up and down her spine at his touch. She wondered if this was what Pearl was talking about when she first told her about Wil.

The restaurant wasn't very busy, and they were taken to a booth right away. The young lady told them that their waiter would be with them in a few minutes and disappeared. Almost immediately an older lady came across the floor, gave them a menu, and asked what they'd like to drink.

"Do you have champagne?" Flint asked.

"I'd rather have a beer," Jasmine piped up before the waitress could answer. "I'm a cheap date. Never did like champagne, but if you want it, that's fine."

Flint chuckled. "Then we'll have two beers. What's your favorite?"

"Longneck Coors," Jasmine answered.

"Same here," Flint told her.

The waitress nodded. "I'll give you time to look over the menu and be back in a minute with your beers."

"I still want a barbecue sandwich with fries," Jasmine said and laid the menu on the edge of the table.

Flint closed his menu and laid it on top of Jasmine's. "Me too. We really should be in a fancy place, having a steak and at least a drink with an umbrella in it to celebrate."

"Like I said, I'm a cheap date"—she smiled across the table at him—"and I can cook a good steak and make a drink with an umbrella at home. I don't do so hot on barbecue. Just never have found the right recipe for sauce to suit me."

"Hey, I'm good at that job," Flint said. "When the movers get here with my stuff, they'll be bringing in a smoker, and I make a fine barbecue sauce. Looks like between the two of us, we'll have the food end of living on the ranch pretty well covered."

Jasmine inhaled deeply and let it out slowly. "Is all this moving too fast?"

"Yes, it is, but then that's where trust comes in. I've had trouble trusting anyone since my ex broke up with me for my cousin. Seems like she didn't like ranching life and just didn't want to tell me. I hope that you will tell me exactly what you like and don't like," Flint said.

Jasmine nodded. "You can depend on that. I have trust issues too. My ex cheated on me more than once."

"You don't seem like the kind of woman to put up with that," Flint said.

"You don't see what you don't want to see. I had my head buried so deep in the sand that my ears were full of it. That's why I couldn't hear my best friends telling me what he was doing," Jasmine told him. "Did anyone warn you?"

"No," he answered, "but looking back, I should have seen the signs. Enough about our exes, though. This is a date, remember, so let's talk about these cookbooks you're writing, or I could just sit here and tell you how pretty you are, or maybe how the temperature rose ten degrees when you walked into the casino."

The waitress brought their beers, took their orders, and rushed off to wait on more folks coming into the restaurant.

Jasmine took a long drink of her beer and then said, "I've heard about every pickup line in the world."

"Do you go out to bars for a night of dancing on Saturday nights?" Flint turned up his bottle and took a drink.

"Not just no, but hell no! I'm tired enough by Saturday night that the only dancing I do is across the floor and up the stairs so I can prop up my feet." Jasmine might not have to worry about a good-night kiss on the second date. When Flint realized how boring she was, there might only be one date and this was it. Tonight would be the first and last.

"Is the café open on Sunday?" Flint asked.

"Nope, and on my one day off, I catch up on laundry and housecleaning," she told him. "I live such an exciting life that coming up here for a sandwich and fries is a big deal."

"That's kind of like ranch life," Flint said. "Work all week. Get off at noon on Saturday unless you own the ranch, then you work until dark that day too. Sunday is church and playing catch-up with the household duties. Grandpa said that if you love what you work at, be it digging ditches, fixing fences, or working cattle, or even sitting in the Oval Office up there in the White House, then you are a success. I guess we're both a success."

"I'll drink to that." She held her bottle up.

"Me too." He clinked his bottle against hers.

———

Jasmine wished she could hang on to the feeling she had when she and Flint were visiting over supper at the casino. But it all faded quickly when she unlocked the back door of the café and realized that now they had to clean up the place for the next morning.

"I'll grab the broom and mop and come help you as soon as I get the dining room put to rights." Flint opened the door to the utility room. "Looks like we've got a full basket of café laundry in here too. I'll just pitch it in the washer."

"And so ends a perfect date," Jasmine muttered as she slipped an apron over her head, tied it in the front, and went to work.

But give thanks that you had a lovely evening to think about while you clean up this place, the voice in her head said.

Jasmine nodded in agreement and got busy. *At least I've got good help. I hope Diana's new hired hands are willing to work as hard as Flint.*

In an hour they had the whole place ready for the next morning and started up the stairs.

"I want to call Sam and talk to him some more." Flint followed behind her.

"I'm going straight for a shower and then to bed." Jasmine didn't even slow down at the top of the steps but headed straight to the bathroom at the end of the hall. She had just passed Flint's bedroom door when she caught something out of the corner of her eye that she thought was a mouse. She tried to get both feet off the floor at the same time, but only succeeded in falling backward and landing in Flint's arms.

"Mouse!" She could barely speak.

"No, just a big old wolf spider that jumped onto my boot and is now dead." Flint held her close to his chest. "No need to get the sawed-off shotgun. The varmint is dead. Open your eyes and see his poor old, squashed body."

"You're sure it's not a mouse?" She shivered.

"Positive. Just a spider the size of a baby mouse," he assured her. "Good thing neither of us are afraid of eight-legged critters."

Jasmine slid one eye open enough to see the remains of the spider on the hardwood floor and started to take a step back, but Flint held her tighter. She shifted her focus from the floor to his face just as his thick eyelashes slowly came to rest on his high cheekbones. She barely had time to moisten her lips and tiptoe before his mouth found hers in a kiss that made her forget that there was a world around them.

Jasmine felt as if she and Flint were wrapped in an over-sized cocoon made of plush velvet. Then suddenly, it was entirely too warm, and heat filled her body. When the kiss ended, he kissed her again, this time on her forehead, and even that was scorching hot.

"Oh! My!" she gasped.

"I know." Flint's drawl was lower and huskier than usual.

She took a step back even though she wanted to stay in his arms all night. "That was..." She searched for the right words.

"Amazing. Awesome. Hot as hell." He filled in the words for her.

"The latter is more what I was thinking. I need a cool shower," she whispered.

"Me too"—Flint nodded—"but you go first. I'll clean up the spider mess." That sounded stupid, he realized, after a kiss that nearly knocked his cowboy boots off. He was almost forty years old, and he had never had trouble sweet-talking the ladies. Where had his game gone?

"Thank you," Jasmine whispered. "Now I feel all awkward, like that was my first kiss, and I don't know what to do."

"I know exactly what you mean." He finally smiled. "That was *our* first kiss, and maybe…" He drew her back into his arms and tipped up her chin with his knuckles. The second kiss was even fiercer than the first, and when it ended, he said, "Nope, it's not beginner's luck or heat or whatever. That one was just as hot as the first one."

"We'd have to call the fire department if we chanced a third one." She stepped out of his reach and headed toward the bathroom. At the door, she turned and smiled at Flint.

"Thank you for a wonderful first date, but I usually don't kiss until the second date."

"I'll consider myself special, then." He blew a kiss her way and went into the sitting room where he sank down on the sofa and fanned himself with a catalog that he picked up from the end table.

Just as he pulled his phone from his shirt pocket, it rang. He chuckled when Sam's name popped up on the screen. "Great minds really do think alike," he answered. "I was just about to call you."

"Please, tell me you haven't changed your mind." Sam's voice was full of concern. "I've already told Gator that we were back in the ranching business."

"If anything, I'm even more sure that this is what I want to do." Flint touched his lips to see if they were as hot as they felt. "The guy who's handling this sale says that when I decide, I can begin to move in. So, when you get here, the cabin is yours—empty but ready for you."

"I called a moving company that I know, and they can pack up the storage unit by tomorrow night. I'll follow the truck to the ranch Friday. This is divine intervention, son. I feel it in my old bones." Sam sighed. "God himself is looking out for you and me."

Flint heard a deep growl in the background.

"And Gator." Sam laughed. "He says that he's bored with this place and needs a little more room and some fences to patrol. Now, about Jasmine. Is she really considering moving to the ranch and cooking for us? Are you sweet-talkin' her yet?"

"Yes, and yes," Flint answered. "There's something about her, Sam. I feel like I've known her forever, and that I can trust her."

"Well, that's an amazing start, especially after what you've been through," Sam said.

"Yep, it sure is," Flint agreed. "I'm talking to Clark in the morning. I'm even hoping to get the paperwork started tomorrow. He says since it's a cash deal, it doesn't take as long to put the deed in my hands as it would if we had to go through the bank."

"As long as we've got free rein on the ranch, the paperwork is just a formality," Sam said. "Me and Gator have some more packing to do. Just think! By Monday morning me and you can be working on fences, or…" He paused. "Monday is Valentine's Day. Have you asked Jasmine out to dinner yet? And remember to get her flowers and candy, or both."

"Yes, sir." Flint made a mental note to do something really nice for Jasmine on that day.

Chapter 6

As soon as the café closed up on Thursday, Flint and Jasmine headed for Nocona and Clark's office. He must have seen Flint parking out at the curb because he met them at the door.

"Come right on in. I've talked to the Promised Land sellers, and they've agreed to the bid you offered, plus they're glad to leave whatever is in the barn so that they don't have to come back and deal with it. Have a seat"—he motioned to two wingback chairs on the other side of his desk—"and grab a pen from the cup right there. I'll need an escrow check to proceed, and there's several places you need to sign. If we get done in the next half hour, you can go on over to the electric company and get the power turned on out there. I checked the propane tank a few days ago. It's about half-full, and you have well water, so that's taken care of."

Jasmine watched as Flint signed his name on several papers, and then tried not to look as he wrote out a check.

"I don't think I've ever written a check for a quarter of a million dollars before," Flint said as he handed it over to Clark. "But I sure feel good about what I'm buying with it."

"It was meant to be." Clark tucked the check inside an envelope and put all the papers in a safe under his desk. "Delman and Ginger's oldest son is flying into Dallas tomorrow morning and will drive up here to finish the deal. Do you think you could come back around four? He'd like to catch the seven o'clock flight back to Amarillo. Here's your copies of what you signed today."

"No problem with being here at four." Flint nodded and took the papers that Clark passed across the desk to him.

"I got to tell you." Clark stood up and reached across the desk to shake hands with Flint. "It's been a long time since I've sold anything on a cash deal. Usually, we have to get banks and lawyers involved."

"My grandpa always taught me the best way to do business is to leave banks and lawyers out of it." Flint shook hands with him, and then turned toward Jasmine. "We'd better get a hustle on if we're going to make it to the electric company before they close." Then he smiled at Clark. "Thank you for making all this happen so quick. My foreman and my moving van will be here tomorrow."

"Almost forgot something." Clark tossed a key ring toward him. "There's two more sets of keys. And if you need help getting that name and brand transferred over into your name, just holler. I can take care of that for you too. It takes a little while, but I've got all the paperwork here in the office."

"Will do, and thanks again." Flint tucked his checkbook into his shirt pocket and draped an arm around Jasmine's shoulders.

"How do you feel right now?" she asked as they walked out of the warm office and into the cold wind.

When they reached his truck, he caged her against the passenger door with a hand on each side of her. Then he kissed her right there in public. "I feel like I just won the lottery," he whispered as he stepped back and opened the door for her. "How do you feel?"

"Kind of hot right now in spite of the cold wind," she answered.

"Let's go have ice cream to celebrate the first step," he suggested. "How about a Peanut Buster parfait from the Dairy Queen down the street?"

"How about some of their tacos before ice cream? But first we better see about getting some electricity at the Promised Land," she reminded him. "Sam might like to have something other than just an oil lamp and the fireplace to see by."

"We're going to make a good team." Flint closed the door and whistled all the way around the back of the truck.

He slid under the wheel and started the engine, then just sat there for a few moments. "Sam told me last night that this was divine intervention, and I kind of believe that he's right."

"I'd say more like Max intervention," Jasmine told him.

"Whatever it was, I'm grateful," Flint said. "I've said it before, but I never thought for one minute I'd have enough money to buy a place and not have to get a loan. If I'm dreaming, don't pinch me. I don't want to wake up."

"Honey, you're not dreaming." Jasmine fastened her seat belt. "Those kisses we've shared are too hot to come from a dream."

"What are we going to do about this chemistry between us?" Flint asked.

"We're going to take it slow and be sure that it's not a flash in the pan. We'll be living in the same house, so we'll see if we endure disagreements and spending lots of time together in the same place," she answered.

He backed the truck out and headed down the street a couple of blocks to the electric company. "Sounds fair to me."

Jasmine waited in the truck while he ran in and gave them the information that they needed to get power turned on out at the ranch. Her phone rang and startled her so badly that she jumped, then fumbled with it when she tried to get it out of her purse. By the time she had it in her hands, she had missed a call from Diana. She hit the right button, and her cousin answered on the first ring.

"Surprise!" Diana said. "I'm loaded and headed that way from Sherman. I got things taken care of here earlier than I planned. Aunt Wynona told me that you've got a good-lookin' cowboy workin' for you."

"That's right, but he's buying a ranch a few miles south of Ringgold, so he's probably only going to be around until you get here," Jasmine said.

"Oh, really!" Diana's voice perked right up. "Tell me more."

"I can only talk but a few minutes. You'll never believe what has happened since Monday." Jasmine ended with, "I'll give you the short version, and as soon as you're comfortable I'm going to leave the café with you."

"My two friends who'll be helping me will be in Sunday evening. They're going to live in the upstairs with me, so if you're ready to let go of the café, Saturday can be your last day. If not, my friends said they'll share a room until you're ready to leave. I know how much that place means to you," Diana said. "And honey, our Granny Thurman used to tell us to answer when opportunity knocks, that it's easier to invite it in for a glass of sweet tea than it is to chase it when it's a mile down the road. So if you don't want to have a footrace with that cowboy, then invite him in."

Flint came out of the office with another bunch of papers in his hand and waved at her.

"I'm going to have ice cream with Flint to celebrate, but we should be back at the café when you get there, and Diana, I think I'll be just fine to move out on Sunday," Jasmine said.

"No rush, now," Diana told her. "This is all happening so quick that your head probably feels like it's spinning out of control."

"Yep, but it feels right and good," Jasmine said. "See you in a couple of hours."

Flint ducked so that he wouldn't knock his hat off when he got in behind the wheel. "There will be electricity by noon tomorrow. Everything is falling into place so well that it's kind of scary. It feels like any minute now the other shoe is going to drop."

Jasmine was slightly superstitious and had been thinking the exact same thing. "I just got a call from my cousin who's buying the café. There's more good news." She told him what Diana had said. "Let me ask one more time..." She paused and then went on. "Are you sure you want to let me have those two other rooms? I sold Chicken Fried as is, with the upstairs intact. I had planned on renting something furnished and just working on my cookbooks."

"I'm very sure." Flint leaned across the console and kissed her on the cheek. "And honey, you will have two furnished rooms. We'll just have to decide what we want in the house and what to donate to a charity or put in storage when it gets here. Grandpa had a really big house."

"How big?" Jasmine asked.

"Maybe three times as big as the house the café is in," Flint answered. "Let's go have tacos and then ice cream to celebrate what all we've gotten done today."

She shot a smile over toward him. "If we celebrate everything that happens, I might have to jog around the fence line every day to keep from gaining fifty pounds."

"If you cook for me and Sam like you do at the café, I'll be right there beside you when you run around the fences," he said.

Chapter 7

JASMINE HAD JUST CRAWLED BENEATH THE COVERS THAT night when she heard a faint knock on her door. *Lord, what will I do if that's Flint?* she wondered as she threw back the sheet and quilt and padded barefoot across the floor. She eased the door open a crack and heaved a sigh of relief when she saw Diana standing there.

"Can I come in for a minute? I'm too excited to sleep," Diana said.

Jasmine opened the door wide. "Of course. I'm having trouble settling down too."

Diana crawled up in the middle of Jasmine's bed. "I can feel the vibes between you and Flint. I knew within a week of the day I met Roger that he was the one, and we were married three months later. Your mama and mine almost had heart failure. They took me on a weekend trip to Vegas and tried to talk me out of getting married so soon. I liked the place so well that I invited Roger to fly out, and we went to one of those chapels right there."

"Why are you telling me this?" Jasmine climbed onto the bed and propped pillows against the headboard to lean on.

Diana raked her hand through her spiky gray hair. "Because I didn't listen to everyone, and Roger and I had thirty wonderful years together before he died. We had two great daughters who have done well in life. Now that I'm retired from the post office, I'm embarking on another journey, something that I've wanted to do for years. I can feel Roger's blessing on my decision to do this, and my two dear friends will have a job too."

She stopped and wiped a tear from her eye. "I'm telling you this because I almost let our mothers talk me out of marrying Roger, and I've felt guilty about it ever since. My mother will tell you that since she's twenty years older than Aunt Wynona, she's so much wiser. Aunt Wynona will say that even if she's the youngest daughter in the family, she's lived long enough to learn a few things. Don't let either of them tell you what to do with your life. Follow your heart, and you'll never go wrong."

Jasmine had always had a close connection with Diana,

even though she was the same age as her cousin's youngest daughter. "Thank you for that, but..."

Diana put a finger over Jasmine's lips. "Don't ever have any *buts* in your life. Do what your heart tells you to do and be damned to the rest of the world. Now that I've spoken my piece, I think I can sleep. Good night, sweetie." She slid off the bed and left the room.

"Wow!" Jasmine muttered. "That was quite a pep talk."

What do you intend to do with it? Granny Thurman's husky voice popped into her head.

"Have no *buts*." Jasmine turned out the bedside light and snuggled down beneath the covers again. She closed her eyes and dreamed that she and Flint were sitting in the sunroom at the ranch. In her dream, Flint had a little silver in his dark hair, and he was telling her all about a heifer that had just had her first calf. It would be perfect for their son to show at the county fair the next spring, he said.

When she awoke the next morning, she sat straight up in bed and looked in the mirror to be sure she hadn't aged at least ten years. "It was just a dream," she muttered. "But..." She stopped and slid out of bed. "No! No *buts*, only *ands* for the rest of my life."

Marcus and Clark were already signing papers when Flint made it to the office on Friday afternoon. Marcus stood up and stretched out a hand. "I'm Delman and Ginger's son, and I want to thank you for buying this ranch. Dad doesn't know much anymore, but sometimes he frets about the tractor or the fences. Now we can tell him that it's all being taken care of."

"Thank you for accepting my offer." Flint shook hands with Marcus and then sat down in the empty chair. "My foreman and movers are about fifty miles east of here at the moment, so it will be good to get everything taken care of before we actually move into the house."

"Is your foreman going to live in the cabin?" Marcus had a wicked gleam in his eyes.

"That's what we plan, but from your expression, I'd guess you have some memories there," Flint said.

"Our foreman used to go visit his kids for a couple of weeks at Christmas, but I'll plead the Fifth on saying anything more than that," Marcus said.

Flint could have liked this guy, even if he wasn't a rancher, had he lived closer to Ringgold. "I understand." He nodded as he picked up a pen and began to sign all the places that had little yellow tags beside the lines. When he got to the page concerning mineral rights, he glanced over at Marcus. "You're selling the mineral rights with the land?"

"That's what Mama wants," Marcus said. "They had a company come out and check most of the land when I was a little kid and they said there was no oil on the place, and she doesn't want to deal with it if there is."

"Thank you." Flint continued signing. "I'm not sure that I'd ever want a pumper on my land anyway, but it's good to know that I own what's under the dirt as well as what's above it."

"You are welcome," Marcus said.

They finished their business in an hour, and Flint went straight out to the ranch. He opened the door to the house with one of his keys and walked through the place. He decided that Jasmine should have the master suite. It wasn't any bigger than the other two bedrooms but it did have a private bathroom, and that would give Jasmine a little more privacy. He would take one of the other two bedrooms and use the bathroom off the hallway. The third bedroom could be set up with a desk and a file cabinet for her to work on her cookbooks.

"Anybody home?" Jasmine knocked on the door and came in without waiting.

Flint hurried down the hallway, picked her up, and swung her around until they were both dizzy and laughing like children. "I have a ranch," he said. "It's all mine now. Signed, sealed, and delivered. I can't believe it."

"I hope it's okay, but I brought a few things since I was coming this way." Jasmine was completely out of breath when he set her down.

"That's great!" he said and planted one of those steamy kisses on her lips. "I'll help you get it into the house. I'm so glad you're here to help organize things when the movers get here."

He tucked her hand into his, and together they walked out to her van. Just that much contact made him want to rush things, but she was right. They should see how they did in all situations before they took their relationship to the next level.

Relationship? His grandfather chuckled so loudly that Flint looked over his shoulder to see if he was standing on the porch. *I'm glad to see you even know how use that word.*

"Me too," he whispered.

"You too what?" Jasmine asked.

"Do you ever hear someone that has passed on talking to you in your mind?" Flint asked as he picked up two boxes and headed toward the house.

"Oh, yeah," Jasmine answered. "Were you agreeing with someone?"

"Yep, with my grandpa," Flint replied, "and do you hear what I hear? That's the sound of trucks coming down the lane."

"Looks like your movers are here." She grabbed the last box from her van and hurried inside the house. "Where do I put this stuff?"

"The bedroom with the bathroom is yours. We'll put all this in the closet." Flint led the way.

"This should be your room," Jasmine protested.

"Maybe it will be someday, but right now it belongs to you. The room right across the hall is your office." He rushed out to the porch and across the yard. When he opened Sam's truck door, Gator bailed out, hiked his leg on a dormant rosebush, and then stretched out on the porch.

Sam got out and wrapped Flint up in a bear hug. "Looks like we've got some mesquite to clear off this place."

Flint patted Sam on the back. "Welcome to the Promised Land."

"I'm glad to be here." Sam took a step back. "Please tell me that van sitting over there belongs to Jasmine. I can't wait to meet her."

"Did I hear my name?" Jasmine stepped out on the porch.

"Yes, you did, and that picture Flint sent me didn't do you justice." Sam took the steps two at a time and stuck out his hand. "I'm right pleased to meet you, and even more pleased that you'll be staying here on the ranch. Me and Flint can both put together a meal, but that ain't sayin' it tastes good." He winked.

"Those two trucks comin' up the lane right now are going to back in here, and you kids will need to tell them what to do with things. When they get done fillin' up this house, then we'll take the rest to the barn, and me and Flint can use our pickups to take my things to the cabin." Sam talked as he walked through the house. "And just so you know, Miz Jasmine, I'm a man of few words unless I'm all excited like I am right now, and then you can't turn me off."

"What do you think?" Flint followed along behind him.

"I think it's a fine place with plenty of room to build on either way if you ever want to," Sam said. "It'll be plenty big to raise a couple of boys in, but if you was to have a big family, you might need a little more space. The trucks are here. Let's get busy. We've got work to do while there's still a sliver of daylight left."

Flint found Jasmine standing in the middle of the kitchen

floor and drew her close to his side. "Think we'll ever have to build on to this house?"

"I read a quote this morning in one of my books. It said: 'The past is your lesson. The present is your gift. The future is your motivation.' I can sure agree with that. I've learned a lot from my past." She raised on her tiptoes and kissed him on the cheek. "Let's enjoy the gift that we have right now."

"And be motivated to have a great future," he said.

Chapter 8

Saturday was a bittersweet day for Jasmine. For more than ten years, her life had revolved around Chicken Fried. Her regular customers had become her friends, and now she was leaving them behind. Sure, Diana would take good care of them. Her cooking was every bit as good as Jasmine's, and her two sweet friends would make everyone who stopped by the café feel welcome and loved.

"How can everything change so drastically in only a week?" she asked Diana as they worked side by side on breakfast orders.

"Seems strange to me too," Diana said. "My dream is happening."

"What if I can't live in the same house with Flint, or what if in a few weeks I find out that Sam drives me crazy?" Jasmine whispered.

"Then move out," Diana answered. "There's no anchor on your butt, girl. If you ain't happy after a week or a month or even six months, pack it up and leave. You're still young, and there's places to live all over the world. But honey, I see the way that Flint looks at you with those love-at-first-sight eyes. I think y'all are goin' to get along just fine."

Jasmine sucked in a lungful of air, but Diana shook an egg turner at her. "Don't argue with me. I know the look because my sweet husband looked at me the same way. It's a miracle that doesn't come along very often."

"Trust isn't easy for me after..." Jasmine hesitated.

"I understand. We all remember what you went through with that sumbitch." Diana gritted her teeth on the last word. "But it's way past time for you to move on."

Pearl poked her head in the back door. "Hey, hey!"

Jasmine stopped stirring a slow cooker full of oatmeal and met her friend halfway across the kitchen. They wrapped their arms around each other for a long hug, and then Pearl stepped back and smiled.

"You are glowing almost as much as you did on your first day here at the café," Pearl said.

"I'm so glad you came today," Jasmine said.

Pearl poured herself a cup of coffee and set it on the

worktable. Then she removed her coat, hung it on the back of a chair, and tucked an errant strand of curly hair behind her ear. "It's good to see you, Diana. You never age. What's your secret?"

"A good life," Diana answered. "Must be ten years since I've seen you, girl, and you haven't changed a bit."

Pearl sat down at the worktable and took a sip of her coffee. "Thank you, but two kids and ranchin' work has taken its toll on me. I wanted to stop by today since I was here on the day Jasmine took over way back when. I wanted to be here when she passed her apron over to you."

"That's so sweet." Diana finished an order, set it on the shelf, and yelled "Order up!"

"That's my cue today," Jasmine said. "I'm doing double duty. Diana's two friends will arrive either late this evening or tomorrow, but today, I'm her waitress. Don't go away, Pearl. I'll be right back."

"I'm not going anywhere for a little while." Pearl waved her away with a flick of her wrist.

Jasmine carried a tray of food to Amos and Elvis and set the two Saturday-morning specials on the table. "You guys have been such amazing customers that this morning's breakfast is on the house."

"Thank you, but we're goin' to miss you." Amos sighed.

Jasmine patted him on the back. "I'm not leaving the state or even the county. We're going to be neighbors."

"That don't mean I can come over to your house every day for breakfast," Elvis said. "But I might make a few deals with Flint. I can loan him a hay baler for a free meal once a week."

Jasmine just smiled and gave Elvis a quick pat on the shoulder. No way was she going to start that kind of thing, or pretty soon she would be running another café out of the ranch house. "Y'all enjoy the Saturday special. You'll find that Diana and I cook just alike."

The bell above the door rang, and she whipped around to see Sam and Flint coming in. Flint caught her eye across the room and flashed a brilliant smile. Her pulse jacked up a few notches and her breath caught in her chest.

"Hey, Flint!" Amos yelled. "Come on over and sit with us. We missed you being the waiter today."

"Thanks for the invitation." Flint and Sam hung up their coats and hats. "I wanted y'all to meet Sam anyway."

Pearl was fanning herself with one of the menus when Jasmine made it back to the kitchen. "Oh. My. Sweet. Jesus!" she gasped.

"What?" Jasmine asked.

"He's even taller and sexier in the flesh than he was in the picture you sent," Pearl whispered. "Before I leave, you'll have to introduce us. How in the world are you going to keep from tiptoeing over to his bedroom and crawling into bed with him?"

Jasmine lowered her chin and looked up at Pearl. "Who says I'll tiptoe?"

Pearl giggled. "In all seriousness, now, I'm happy for you, but if things don't work out, remember that Wil and I have an empty bunkhouse you are welcome to use for as long as you like."

Jasmine stopped long enough to give her a hug. "Thanks for that. Now I've got to get back out there and wait on Flint and Sam."

She poured two cups of coffee, carried them to the table, and whipped out her order pad. "What can I get you guys this morning?"

"Whatever they're having looks mighty fine," Sam answered.

"Looks good to me too," Flint nodded. "Need some help while I'm here?"

"Thanks, but we're managing. How are things at the ranch?" she asked.

"That place is sure named right," Sam answered. "Me and

old Gator feel like we've done got to the promised land. The cabin is just perfect, and Gator has already had him a swim in the pond. Came back to the cabin and shook enough water off hisself that it looked like it was rainin'. You got the last of your stuff packed up and ready to move this evenin'?"

"Yes, I do," Jasmine answered.

"I'll be here about four to load it up for you." Flint reached out and gently squeezed her free hand.

She thought of what Pearl had said about tiptoeing across the hallway and bit back a giggle. Along with the sparks dancing across the table, she got a vision of herself cuddling up next to Flint after a night of steamy, hot sex.

"You okay?" Elvis asked.

Jasmine was jerked back to reality in a split second. "I'm fine," she answered. "I was just trying to think if there was anything I'd forgotten to pack. And now I'm going to go put your order in for Diana to get ready."

"Hello," Pearl said right behind her. "I'm Pearl. Jasmine and I've been friends since we were toddlers."

Both Sam and Flint pushed back their chairs and stood up. Flint stretched out his hand. "Pleasure to meet you. Jasmine has talked about you and your husband, Wil. Come see us at the Promised Land."

Pearl shook with him and then with Sam. "We'd love to, and you all have an open invitation to drive over to Henrietta to see us. We'll be seeing each other before then, but we have a big Fourth of July ranch party. We'd love to have you come spend the day with us."

"Whoa, now, girlie," Amos said. "I have a party on my ranch that day too and…"

"Pretty nice to have folks fightin' over us." Sam chuckled.

"We'll see who wins." Pearl shot a broad wink at Jasmine. "We'd better get on back in the kitchen before these two handsome cowboys starve plumb to death."

"Awww, shucks." Sam grinned. "Been years since I been called handsome. I really have made it to the promised land."

Jasmine shot a smile his way and followed Pearl back to the kitchen.

"You're goin' to have trouble," Pearl whispered.

"Why do you say that?" Jasmine asked.

"Flint's deep Southern drawl is as sexy as he is," Pearl answered.

"Why's that trouble?" Diana asked.

"With that voice, he could sweet-talk a holy woman's underpants right off her body," Pearl teased.

"Thank God I'm not a holy woman, then." Jasmine broke

six eggs into a bowl and whipped them up. "You want a stack of pancakes?"

"Thought you'd never ask," Pearl answered. "I got the kids off to school and Wil out to work on fences, but I didn't have time for anything but a piece of leftover toast this morning. What can I do to help?"

"Just sit tight and I'll have it ready in a second. I can do that while the bacon fries up for this order," Diana said.

"Thank you," Pearl said and then turned to Jasmine. "Now, back to Flint. Are you going to be able to focus on your cookbooks with him around?"

"I hope so," Jasmine said, but down deep in her heart, she had wondered the exact same thing.

_____

Flint and Sam drove around the fence line, checked out the ponds and the barn that morning, and then they went into the barn. The truck started on the first try but had a rattle that Sam said he could fix in a couple of days. The tractor was more stubborn, and after checking it out, Flint decided the first thing it needed was a new starter.

"So, you think we need to start out by getting the equipment in order?" Flint asked.

"Yep, and then we need to clear out the little mesquite trees popping up in the pastures. We should be able to do some plowing this spring and get some alfalfa in the ground for hay. That way when we start to bring the cattle onto the ranch, we'll have a barn full of good hay." Sam talked as he checked out the tack room and stalls. "This is a fine start, and it'll hold a lot of small bales. Amos said he's got a baler for sale. We might take a look at it toward the end of the week."

"Do you think the folks in the Bible who finally made it to the promised land ever felt like the other shoe was about to drop?" Flint asked.

Sam shook his head. "Nope. They had reached the land of milk and honey, but they had to fight to keep it. We'll have to fight mesquite and fight the heat and weather and everything that can get thrown at us if we want to keep this ranch. The name is pretty, but the work is going to make us both cuss and sweat."

"Bring it on." Flint grinned.

"Are you ready to work that hard to get and keep Jasmine?" Sam asked.

"I think I am," Flint answered. "I don't think I've ever felt this strong for any woman."

"Well, son." Sam rubbed his chin. "If you need some help along those lines, me and Gator are here to help you out. It's the least we can do after you letting us come live here."

"I appreciate that," Flint said, "but I reckon I can fight that battle myself. And Sam, I don't want you to overdo it. You are supposed to be retired and taking it easy."

"I can take it easy for a long time when I'm dead. I was so bored this past week I thought they'd have to call you to come make the arrangements for my funeral." Sam backed up and sat down in an old lawn chair.

"Don't talk like that," Flint said. "You're going to live to be a hundred."

"Or die tryin'." Sam chuckled. "With this new lease on life, I just might make it. You ready to drive to wherever we need to go for some tractor and truck parts? We've got a few hours until you bring your woman to the ranch."

"She's not my woman yet, Sam," Flint answered. "But I can always hope for someday."

"Hope is a powerful thing, son." Sam popped up from the chair.

"And sometimes it brings something to you a helluva lot faster than you think it will." Flint led the way out of the barn and down the path toward the house. "Who'd have ever thought that I'd brake to keep from hitting a dog and wind up with all this in a week's time?"

"Fate, boy!" Sam said seriously. "It's all Fate."

———————

Jasmine had never been a hoarder, but she didn't realize she had so much stuff until she and Flint began to load her van and his truck.

"Good Lord!" Diana said. "If you had one more shoebox, you would have to come back for it."

"Ten years' accumulation." Jasmine sighed. "I'm glad there's a spare room at the ranch for me to unload all this."

"And the better part of a barn. We put everything we didn't need for the house in the two stalls," Flint reminded her. "Ready to go, or do you need a minute or two alone?"

Jasmine shook her head. "I've made my peace with leaving, and I'm ready to start a new chapter." She gave Diana a hug on the front porch. "Call me if you need anything, or call me just because. We'll be in for dinner sometime next week."

"I will, and I'll be lookin' for you." Diana wiped away a tear. "Now, get on out of here before I start crying in earnest.

My friends will be here in another hour, and I don't want them to see me all weepy."

"Holy hell!" Jasmine muttered as she drove east out of Ringgold. "This has to be the craziest thing I've ever done. I'm about to move in with a man I've known one week."

Oh, hush! The voice in her head said. *Flint has lived in the same house as you all week. You've spent twenty-four hours a day with him, and he's been nothing but a gentleman.*

"But the kisses are so hot," she groaned.

She turned into the driveway, looked up at the sign swinging from two huge posts, and suddenly peace filled her heart. She was doing the right thing, and no amount of second-guessing herself was going to change that.

She backed her van as close to the porch as she could get it and opened the back. She had just picked up the first box when Flint parked beside her and rushed over to help.

"I can bring all this inside," he said. "You can tell me which room to put it in."

"Thanks," she said.

She was blown away when she walked into the house and found it fully put together. When she'd left two nights ago, there was barely room to walk between boxes and furniture. A well-worn but comfortable-looking leather sofa faced the fireplace in the living room. Recliners flanked the ends, and a massive wood coffee table that looked like it had seen lots of boots propped on it sat in front of the sofa.

"I'll just put the clothes all in the bedroom and you can arrange them later, if that's all right."

"Perfectly fine." She carried her one little box that was marked COOKBOOKS on the side into the third bedroom and gasped when she saw an antique oak desk against one wall, with a leather office chair behind it and a tall four-drawer filing cabinet in the corner.

She set the box down and went across the hallway to find a four-poster bed all made up and ready for her to crawl into that night. The matching dresser had a huge mirror above it, and a rocking chair had been placed under the window.

"I feel like I'm moving into a five-star hotel," she said.

Flint beamed. "If there's anything you want moved or rearranged, just let me know and I'll fix it for you."

"It's all perfect," she whispered, "more than I ever dreamed about."

Flint drew her close to his chest, then kissed her long and passionately. "Welcome home, Jasmine Thurman. I hope you're as happy as I am here on the Promised Land."

"My heart tells me that I will be," she said.

Epilogue

One year later

"WHAT DID FLINT GIVE YOU THIS YEAR FOR VALENTINE'S?" Pearl asked.

"It was tough to outdo last year's present, when he gave me a set of keys to the house, the barn, and all the vehicles, and a bouquet of wildflowers," Jasmine said as she looked into the makeup mirror on the worktable in the tack room. "This year's gift is going to be his wedding vows. I'm giving him the same thing."

Pearl removed the rollers from Jasmine's hair while she put on her makeup. "I can't believe y'all waited a whole year to tie the knot."

"I wanted to be sure, not just for myself but for Flint." Jasmine finished the last touch and twisted her hair up into a bunch of curls. "Now you can put the ringlet of baby roses on for me and pin it down."

"We've only got about thirty minutes until…" Pearl said.

Jasmine's sister, Kathleen, came into the tack room with a disgusted look on her face. "I can't believe you're getting married in a barn, of all things, and getting ready in a nasty room like this."

"I'll have you know"—Jasmine shook her finger at Kathleen—"Flint scrubbed this room until there's not a speck of dirt or dust anywhere, and why wouldn't a rancher get married in a barn?"

"But you have arrived." Kathleen set her mouth in a firm line. "Your first cookbook hit the market in a big way, and you've been on television talk shows. I hated that title, but it's growing on me. *Chicken Fried* just didn't seem like a decent thing to name your first book, but who am I to argue with success?" She sighed. "Even if you are too stubborn to go on a book tour."

"The second one will be out by Easter, and it's called *The Promised Land Ranch Cookbook*," Pearl told Kathleen.

"Well, it's your life, but you could be a lot bigger than you are if you'd do a little more with your life than live on this godforsaken…"

Jasmine took a couple of steps back, put her hand over her heart, and rolled her eyes toward the rafters. "Be careful. There's not a dark cloud in the sky today, but honey, I don't want to be standing beside you right here on the Promised Land when you say it's godforsaken. If lightning comes through that ceiling, I might even run out there to the barn and hurry up and marry Flint in this robe before the place burns down."

"Hmphhh!" Kathleen huffed. "You always were a smart-ass. Get your dress on."

"Have you talked to Flint?" Jasmine asked.

"He's nervous, and good grief, Jasmine, where are your shoes?" Kathleen pointed to the dress hanging on the door leading into the small bathroom and the cowboy boots sitting on the floor.

"I'm wearing boots." Jasmine dropped her robe and slipped into the straight champagne-colored dress that was covered with lace.

Pearl zipped it up the back and then dropped to her knees to help Jasmine put on the boots. "You look amazing, girlfriend."

"Thank you." Jasmine smiled and shot a look over at her sister.

"If you like the flower-child look, I suppose you do look

all right." Kathleen sighed. "I had eight bridesmaids and a designer dress that had a twelve-foot train. Mama still shows off the pictures every chance she gets."

"Sister, you wanted a wedding." Jasmine crossed the room and gave her an air kiss on the cheek. "I want a marriage, and"—she lowered her voice—"I'm sure that when the baby gets here, Mama will have plenty of pictures to show off."

"You're pregnant?" Kathleen's eyes got so wide that Jasmine thought for a minute they would pop out and roll around on the floor. "I'm the oldest. I should have the first grandchild."

"Too bad, honey," Jasmine said. "This little rancher is due the first of September. He or she will be just the right size for cute Christmas pictures. Don't be upset. You are going to be an aunt."

"Does Mama know?" Kathleen asked.

"Not yet, but she will right after the wedding. I'll tell her at the reception, and if you say a word before I get to tell her, I won't ever speak to you again," Jasmine said.

Pearl put Jasmine's bouquet in her hand just as the music started playing. "It's time for me and Kathleen to lead the way for you. Be as happy as I am, and, FYI, I'm going to be an aunt too."

"Thank you." Jasmine took the bouquet.

Sam poked his head in the door. "I hear there's a beautiful bride waiting for this homely old cowboy to walk her down the aisle."

"No, sir, she's waiting on a handsome cowboy who will never be old in her eyes to escort her down the aisle." Jasmine looped her arm in his. "Thank you for doing this for me, Sam. I hope my dad is looking down through the holes in the floors of heaven and can see how happy I am."

"I'm sure he is, darlin' girl," Sam said, "and I'm downright honored to get to do this."

―――――――――

Flint had been so nervous he could hardly stand still, right up until the time he could see Jasmine coming down the aisle. Then, a peace settled over him, and everyone in the room seemed to disappear. Like it had been for the last year, if he was with her, everything was fine.

"Who gives this woman to be married to this man?" the preacher asked.

"I do, with honor and pride," Sam answered as he took Flint's hand and put Jasmine's in it. "Love each other. Trust each other. Lean on each other. Just like you've done this past year."

"Yes, sir," Jasmine and Flint said in unison.

Flint didn't wait for the preacher to go on, but drew Jasmine a little closer, looked deep into her eyes, and said, "I didn't believe in fate or love at first sight until a year ago, but I do now. I think I fell in love with you when I came close to plowing right into the café porch and you stepped outside. I'm convinced that fate caused that dog to make me stop in Ringgold, and I'm so glad it did. Jasmine, without you my life would be empty and my heart nothing but a shell. I love you with my whole being and will forever."

Jasmine handed her bouquet off to Pearl, slipped her free hand into Flint's so that she was holding both of his hands, and said, "Flint, if someone would have told me a series of events was about to happen that day that would turn my life and my heart around, I would have thought they'd been sippin' too much moonshine," she said.

Everyone in the barn chuckled.

"But I'm so glad it did because I'm just reaffirming that you have my whole heart today and forever. You've had it since the morning you said you'd stay and work for me until the new owner of my café arrived. I love you and this life we are building right here on the Promised Land Ranch."

"Well, I don't know if there's much more I need to say,"

the preacher said, "but I would like to read a verse from Romans: 'Be devoted to one another in love. Honor one another above yourselves.'" He went on with the traditional giving and taking of the rings and the rest of the ceremony and ended with "Flint, you may kiss your bride."

Flint bent her backward in a true Hollywood kiss and whispered, "I love you, Mrs. Walker." He straightened her up and pulled her close with his arm around her waist.

"I'd like to introduce to all of you for the first time ever Mr. and Mrs. Flint Walker," the preacher said.

Amid the applause, they walked together down the aisle and to the other side of the barn where the reception was set up.

"Happy Valentine's Day." Flint kissed her again. "And darlin', you are the most beautiful bride in the whole world. I love the dress, the boots, your hair, and everything about you."

"You look pretty sexy yourself, all fancied up in your black suit and your shiny boots"—she leaned in to whisper—"but I'd rather be naked with you in our big bed than be all dolled up in our fancy wedding clothes."

Flint laughed out loud. "Darlin', you read my mind."

Can't get enough of Carolyn Brown's
hilarious Southern fiction? Read on for
an excerpt from *The Sisters Café*.

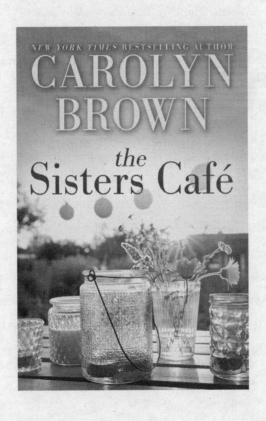

Chapter 1

IF PRISSY PARNELL HADN'T MARRIED BUSTER JONES AND LEFT Cadillac, Texas, for Pasadena, California, Marty wouldn't have gotten the speeding ticket. It was all Prissy's damn fault that Marty was in such a hurry to get to the Blue-Ribbon Jalapeño Society monthly meeting that night, so Prissy ought to have to shell out the almost two hundred dollars for that ticket.

They were already passing around the crystal bowl to take up the voting ballots when Marty slung open the door to Violet Prescott's sunroom and yelled, "Don't count 'em without my vote."

Twenty faces turned to look at her and not a one of them, not even her twin sister, Cathy, was smiling. Hell's bells, who had done spit on their cucumber sandwiches before she got there, anyway? A person didn't drop dead from lack of punctuality, did they?

One wall of the sunroom was glass and looked out over lush green lawns and flower gardens. The other three were covered with shadow boxes housing the blue ribbons that the members had won at the Texas State Fair for their jalapeño pepper entries. More than forty shadow boxes all reminding the members of their history and their responsibility for the upcoming year. Bless Cathy's heart for doing her part. She had a little garden of jalapeños on the east side of the lawn and nurtured them like children. The newest shadow box held ribbons that she'd earned for the club with her pepper jelly and picante. It was the soil, or maybe she told them bedtime stories, but she, like her mamma and grandma, grew the hottest jalapeños in the state.

"It appears that Martha has decided to grace us with her presence once again when it is time to vote for someone to take our dear Prissy's place in the Blue-Ribbon Jalapeño Society. We really should amend our charter to state that a member has to attend more than one meeting every two years. You could appreciate the fact that we did amend it once to include you in the membership with your sister, who, by the way, has a spotless attendance record," Violet said.

Violet, the queen of the club, as most of the members called it, was up near eighty years old, built like SpongeBob SquarePants, and had stovepipe jet-black hair right out of the bottle. Few people had the balls or the nerve to cross her, and those who did were put on her crap list right under Martha, aka Marty, Andrews's name, which was always on the top.

Back in the beginning of the club days, before Marty was even born, the mayor's wife held the top position on the crap list. When they'd formed the Blue-Ribbon Jalapeño Society, Loretta Massey and Violet almost went to war over the name of the new club. Loretta insisted that it be called a society, and Violet wanted it to be called a club. Belonging to a club just sounded so much fancier than saying that one belonged to a society. Loretta won when the vote came in, but Violet called it a club anyway and that's what stuck. Rumor had it that Violet was instrumental in getting the mayor ousted just so they'd have to leave Grayson County and Loretta would have to quit the club.

Marty hated it when people called her Martha. It sounded like an old woman's name. What was her mother thinking anyway when she looked down at two little identical twin baby daughters and named them after her mother and aunt— Martha and Catherine? Thank God she'd at least shortened their names to Marty and Cathy.

Marty shrugged, and Violet snorted. Granted, it was a ladylike snort, but it still went right along with her round face and three-layered neck. Hell, if they wanted to write forty amendments to the charter, Marty would still do only the bare necessities to keep her in voting standing. She hadn't even wanted to be in the damned club and had only done it because if she didn't, then Cathy couldn't.

Marty slid into a seat beside her sister and held up her ballot.

Beulah had the bowl in hand and was ready to hand it off to Violet to read off the votes. But she passed it to the lady on the other side of her and it went back around the circle to Marty, who tossed in her folded piece of paper. If she'd done her homework and gotten the numbers right, that one vote would swing the favor for Anna Ruth to be the new member of the club. She didn't like Anna Ruth, especially since she'd broken up her best friend's marriage. But hey, Marty had made a deathbed promise to her mamma, and that carried more weight than the name of a hussy on a piece of paper.

The bowl went back to Violet, and she put it in her lap like the coveted jeweled crown of a reigning queen. "Our amended charter states that only twenty-one women can belong to the Blue-Ribbon Jalapeño Society at any one time, and the only time we vote a new member in is when someone moves or dies. Since Prissy Parnell got married this past week and moved away from Grayson County, we are open for one new member. The four names on the ballet are: Agnes Flynn, Trixie Matthews, Anna Ruth Williams, and Gloria Rawlings."

Even though it wasn't in the fine print, everyone knew that when attending a meeting, the members should dress for the occasion, which meant pantyhose and heels. Marty could feel nineteen pairs of eyes on her. It would have been twenty, but Violet was busy fishing the first ballot from the fancy bowl.

Marty threw one long leg over the other and let the bright red three-inch high-heeled shoe dangle on her toe. They could frown all they wanted. She was wearing a dress, even if it only reached mid-thigh, and had black spandex leggings under it. If they wanted her to wear pantyhose, they'd better put a second amendment on that charter and make it in big print.

God Almighty, but she'd be glad when her great-aunt died and she could quit the club. But it looked like Agnes was going to last forever, which was no surprise. God sure didn't want her in heaven, and the devil wouldn't have her in hell.

"One vote for Agnes," Violet said aloud.

Beulah marked that down on the minutes and waited.

Violet enjoyed her role as president of the club and took

her own sweet time with each ballot. Too bad she hadn't dropped dead or at least moved to California so Cathy could be president. Marty would bet her sister would get those votes counted a hell of a lot faster.

There was one piece of paper in the candy dish when Beulah held up a hand. "We've got six each for Agnes, Trixie, Anna Ruth, and two for Gloria. Unless this last vote is for Agnes, Trixie, or Anna Ruth, we have a tie, and we'll have to have a runoff election."

"Shit!" Marty mumbled.

Cathy shot her a dirty look.

"Anna Ruth," Violet said and let out a whoosh of air.

A smile tickled the corner of Marty's mouth.

Saved, by damn!

Agnes was saved from prison.

Violet was saved from attending her own funeral.

The speeding ticket was worth every penny.

―――――――――――

Trixie poked the black button beside the nursing home door and kicked yellow and orange leaves away as she reached for the handle. She heard the familiar click as the lock let go and then heard someone yell her name.

"Hey, Trixie. Don't shut it. We are here," Cathy called out.

Trixie waved at her two best friends: Cathy and Marty Andrews. Attitude and hair color kept them from being identical. They were five feet ten inches tall and slim built, but Cathy kept blond highlights in her brown hair and Marty's was natural. In attitude, they were as different as vanilla and chocolate. Cathy was the sweet twin who loved everyone and had trouble speaking her mind. Marty was the extrovert who called the shots like she saw them. Cathy was engaged, and Marty said there were too many cowboys she hadn't taken to bed to get herself tied down to one man.

Marty threw an arm around Trixie's shoulder as they marched down the wide hall. Trixie's mother, Janie Matthews, had checked herself into the nursing home four years before when her Alzheimer's had gotten so bad that she didn't know Trixie one day. Trixie had tried to talk her mother into living with her, but Janie was lucid enough to declare that she couldn't live alone and her daughter had to work.

"Congratulations, darlin', you did not make it into the club tonight. Your life has been spared until someone dies or moves away and Cathy nominates you again," Marty said.

"Well, praise the Lord," Trixie said.

"I know. Let's string Cathy up by her toenails and

force-feed her fried potatoes until her wedding dress won't fit for even putting your name in the pot." Marty laughed.

"Trixie would be a wonderful addition to the club. She wouldn't let Violet run her around like a windup toy. That's why I keep nominating her every chance I get," Cathy said. "Anna Ruth is going to be a brand-new puppet in Violet's hands. Every bit as bad as Gloria would have been."

Trixie stopped so fast that Marty's hand slipped off her shoulder. "Anna Ruth?"

"Sorry." Cathy shrugged. "I'm surprised that she won, and she only did by one vote."

Trixie did a head wiggle. "Don't the world turn around? My mamma wasn't fit for the club because she had me out of wedlock. And now Anna Ruth is living with my husband without a marriage certificate, and she gets inducted. If she has a baby before they marry, do they have a big divorce ceremony and kick her out?"

"I never thought she'd get it," Cathy said. "I don't know how in the world I'm going to put up with her in the club, knowing that she's the one that broke up your marriage."

Trixie paled. "Who's going to tell Agnes that she didn't get it again? Lord, she's going to be an old bear all week."

"That's Beulah's job. She nominated her. I'm just damn

glad I have a class tonight. Maybe the storm will be over before I get home," Marty said.

Cathy smiled weakly. "And I've got dinner with Ethan back at Violet's in an hour."

"I'm not even turning on the lights when I get home. Maybe she'll think I've died." Trixie started walking again.

"You okay with the Anna Ruth thing?" Marty asked.

Trixie nodded. "Can't think of a better thing to happen to y'all's club."

"It's not my club," Marty said. "I'm just there so Cathy can be in it. I'm not sure Violet would let her precious son marry a woman who wasn't in the al-damn-mighty Blue-Ribbon Jalapeño Society. I still can't believe that Violet is okay with her precious son marrying one of the Andrews twins."

Cathy pointed a long slender finger at her sister. "Don't you start with me! And I'm not the feisty twin. You are. I can't see Violet letting Ethan marry you for sure."

"Touchy, are we? Well, darlin' sister, I wouldn't have that man, mostly because I'd have to put up with Violet." Marty giggled.

"Shh, no fighting. It'll upset Mamma." Trixie rapped gently on the frame of the open door and poked her head inside a room. "Anyone at home?"

Janie Matthews clapped her hands, and her eyes lit up. She and Trixie were mirror images of each other—short, slim built, light brown hair, milk chocolate-colored eyes, and delicate features. Trixie wore her hair in a chin-length bob, and Janie's was long, braided, and wrapped around her head in a crown. Other than that and a few wrinkles around Janie's eyes, they looked more like sisters than mother and daughter.

"Why, Clawdy Burton, you've come to visit. Sit down, darlin', and let's talk. You aren't still mad at me, are you?"

Marty crossed the room and sat down beside Janie on the bed, leaving the two chairs in the room for Cathy and Trixie. It wasn't the first time Janie had mistaken her for Claudia, the twins' mother, or the first time that she'd remembered Claudia by her maiden name either.

"I brought some friends," Marty said.

"Any friend of Clawdy's is a friend of mine. Come right in here. You look familiar. Did you go to school with me and Clawdy?" Janie looked right at her daughter.

"I did," Trixie said.

Janie's brow furrowed. "I can't put a name with your face."

"I'm Trixie."

Janie shook her head. "Sorry, honey, I don't remember you. And you?" She looked into Cathy's eyes.

"She's my sister, Cathy, remember?" Marty asked.

"Well, ain't that funny. I never knew Clawdy to have a sister. You must be older than we are, but I can see the resemblance."

"Yes, ma'am, I didn't know you as well as"—Cathy paused—"my little sister did, but I remember coming to your house."

"Did Mamma make fried chicken for you?"

"Oh, honey, I've eaten fried chicken more than once at your house," Cathy said.

"Good. Mamma makes the best fried chicken in the whole world. She and Clawdy's mamma know how to do it just right. Now, Clawdy, tell me you aren't mad at me. I made a mistake runnin' off with Rusty like that, but we can be friends now, can't we?"

Marty patted her on the arm. "You know I could never stay mad at you."

"I'm just so glad you got my letter and came to visit." Janie looked at Trixie and drew her eyes down. "You look just like a girl I used to know. It's right there on the edge of my mind, but I've got this remembering disease. That's why I'm in here, so they can help me." She turned her attention back to Marty. "You really aren't mad at me anymore?"

"Of course not. You were in love with Rusty, or you wouldn't have run off with him," Marty said. They had this conversation often, so she knew exactly what to say.

"I did love him, but he found someone new, so I had to bring my baby girl and come on back home. How are your girls?" She jumped at least five years from thinking she and Claudia were in school to the time when they were new mothers.

"They're fine. Let's talk about you," Marty said.

Janie yawned. "Clawdy, darlin', I'm so sorry, but I can't keep my eyes open anymore."

It was always the same. On Wednesday nights, Trixie visited with Janie. Sometimes, when they had time between closing the café and their other Wednesday evening plans, Marty and Cathy went with her. And always after fifteen or twenty minutes, on a good night, she was sleepy.

"That's okay, Janie. We'll come see you again soon," Marty said.

Trixie stopped at the doorway and waved.

Janie frowned. "I'm sorry I can't remember you. You remind me of someone I knew a long time ago, but I can't recall your name. Were you the Jalapeño Jubilee queen this year? Maybe that's where I saw you."

"No, ma'am. They don't crown queens anymore. But it's okay. I remember you real well," Trixie said.

━━━━━━━━━━

Less than half an hour later, Trixie parked beside a big two-story house sitting on the corner of Main and Fourth in Cadillac, Texas. The sign outside the house said *Miss Clawdy's Café* in fancy lettering. Above it were the words: *Red Beans and Turnip Greens.*

Most folks in town just called it Clawdy's.

It had started as a joke after Cathy and Marty's mamma, Claudia, died and the three of them were going through her recipes. They'd actually been searching for "the secret," but evidently Claudia took it to the grave with her.

More than forty years ago, Grayson County and Fannin County women were having a heated argument over who could grow the hottest jalapeños in North Texas. Idalou Thomas, over in Fannin County, had won the contest for her jalapeño corn bread and her jalapeño pepper jelly so many years that most people dropped plumb out of the running. But that year, Claudia's mamma decided to try a little something different, and she watered her pepper plants with the water she used to rinse out her unmentionables. That was the very year that Fannin County lost their title in all of the jalapeño categories to Grayson County at the Texas State Fair. They brought home a blue ribbon in every category that had anything to do with growing or cooking with jalapeño peppers. That was also the year that Violet Prescott and several other women formed the Blue-Ribbon Jalapeño Society. The next fall, they held their First Annual Blue-Ribbon Jalapeño Society Jubilee in Cadillac, Texas.

The Jubilee got bigger and bigger with each passing year. They added vendors and a kiddy carnival with rides and a Ferris wheel, and people started marking it on their calendar a year in advance. It was talked about all year, and folks planned their vacation time around the Jalapeño Jubilee. Idalou died right after the first Jubilee, and folks in Fannin County almost brought murder charges against Claudia's mamma for breaking poor old Idalou's heart. Decades went by before Claudia figured out how her mother grew such red-hot peppers, and when her mamma passed, she carried on the tradition.

But she never did write down the secret for fear that one of the Fannin County women would find a way to steal it. The one thing she did was dry a good supply of seeds from the last crop of jalapeños just in case she died that year. It wasn't likely that Fannin County would be getting the blue ribbon back as long as one of her daughters grew peppers from the original stock and saved seeds back each year.

"If we had a lick of sense, we'd all quit our jobs and put a café in this big old barn of a house," Cathy had said.

"Count me in," Marty had agreed.

Then they found the old LP albums in Claudia's bedroom, and Cathy had picked up an Elvis record and put it on the turntable. When she set the needle down, "Lawdy, Miss Clawdy" had played.

"Daddy called her that, remember? He'd come in from working all day and holler for Miss Clawdy to come give him a kiss," Marty had said.

Trixie had said, "That's the name of y'all's café—Miss Clawdy's Café. It can be a place where you fix up this buffet bar of Southern food for lunch. Like fried chicken, fried catfish, breaded and fried pork chops, and always have beans and greens on it seasoned up with lots of bacon drippings. You know, like your mamma always cooked. Then you can serve her pecan cobbler, peach cobbler, and maybe her black forest cake for dessert."

"You are making me hungry right now just talkin' about beans and greens. I can't remember the last time I had that kind of food," Marty had said.

Trixie went on, "I bet there's lots of folks around here who can't remember when they had it either with the fast-food trend. Folks would come from miles and miles to get at a buffet where they could eat all they wanted of good old Southern fried and seasoned food. And you can frame up a bunch of those old LP covers and use them to decorate the walls. And you could transfer the music from those records over to CDs and play that old music all day. You could serve breakfast from the menu and then a lunch buffet. It would make a mint, I swear it would."

That started the idea that blossomed into a café on the ground floor of the big two-story house. The front door opened into the foyer where they set up a counter with a cash register. To the left was the bigger dining area, which had been the living room. To the right was the smaller one, which had been the dining room. What had been their mother's sitting room now seated sixteen people and was used for special lunch reservations. Their dad's office was now a storage pantry for supplies.

Six months later and a week before Miss Clawdy's Café had its grand opening, Trixie caught Andy cheating on her, and she quit her job at the bank to join the partnership. That was a year ago, and even though it was a lot of work, the café really was making money hand over fist.

"Hey, good lookin'," a deep voice said from the shadows when she stepped up on the back porch.

"I didn't know if you'd wait or not," Trixie said.

Andy ran the back of his hand down her jawline. "It's Wednesday, darlin'. Until it turns into Thursday, I would wait. Besides, it's a pleasant night. Be a fine night for the high school football game on Friday."

Trixie was still pissed at Andy and still had dreams about strangling Anna Ruth, but sex was sex, and she was just paying Anna Ruth back. She opened the back door, and together they crossed the kitchen. He followed her up the stairs to the second floor, where there were three bedrooms and a single bathroom. She opened her bedroom door, and once he was inside, she slammed it shut and wrapped her arms around his neck.

"I miss you," he said.

She unbuttoned his shirt and walked him backward to the bed. "You should have thought about that."

"What if I break it off with Anna Ruth?"

"We've had this conversation before." Trixie flipped a couple of switches, and those fancy no-fire candles were suddenly burning beside the bed.

He pulled her close and kissed her. "You are still beautiful."

She pushed him back on the bed. "You are still a lyin', cheatin' son of a bitch."

He sat up and peeled out of his clothes. "Why do you go to bed with me if I'm that bad?"

"Because I like sex."

"I wish you liked housework," Andy mumbled.

"If I had, we might not be divorced. If my messy room offends you, then put your britches back on and go home to Anna Ruth and her sterile house," Trixie said.

"Shut up and kiss me." He grinned.

She shucked out of her jeans and T-shirt and jumped on the bed with him. They'd barely gotten into the foreplay when a hard knock on the bedroom door stopped the process as quickly as if someone had thrown a pitcher of icy water into the bed with them. Trixie grabbed for the sheet and covered her naked body; Andy strategically put a pillow in his lap.

"I thought they were all out like usual," he whispered. "If that's Marty, we are both dead."

"Maybe they called off her class for tonight," Trixie said.

"Cadillac police. Open this door right now, or I'm coming in shooting."

Trixie groaned. "Agnes?"

Andy groaned and fell back on the pillows. "Dear God!"

And that's when flashing red, white, and blue lights and the mixed wails of police cars, sirens, and an ambulance all screeched to a halt in front of Miss Clawdy's.

Trixie grabbed her old blue chenille robe from the back of a rocking chair and belted it around her waist. "Agnes, is that you?"

"It's the Cadillac police, I tell you, and I'll come in there shooting if that man who's molesting you doesn't let you go right this minute." Agnes tried to deepen her voice, but there was just so much a seventy-eight-year-old woman could do. She sounded like a prepubescent boy with laryngitis.

"I'm coming right out. Don't shoot."

She eased out the door, and sure enough, there was Agnes, standing in the hallway with a sawed-off shotgun trained on Trixie's belly button.

The old girl had donned her late husband's pleated trousers and a white shirt and smelled like a mothball factory. Her dyed hair, worn in a ratted hairdo reminiscent of the sixties, was crammed up under a fedora. Enough curls had escaped to float around the edges of the hat and remind Trixie of those giant statues of Ronald McDonald. The main difference was that she had a shotgun in her hands instead of a hamburger and fries.

Trixie shut her bedroom door behind her and blocked it as best she could. "There's no one in my bedroom, Agnes. Let's go downstairs and have a late-night snack. I think there are hot rolls left and half of a peach cobbler."

"The hell there ain't nobody in there! I saw the bastard. Stand to one side, and I'll blow his ass to hell." Agnes raised the shotgun.

"You were seeing me do my exercises before I went to bed."

Agnes narrowed her eyes and shook her head. "He's in there. I can smell him." She sniffed the air. "Where is the sorry son of a bitch? I could see him in there throwing you on the bed and having his way with you. Sorry bastard, he won't get away. Woman ain't safe in her own house."

Trixie moved closer to her. "Look at me, Agnes. I'm not hurt. It was just shadows, and what you smell is mothballs. Shit, woman, where'd you get that getup, anyway?"

Agnes shook her head. "He told you to say that or he'd kill you. He don't scare me." She raised the barrel of the gun and pulled the trigger. The kickback knocked her square on her butt on the floor, and the gun went scooting down the hallway.

"Next one is for you, buster," she yelled as plaster, insulation, and paint chips rained down upon her and Trixie.

Trixie grabbed both ears. "God Almighty, Agnes!"

"Bet that showed him who is boss around here, and if you don't quit usin' them damn cussin' words, takin' God's name in vain, I might aim the gun at you next time. And I don't have to tell a smart-ass like you where I got my getup, but I was tryin' to save your sorry ass so I dressed up like a detective," Agnes said.

Trixie grabbed Agnes's arm, pulled her up, and kept her moving toward the stairs. "Well, you look more like a homeless bum."

Agnes pulled free and stood her ground, arms crossed over her chest, the smell of mothballs filling up the whole landing area.

"We've got to get out of here in a hurry," Trixie tried to whisper, but it came out more like a squeal.

"He said he'd kill you, didn't he?" Agnes finally let herself be led away. "I knew it, but I betcha I scared the shit out of him. He'll be crawling out the window and the police will catch him. Did you get a good look at the bastard? We'll go to the police station and do one of them drawin' things, and they'll catch him before he tries a stunt like that again."

They met four policemen, guns drawn, serious expressions etched into their faces, in the kitchen. Every gun shot up and pointed straight at Agnes and Trixie.

Trixie threw up her hands, but Agnes just glared at them.

"Jack, it's me and Agnes. This is just a big misunderstanding."

Living right next door to the Andrews house his whole life, Jack Landry had tagged along with Trixie, Marty, and Cathy their whole growing-up years. He lowered his gun and raised an eyebrow.

"Nothing going on upstairs, I assure you," Trixie said, and she wasn't lying. Agnes had put a stop to what was about to happen for damn sure.

Trixie hoped the old girl had an asthma attack from the mothballs as payment for ruining her Wednesday night.

"We heard a gunshot," Jack said.

"That would be my shotgun. It's up there on the floor. Knocked me right on my ass. I forgot that it had a kick. Loud sumbitch messed up my hearing." Agnes hollered and reached up to touch her kinky hair. "I lost my hat when I fell down. I've got to go get it."

Trixie saw the hat come floating down the stairs and tackled it on the bottom step. "Here it is. You dropped it while we were running away."

Agnes screamed at her. "You lied! You said we had to get away from him before he killed us, and I ran down the stairs, and I'm liable to have a heart attack, and it's your fault. I told

Cathy and Marty not to bring the likes of you in this house. It's an abomination, I tell you. Divorced woman like you hasn't got no business in the house with a couple of maiden ladies."

"Miz Agnes, one of my officers will help you across the street." Jack pushed a button on his radio and said, "False alarm at Miss Clawdy's."

A young officer was instantly at Agnes's side.

Agnes eyed the fresh-faced fellow. "You lay a hand on me, and I'll go back up there and get my gun. I know what you rascals have on your mind all the time, and you ain't goin' to skinny up next to me. I can still go get my gun. I got more shells right here in my britches' pockets."

"Yes, ma'am. I mean, no, ma'am. I'm just going to make sure you get across the street and into your house safely," he said.

Trixie could hear the laughter behind his tone, but not a damn bit of it was funny. Andy was upstairs. The kitchen was full of men who worked for him, and if Cathy and Marty heard there were problems at Clawdy's, they could come rushing in at any time.

"Maiden ladies my ass," Trixie mumbled. "I'm only thirty-four."

Darla Jean had finished evening prayers and was on her way back down the hallway from the sanctuary to her apartment. Her tiny one-bedroom apartment was located in the back of the old convenience store and gas station combination. Set on the corner lot facing Main Street, it had served the area well until the Walmart Supercenter went in up in Sherman. Five years before when business got too bad to stay open, her uncle shut the doors. Then he died and left her the property at a time when she was ready to retire from her "escort" business. She had been worrying about what to listen to: her heart or her brain. The heart said she should give up her previous lifestyle and start to preach like her mamma wanted her to do back when she was just a teenager. Her brain said that she'd made a good living in the "escort" business and she would be a damn fine madam.

The gas station didn't look much like a brothel, but she could see lots of possibilities for a church. It seemed like an omen, so she turned it into the Christian Nondenominational Church and started preaching the word of God. Main Street ran east and west through Cadillac and north and south streets were numbered. The church sat on the corner of Fourth and Main streets, facing Main. Straight across Main was the Cadillac Community Building, and across Fourth was Miss Clawdy's Café.

She hadn't even made it to her apartment door when the noisy sirens sounded like they were driving right through the doors of her church sanctuary. She stopped and said a quick prayer in case it was the rapture and God had decided to send Jesus back to Earth with all the fanfare of police cars and flashing lights. The Good Book didn't say just how he'd return, and Darla Jean had an open mind about it. If he could be born in a stable the first time around, then he could return in a blaze of flashing red, white, and blue lights the second time.

She pulled back the mini blinds in her living room. The police were across the street at Miss Clawdy's. At least Jesus wasn't coming to whisk her away that night. There was only one car in the parking lot, like most Wednesday nights, and she knew who drove that car. Hopefully, the hullabaloo over there was because Trixie had finally taken her advice and thrown the man out.

God didn't take too kindly to a woman screwing around with another woman's man. Not even if the woman had been married to him and the "other woman" wasn't married to him yet. Maybe it was a good thing that Jesus wasn't riding in a patrol car that night. She'd hate for her friend Trixie to be one of those *Left Behind* folks.

"Got to be a Bible verse somewhere to support that. Maybe I could find something in David's history of many wives that would help me get through to her," she muttered as she hurried out a side door and across Fourth Street toward the café.

"Holy Mother of Jesus, has Marty come home early and caught Andy over there and murdered him?" Darla Jean mumbled.

Had the cops arrived in all the noisy fanfare to take her away in handcuffs?

Then she saw a policeman leading Agnes across the street. So it hadn't been Marty but Agnes who'd done the killing. That meant Trixie was dead. Agnes had never liked her, and she'd threatened to kill her on more than one occasion. Now the policeman was leading her across Main Street to her house, probably so she could get out of that crazy costume and back into her regular clothes. Lord, have mercy! The twins were going to faint when they found out.

It looked like an old man, but it had to be Agnes. There wasn't another person in the whole town of Cadillac that had hair like that. Darla Jean stopped so quick in the middle of Fourth Street that she pulled the toe piece out of a flip-flop, got tangled in the rubber strap, and fell right on her butt, with the fall leaves from the trees around Clawdy's blowing all around her. She shook her head and didn't blink for several seconds. What in the world was Agnes doing in that getup? It wasn't Halloween for another three weeks.

———————

The minute the police were out of Clawdy's kitchen, Trixie melted into a chair and slapped both hands over her ears. Was she doomed forever to hear pigs squealing every time her heart beat? A shotgun blast in the small confines of a hallway was worse than the noise from the local boys' souped-up stereo systems in their fancy little low-slung pickup trucks chasing up and down Main Street on Saturday night.

"Shit!" she mumbled, but even that word sounded like it came out of a deep, dark tunnel.

When she looked up, her ex-husband was standing at the bottom of the stairs wearing a sheepish grin. He was fully dressed in his dark blue policeman's uniform, gun holstered, radio on his shoulder, and bits of her last scrapbook paper job stuck to his shiny black shoes. His hair was a nondescript brown and he wore it short; his eyes hazel with flecks of gold; his build solid on a five-foot-ten-inch frame. He'd missed being handsome by a frog hair, but he made up for it in pure sex appeal and charm. When he walked into a room, he brought a force with him that said, "Look at me and just wish you were with me," and when he poured on the charm, there wasn't a woman in the world who wouldn't drop her under-britches for him.

She bent down and swiped the paper remnants from his shoes. Anna Ruth would go up in flames if he tracked paper into her perfect house.

"You could vacuum," he said.

"Yes, and you could have been a good husband and not cheated on me." She followed him to the back door, picking more paper from the butt of his uniform.

He brushed a kiss across her forehead. "See you next week," he whispered before he slipped out the back door and quickly blended into the mass of milling men in uniforms.

"What happened around here? I was on my way home. Heard it on the radio. Parked over in the church lot since everything was full here," Andy asked Jack.

Jack shook his head slowly. "Agnes thought she saw someone up there fightin' with Trixie, but it wasn't nothing. Agnes told my officer that she could see shadows behind the window shades and the man threw Trixie down on the bed and was raping her."

Trixie made out every word even though it was muddled.

So it had been the candles that had brought the mothball queen across the street with her fedora and shotgun. Lord, Agnes Flynn was a meddlesome old witch. Claudia Burton Andrews had taken care of Agnes like she was her mother instead of her aunt, and she'd passed the legacy of looking after her on down to Cathy and Marty. But Trixie damn sure hadn't taken on the job of taking care of the nosy old toot, so she could keep her hair, stinky getup, and shotgun across the street.

"She wasn't defending a damn thing for me. She was just making sure nobody was getting something that she couldn't. If it had been a rapist, she would have probably insisted I share with her," Trixie muttered.

Next week she was buying blackout drapes. No telling what would happen if Anna Ruth, Andy's live-in girlfriend, found out he spent Wednesday nights in Trixie's bed. And if Agnes ever discovered it, heaven help everyone, because the whole town of Cadillac, all 1,542 people, would know about it by breakfast the next morning. Agnes had a gossip hotline that worked faster than a sophomore boy his first time.

Trixie heaved a sigh of relief when all the cop cars and the ambulance were finally gone. She'd deal with the shotgun and the hole in the ceiling later. Right then she needed a good stiff drink. She pushed the chair back, rustled around in the cabinet, and found the whiskey. She poured two fingers of Jack Daniel's in a jelly glass, added one ice cube, brushed plaster dust from her chenille robe and hair, and sat back down at the table. It was a poor substitute for a bout of good old passionate sex, but at least it warmed her insides.

Chapter 2

ANDY WAS ALMOST ACROSS FOURTH STREET WHEN, FROM the corner of his eye, he saw someone smack in the middle of the pavement. Surely some bum hadn't passed out cold. It was Wednesday, not Saturday when all the drunks came out of the mesquite and woodwork. Dammit! Had there been someone hiding in the attic and Agnes's shotgun blast wounded them? Then the person sat up and brushed leaves from their hair and clothing.

Tall and thin, she had dark hair that fell to her waist and brown eyes. In her best earning days, she'd been the cream of the crop, but gravity had begun to work on her face, and at forty, she had hung up her hooker shoes and her suitcase of sex toys.

"Good evening, Andy," Darla Jean said.

Andy extended a hand. "What in the hell are you doing sitting there? I thought you were a drunk or a dead man."

She reached up and took his hand. "I was on my way to see if you were dead, and I fell down."

He pulled her up. "Why would you think I'm dead?"

"Thanks for the hand. Figured Marty came home early from her classes, caught you, and killed you."

The woman had always intimidated the hell out of Andy. He cleared his throat. "It was Agnes, and she shot the ceiling. I got away without a scratch. I got to admit I ducked when that blast went off, though."

Darla reached out and brushed a bit of paper from his shoulder.

"Trixie all right?"

"She might appreciate you dropping by," Andy said.

"That's where I'm headed." Darla Jean kicked off the other flip-flop, leaving them both on the street.

"That is littering, and it's too late in the year to be wearing flip-flops," Andy said.

"What you were doing might be adultery, and what kind of shoes I wear is none of your business," Darla Jean said.

"I'm not married to Anna Ruth," Andy said defensively.

"But you were married to Trixie when you started sleeping

with Anna Ruth, weren't you?" Darla Jean shot over her shoulder.

Andy picked up the flip-flops and tossed them in his trunk before he drove out of the church parking lot.

———————

Trixie poured a second shot. She couldn't remember when she didn't know Marty and Cathy Andrews. Their mothers had grown up in Cadillac and were friends. Then she and the twins—and Jack Landry—had grown up together. First as toddlers in church, then as rambunctious kids, and later as teenagers. After graduation, Jack went into the Army, leaving Trixie, Cathy, and Marty to share everything: joys, tears, PMS, boyfriend troubles, divorce, sex stories, and everything in between.

Through it all, they had each other. They'd been her bridesmaids when she married Andy right out of high school. They'd been her support system when she divorced him. And now they were business partners.

Marriage to Andy had not been easy for either of them, but they'd been young and foolish. If they'd been older and wiser, they would have known that his obsession with neatness and her I-don't-give-a-shit-about-keeping-things-in-order attitude would never work. The only thing that kept their marriage together was wild, passionate sex, and his affair with Anna Ruth was the thing that ended it.

A month after the divorce was final, Trixie had run into Andy at the Walmart in Sherman, six miles north of Cadillac. His hand brushed hers, and it was all downhill from there. They couldn't keep their hands off each other any more than they could back when they were in high school.

Yep, she'd shared everything with her friends—except for Wednesday nights with Andy. Marty would kill him graveyard dead if she ever saw him in the house. Cathy was sweet enough that she'd provide the shovels to bury his sorry old ass out under the crape myrtle bushes in the backyard, and they could probably get Darla Jean to say a prayer over his body. But it was Marty who'd do the actual murder because she'd never trusted him. She said from the beginning, back when he and Trixie started dating her senior year in high school, that he'd been a player since he was old enough to talk a girl's skirt up over her belly button and he'd never change. And he'd damn sure proven her right.

"Sorry sumbitch. I'm not going to sleep with him anymore," she declared.

Darla Jean didn't knock. She never did.

"You all right, girl? I just ran into that SOB, and I did hear you say you weren't sleeping with him, didn't I?" she asked as she pushed the door open.

"You did, but I won't stick with it. You know I won't. I never do." Trixie shook her head from side to side. "The blast is still ringing in my ears, but it's getting better. Did the sirens or the shot get your attention?"

"Honey, my first thought was that the rapture had come. I even said a prayer in case Jesus returned," Darla Jean said.

Trixie looked down at Darla's feet.

"Lost 'em out on the street, but Andy couldn't leave them there to litter." She laughed. "The pavement was still warm, and the grass felt pretty good on my feet. October in Texas don't mean a person has to wear shoes, does it?"

"What would you have done if it had been the rapture?" Trixie asked.

"Well, I wouldn't be standing here if it had been. I'd have been on my way to glory. Evidently the good Lord needs me to stay here a spell longer and take care of all y'all over here at Clawdy's. Now tell me what happened and how in the world you got Andy out so slick and how come Agnes looked like she was trick-or-treating."

Trixie raised her head. "That woman is going to be the

death of all of us! Agnes was the one who called the cops and the ambulance. She thought I was being attacked in my room. I swear the old girl has a camera trained on the house. And she had a shotgun, I'm tellin' you, a real, honest-to-God loaded gun. There's a hole in the landing ceiling to prove it. And that's not even the worst of it! She dragged her dead husband's old clothes out of a mothball trunk and put them on so she'd look like a police officer. She had a fedora on top of her ratted-up hair. You should have seen her!"

Darla Jean poured a cup of coffee from the pot and heated it in the microwave while she nibbled on a leftover hot roll from lunch.

"I did see her"—she giggled— "while I was sitting on the street where I fell."

"Are you all right?" Trixie asked.

"I'm fine. Just my pride was hurt and your cheatin' husband even gave me a hand up. Who was she trying to shoot? You or Andy?" she asked.

"She blew a hole in the ceiling, and half the attic floated down on me. But it might have been a different story if I'd been holding that shotgun. We'd moved past the foreplay and were getting ready for the big production when the red, white, and blue strobes hit the window right along with the sirens."

"I wondered what all that dust was doing on you. Figured you'd taken up another hobby. You've got to start giving Andy a brushing before he leaves. He had your scrapbooking bits and pieces on him. They were shinin' on that dark uniform out there in the moonlight. You can bet if I can see them in the dark, they won't get past Anna Ruth." Darla Jean sat down at the table. "You havin' sweet tea?"

Trixie held up her glass. "I've got J.D.'s special brand of tea."

"Whiskey and another woman's man. Been there. Only difference was I got paid," Darla Jean told her.

"Oh, honey, I'm getting paid in more ways than one. I get good sex once a week, and I'm getting back at Anna Ruth at the same time. Why would he want to marry her? She can't be good in bed because if she was, he wouldn't be having sex with me every week," Trixie asked.

"Men marry for reasons other than sex. He don't need it from her long as you are puttin' out. Lord don't look kindly on a woman givin' it away to a married man."

"But it's okay if you sell it to him?" Trixie asked.

Darla Jean smiled, her big brown eyes twinkling. "Don't reckon he looks too kindly on that either or else he would have steered me in the direction of bein' a madam rather than a preacher when I quit the business. But this ain't about my past sins, Trixie Matthews! You almost got caught, girl! God is talkin' to you pretty strong. He's sayin' that if you don't give up your wickedness, he's goin' to stop talkin' and let Agnes take care of things. You want that?"

"Hell no! I'd rather face off with the devil as that old girl. But I'm not giving up my Wednesday nights either. I'll just be more careful." Trixie giggled and felt some of the pressure release in her ears.

"There's lots of men you can have sex with. Why Andy?" Darla Jean asked.

"He drives me crazy. I make him nuts. I'm messy; he's a neat freak deluxe. Perfect is barely good enough for him. Anna Ruth is the same way. But put me and Andy in a bed and, honey, it's worth taking the risk for."

———

Cathy was sitting in the back booth of the Rib Joint, a little barbecue joint in Luella, Texas, when her phone rang.

"Shoot!" she mumbled. She was right at the end of the novel that just came out by Candy Parker, and it was so hot that she actually felt the heat coming through her e-reader. She'd discovered the author four years ago and preordered all her books the day they were available. She always bought them in ebook format. She couldn't have faced Trixie or Marty if they'd known she was reading smut.

Agnes would pitch a hissy if she picked up one of Candy's books. Lord, she might have a coronary and it would be laid to Cathy's charge. Yes, ma'am, it was much easier to keep them on the e-reader. Agnes wouldn't even know how to access a book on it if she did find it lying about.

The phone rang four times, and then there was a pause before it started ringing again. Someone must be in big trouble to need to talk to her that badly.

"Hello," she said sweetly.

"This is Beulah. I called Violet, and she said you were already gone, and I called Marty but she's not answering, and there's not an answer at Clawdy's. And I'm worried plumb out of my mind. There were shots fired and the police cars, the ambulance, and the fire truck are all over at your house. I'm afraid to go outside and Jack won't answer my calls. I can just feel my blood pressure risin'. If someone has shot Jack, I don't know if I can stand it. I'm looking out the window now, and there are policemen everywhere and they're takin' Agnes... My God, what is she wearing? Cathy, she's shot Jack. And I'm afraid his black suit will be too small. Do you think they'll let me bury him in his uniform?" Beulah's voice cracked and she began to sob.

"I'll be home in five minutes, Beulah. Did you tell Agnes about the vote?" Cathy asked.

"Oh, honey, it was awful, just awful. She cussed and carried on and threatened to shoot Violet. Oh my God! Do you think she went over to Clawdy's and shot Trixie? I told her that Anna Ruth got chosen, but she was rantin' about so much that she might've thought it was Trixie who kept her from getting in the club."

"Agnes wouldn't do that even if she was mad. I'll call you. Don't worry, sweetheart—Jack is fine."

Cathy put her e-reader inside her oversized purse and headed for the door. Her high heels sunk into the gravel, and just as she got to her car, one popped clean off. She grabbed the hood to keep from falling. She hobbled around the car, crawled in, and looked longingly at her purse. A few more minutes and she'd have finished reading the chapter. She hated to stop in the middle of a scene, but it would have to wait.

She started up the car and sighed. If only her fiancé, Ethan, could be as passionate as the men that Candy Parker wrote about. It didn't matter if they were cowboys, firemen, Navy SEALS, or even mechanics. They all had one thing in common. They knew how to turn a woman on until all she could think about were their hands and lips on every part of her body.

She muttered as she drove, "So Ethan isn't passionate. He is respectable and he has morals. After we are married, he'll show more emotion. He just doesn't want to get all involved when we've agreed not to have sex until we are married."

Actually, she could read about it every chance she got, but the real thing scared the bejesus out of her. In today's world, women were not virgins at thirty-four—but Cathy was. Marty lost her virginity at the age of fifteen and came home that night to sit on her twin bed and tell Cathy every single detail.

It had all started in high school right after Marty's first bad boy cowboy talked her into a hayloft and Andy talked Trixie into the back seat of his car. It had been easy for Cathy to let them think that she had been doing it as long as either of them. It was the one thing, possibly the only thing, she kept secret from them. Well, that and her appetite for erotic romance. At first it was easy just to let them think she was bonking the guy in the library where she went every night. She never actually said that she had sex, but a little insinuation can go a long way. Like telling them that they should try doing it in between the back two bookshelves because the danger of almost getting caught was so exciting.

Then when she was thirty and they'd gone to a male strip

joint in Dallas to celebrate, she'd let them believe she was going home with Butch, the stripper cowboy in chaps, boots, and a barbed wire tat on his bicep. The next morning, she just rolled her eyes and measured out about a foot between her hands when they asked her how things went with him in the motel room. Sometimes it wasn't what you actually said but what they thought they heard.

She held her breath as she turned off State Highway 11 and down Main Street. She didn't see flashing lights or hear sirens anywhere near the café. Everything was as quiet as it was every Wednesday night when she pulled up in the driveway. She parked her car and hit the back porch in a jog, threw open the door, and there were Trixie and Darla Jean sitting at the table, cool as cucumbers.

Trixie looked at Cathy's feet. "Is this barefoot night?"

"I broke a heel getting here. Beulah called and thought someone had shot Jack in this house. She said there were police cars and even the ambulance. Please tell me they didn't park on the lawn and ruin my flower beds. In the dark I couldn't see a blessed thing and I just put the pansies out last week. They've not even had time to get adjusted to the ground."

"Your lawn is fine. The flower beds didn't lose a single petal, and the trouble was Agnes," Trixie said.

"There were police cars, the ambulance, and the fire truck. But they kept it all on the curb," Darla Jean said.

Cathy's eyes went to the glass Trixie was holding. "Tea with no ice?"

"Jack Daniel's, neat. Want one? You might need it before you go upstairs. Agnes brought her shotgun and blew a hole in the ceiling."

Cathy shook her head. She should be glad that no one was hurt, and it was all a silly mix-up, but she wasn't. She'd wanted to sit in the Rib Joint and finish her book. She'd even begged off from dessert at Ethan's, saying that she had to make sweet potato pies for Clawdy's lunch the next day and she'd best get on home to get a head start on them.

She pulled out a chair and sat down. She pushed the sleeves of her baby blue sweater up to the elbows, reached in her purse for her phone, and poked in some numbers. "I've got to call Beulah before y'all tell me the story. She thinks Jack is lyin' over here dead, and she's frettin' about whether his black suit is goin' to be too tight."

"That's Beulah," Trixie said.

Cathy finished her call and looked up. "I smell mothballs."

"Agnes called in the troops when she thought she saw someone molesting me. I had candles lit and the shades drawn. Who knows what she saw? Probably me putting on or taking off my big chenille robe, and she came over here smelling like mothballs," Trixie said.

"Smelling like what?"

"You heard me. You should have seen her, Cathy. She pulled her husband's old clothes out of a mothball trunk and put them on so the rapist would think she was the Cadillac police." Trixie reached for the whiskey to refill her glass. "Sure you don't want one?"

"After tonight it looks tempting, but no thanks," Cathy said.

"Agnes would drive a holiness preacher to whiskey. Want me to see if Andy can fix that hole in the ceiling over the weekend?"

Cathy grabbed the whiskey from her hands and put it back in the cabinet. "You stay away from that man! He cheated on you and broke your heart. I won't let him drive you into alcoholism. I mean it, Trixie!"

Darla Jean snorted when she giggled.

Trixie shot her a look that said the night wasn't over and the shotgun had not gone home yet. "Hey, don't punish me because you couldn't get me into your club shit. I wouldn't have gone to the meetings anyway, even if they had voted me in. Why in the hell would I put myself into a situation where I had to be in the same room with Anna Ruth?"

"But if you'd won, she wouldn't be there." Cathy rolled her big blue-green eyes toward the ceiling.

Trixie changed the subject. "So did you and Ethan finally get in the horizontal position tonight?"

"I told you Ethan is a gentleman. We are saving sex until our wedding night when I fully well intend to get pregnant with a son, Ethan Prescott the Fifth. Doesn't that sound classy? Ethan's middle name is Edward, so we'll probably call him that, and he's going to have blond hair and big blue eyes."

"It'll be a girl and look and act just like Marty. One of those McCleary genes might surface and she'll look like Agnes," Trixie whispered. She could hear better and her hands weren't shaking anymore. Thank God for Jack Daniel's.

"I've waited..." Cathy hesitated before she spit out anymore.

"Waited for what?" Darla Jean asked.

"A man I can trust. Someone who loves me and won't cheat on me."

Trixie held up the glass with only a few drops of whiskey in the bottom. "Touché, Cathy."

"I'm sorry, that was mean. I'm tired and cranky. I didn't sleep well last night, and I don't want to be in a club with Anna Ruth."

Trixie nodded. "You are forgiven, darlin'. I'd be pissy if I had to go out to that museum called the Prescott house and spend time with Violet every week and had to face off with Anna Ruth once a month."

Cathy fidgeted in the chair. "Violet's not so bad. She just wants the very best for her son. As bad as I want a baby, I can almost understand her, but I'm tellin' you, I'll be glad when Ethan and I are married, have our own place, and don't have to deal with her every time we are together."

"You are a pushover, girl," Trixie scolded.

"No, I'm not. I just try to be fair."

"And do you understand Anna Ruth too?" Trixie asked.

"She is enough to drive me to the whiskey bottle with you."

"And Andy? Do you feel sorry for him?" Trixie pushed.

"He doesn't deserve to be understood. He cheated on you, and I'm not going to like him. I don't want to talk about him or Agnes anymore. You promised to help me plan this wedding even though you aren't fond of Ethan. I helped you plan yours, and I didn't care much for Andy even then. At least I don't have to worry about Ethan cheating on me."

"Bravo," Darla Jean said.

"I'm so sorry. That was ugly. What is the matter with me tonight?" Cathy groaned.

"But it was true. Your mamma and y'all girls did help with my wedding. Besides, Ethan will have his hands full with two women. He wouldn't cheat on you, because that would involve a third woman in his life. He'd stroke out if he tried three," Trixie said.

Cathy raised a perfectly arched eyebrow. "Three?"

"You and Mommy Dearest are about all he'll be able to handle, especially with his campaign going on. No way would he bring in a mistress." Trixie's hearing was almost normal, and the whiskey was mellowing her out. "And, honey, even if I do think he's stuffy, I intend for you to have one helluva wedding. Three months from now you will have the biggest splash Cadillac, Texas, has ever seen. We'll even hire guards to keep the paparazzi back. It'll be bigger than the Christmas Ho-Ho-Ho. I mean, after all, you are marrying Ethan Prescott the Fourth, the richest bastard in Cadillac, Texas."

Cathy smiled. "Not the richest and not a bastard. His mamma and poppa were married."

Marty looked over the top of her laptop computer at the students in her Adult Basic Education class. She only had to lean a little to the left and there he was in the flesh: Derek, the young cowboy who was the hero in her newest work in progress. His hair was dark, his chest was broad, and those biceps were made to hold a woman. She shut her eyes just long enough to get a good solid image of him naked and then she opened them and began to type.

It had begun as an outlet while she was still teaching full time. Nowadays, she used the time she was monitoring her ABE class to catch up on writing. Her students were all full-grown adults brushing up their skills to take the GED test.

That required little actual teaching. She stacked booklets on the end of her desk, and her students picked them up at the beginning of class. They worked at their own speed and raised a hand when they needed one-on-one help. If they finished early, they put their name on the front of the booklet and gave it back to her to grade. If they didn't get it done by the time class ended, they put their name on the front and left it on the other end of her desk so they could work on it again the next week. Eight weeks to complete the class and then they took their GED test. If they passed, she never saw them again. If they didn't need a lot of help, she could get the biggest part of a rough draft done in that time.

When her first book sold and her editor asked her if she was going to write under her name or an assumed one, she made the decision to use the pseudonym Candy Parker. She didn't intend for anyone in Cadillac ever to know that she was writing erotic romance. She'd never do anything to embarrass her sister. So, Candy Parker, the erotic romance writer, was her second secret. The first being keeping Aunt Agnes out of the social club, no matter what the cost.

Class had ended, and she was standing on the sidewalk outside the college classroom building, watching Derek's cute little butt get into his truck when her phone rang. If she was ten years younger she might have a little sample of that cowboy. She didn't mind if her flings were slightly younger, but nineteen was just too danged young.

She answered the phone on the fourth ring just before it went to voicemail. "Hello."

"Marty, I just passed Clawdy's, and something has happened. There's police cars and the ambulance and the fire truck all there," said Christopher Green, a regular at the café.

"Thanks, Christopher. I'm on my way home," she said.

"Sure thing. Hope everything is all right."

"You sure it was my place or Aunt Agnes's? She lives right across the street."

"No, it was yours. They were leading Agnes back across the street. I had to stop and wait for the officer to get her across. Wouldn't have known the old girl, but that red hair can't be missed. She was wearing some kind of weird getup. Reckon she's gone off the deep end?"

"I don't have any idea, but I'm going home to see about it," Marty said.

Dammit! Agnes had never liked Trixie or Janie. Had the old girl snuck in the café and killed Trixie in her sleep? Marty didn't need a second speeding ticket in the same night so she kept a close watch on the speedometer. But when she left the main highway and entered the Cadillac city limits, she stepped on the gas. Andy or any of his town policemen wouldn't stop Marty. Most of them had lunch at Clawdy's on a regular basis, and she was the cook. They'd be afraid to give her a ticket.

She hit the back door in a dead run. "What in the hell happened? I got a call that there was an ambulance here."

"You done missed the excitement," Darla Jean said.

Marty looked at Trixie.

Trixie shrugged. "Aunt Agnes."

"Dammit, Cathy! We ought to put her in a nursing home. What'd she do—get mad over that stupid club vote and come over here to start a fight with Trixie?" Marty asked.

"She threw a fit about the club, but that wasn't the problem. And she ain't never goin' to a nursing home," Cathy said. "Mamma made me promise after Daddy died so sudden that if she went like that, we'd take care of Aunt Agnes."

Marty pulled a cold beer from the refrigerator. She'd promised her mother something about Aunt Agnes too and had gotten a speeding ticket that night, so she knew something about promises, but she damn sure didn't have to like them.

"And you're marrying Mr. Hoity-Toity and leaving me with the job. I didn't make a promise, so my way of putting up with her is to poison the old witch and then shed a fake tear at her funeral. What'd she do?" Marty leaned against the counter and looked at Trixie. "You look like hell rained down on you."

———

Trixie told the story for the third time while Marty drank two beers and swore the whole time.

Trixie pointed to the cabinet. "Cathy won't let me have

another two fingers of Jack, and I deserve it. It rained plaster dust, insulation, and who knows what from the attic. I might die from some kind of antique dust mite poisoning unless I wash all the stuff out of my system with whiskey."

Marty melted into the last chair around the table. "When you start telling jokes that aren't funny, you've had enough. I hope Aunt Agnes is constipated all day tomorrow and can't even come over here. I don't want to see her for a week."

"Marty! She was protecting Trixie. I'd say she gets a gold star for that, because she doesn't even like Trixie," Cathy exclaimed.

"Oh, stop being so nice. You know she's a meddling old woman," Marty said.

"I'm tired of this whole thing. I'm going to bed," Cathy said.

Before she could stand up, the kitchen door flew open without even a knock, and Anna Ruth blew into the room like a whirlwind. She grabbed Cathy around the neck and hugged her so tightly that Cathy's eyes bugged out, and then she headed toward Marty.

"I was so excited that we're going to be club sisters that I had to rush over here and tell you. Isn't it just the most exciting thing ever?" She beamed.

Trixie and Marty locked gazes somewhere between the

table and cabinet. It was one of those times when two life-time friends could speak without using a single word. Marty would help Trixie mop up Main Street with Anna Ruth. All Trixie had to do was nod.

"Anna Ruth, I hardly think it's appropriate for you to be—"

Anna Ruth interrupted before Cathy could finish the sentence. "Oh, don't be silly. Trixie knows that she never had a chance at the club, don't you?"

Marty stepped to one side. "What she's saying is that Clawdy's is closed."

"But we are club sisters now. I have the right to come in the kitchen and talk to my sisters," Anna Ruth protested.

"No, you don't," Trixie said.

"Tell her, Cathy. She's just mad because I won and she lost."

"Well, there is something about breaking up my marriage. Of course, it's a little thing," Trixie said.

Anna Ruth shrugged. "That doesn't count. This is about the club, for God's sake."

"I'm going back to the church. Anna Ruth, I'll walk you out." Darla looped an arm around Anna Ruth's shoulders. The small woman had no choice but to let herself be led outside. "Y'all remember to lock the door," Darla Jean said over her shoulder. "We've had enough excitement for one night on our block."

"Now I'm really going up to my room." Cathy disappeared up the stairs.

"Lord, have mercy! How many times did she shoot the ceiling? It's a mess up here," she yelled in a few seconds.

"I'll clean it up," Trixie called up the stairs.

"Go on to bed. You fended off Aunt Agnes and didn't pick up a butcher knife and kill Anna Ruth. I'll do the cleanup," Marty said.

Trixie covered a yawn with the back of her hand. "Guess I'm off to bed."

Marty nodded. When she was alone, she retrieved her laptop from her truck and opened it at the kitchen table. She only had another five thousand words, and she'd have the rough draft done, but nothing came to mind without her sexy cowboy muse.

She sat there another ten minutes before she shut the laptop. It was all Agnes's fault. She was a busybody who spied on everything that went on in the whole town of Cadillac and especially at Clawdy's. But if Agnes said she saw two people in that bedroom, then she probably did. So who in the hell was Trixie having sex with?

Chapter 3

If Agnes really had shot someone in Clawdy's the night before, they would have had to hire another cook and two more waitresses. Thursday wasn't usually a busy day at Clawdy's, but that morning Marty couldn't keep up with the orders. Cathy had to help in the kitchen, leaving Trixie to do all the waitressing and payouts at the cash register. A ruckus involving a shotgun would have been the talk of the town no matter where it happened, but Miss Clawdy's Café offered a place to sit, damn fine food, and unlimited refills on coffee. And it also gave the folks in Cadillac the opportunity to weasel more information out of Trixie. Not a bad deal for less than five dollars.

Rumor had it that Trixie and Agnes got into an argument over the voting at the social club and Agnes tried to kill her. Beulah said the cops and the ambulance were called out and that she feared that her precious son, Jack, had survived two tours of Iraq only to come home and be killed—and all because Agnes Flynn thought Trixie had gotten into the social club and she had gotten left behind for the twentieth time.

That morning, Clawdy's customers went through two extra pans of biscuits and a second gallon of sausage gravy, and Marty completely ran out of bacon and ham steaks. Everyone left full and unsatisfied, because all Trixie would say was that Agnes thought she saw someone hurting her and rushed across the street to protect her. Now that was a big crock of bullshit. Everyone knew there wasn't a smidgen of love lost between Trixie and Agnes, and there was no way in hell she would protect Trixie from anything or anyone. No, sir, that was a lie, but never fear, the gossipmongers would ferret out the truth if it absolutely killed them.

It was ten thirty when Trixie finally had time for a five-minute break and poured herself a cup of coffee. She sat down at the kitchen table with Cathy and Marty and buttered a leftover biscuit. She'd barely gotten the first bite when the back door flew open, and the faint aroma of mothballs filled the room.

"Good mornin', Aunt Agnes," Cathy said. "You had breakfast?"

"Hell yes, I've had breakfast, but that was hours ago. I wish y'all had the buffet up and ready. Now I'm ready for fried chicken."

"It's not ready, but I've got some leftovers from yesterday. You want me to pop them in the microwave?"

"Got beans and greens?" Agnes asked.

"Maybe a cup full of each."

"Two pieces of dark chicken and whatever beans and greens you've got with pepper jelly on the side for my corn bread," she said.

"You're not mad at me? I figured you'd still be mad because you were wrong last night," Trixie said.

"I don't like you enough to be mad at you, and I wasn't wrong. Somebody was in that room with you. I'm mad at Cathy," Agnes declared.

"What did I do?" Cathy asked.

"You're the one who put Trixie's name in the pot for the social club. If you hadn't done that fool thing, then there would have been the six votes for me that she got."

"And I didn't even want to be in the damned old club," Trixie said.

"How did you vote?" Agnes pointed at Marty. "I figured Cathy wouldn't betray me, but she did. I guess you did too."

Trixie waved to get everyone's attention. "Okay, Agnes, how did you vote in the last presidential election?"

"That is not one damn bit of your business," Agnes huffed.

"Point proven then," Marty said. "Voting is private."

"And Beulah should not have told you how many votes went which way," Cathy chimed in.

Agnes shook her finger at the lot of them. "I'm going to be in that social club before I die. Speakin' of which, Violet is about to put in a miserable year. It'd be in her best interest to shoot a member"—she looked right at Marty—"or find a way to make one move."

"Why don't you shoot Violet? She's the one who doesn't want you to be a member," Trixie said.

"Because I want her to be alive and well the day she has to give me that little club pin to put on my lapel that says I'm a member. Put my food in a to-go box, Marty. I've had all of y'all I want for one day. It's a cryin' damn shame when a woman's nieces treat her this way."

"You can have my pin," Marty said.

"Those are the gaudiest damn things I've ever seen! I don't know why you'd want one of the ugly things," Trixie said.

"I know! Back when Violet and Mamma designed them, they were to show the Fannin County women's club that they had bragging rights to the hottest jalapeños in the whole state. Did you know they only had twenty-one of them made and that's the reason there can't be any more members in the club than that?" Cathy said.

"I thought the original charter said twenty." Marty raised an eyebrow.

"It did, but Grandma wanted an extra one made just in case someone lost theirs. That's why they had the extra one so that we could both get in."

"Hmph," Agnes snorted. "Nobody ever lost one of those ugly things. Hell, Violet would stand at the Pearly Gates and kick them into hell if they lost a club pin."

Trixie giggled. "BR—Bitches Rule—in ruby red letters. Then the little emerald-green jalapeño, which must stand for hot as hell. And after that S in rubies. I heard that in the beginning there was a big argument and the S should be a C for club instead of an S for society."

"It stands for 'stupidity,'" Agnes said.

Brenda Lee was belting out "Sweet Nothin's" when the front door opened, and Trixie left Agnes still fussing, Cathy trying to calm her down, and Marty unloading the dishwasher.

Customers had to be waited on no matter what the kitchen drama of the day was.

"What in the hell are you doing here?" Trixie hissed when she saw Andy.

Andy bypassed the cash register counter and sat down at a table in the old dining room. "A piece of sweet potato pie and a cup of coffee. That's not a very nice line for a waitress. It won't get you a tip, even if you do look like a young version of the woman singing that song. And would you please pour the coffee and cut my slice of pie? Marty might do something evil to it. I figure if Anna Ruth is welcome here, her being a club sister and all, then I should be able to get a good meal here at Clawdy's. Right?"

"The sweet potato pie won't be ready to serve until noon. All we have left from yesterday is pecan cobbler," she said.

"My favorite. Add some of y'all's whipped cream to the top. Not any of that stuff out of the tub or the can either. I know the difference in fake and the real thing," he said.

"Don't bet on it, buster," Trixie said.

Trixie filled a bowl with cobbler, warmed it in the microwave, and then topped it off with the last of yesterday's whipped cream. She poured a cup of coffee, put both on a tray, and carried them out to Andy's table.

Damn the club anyway! She could wring Cathy's neck for putting her name on the ballot. And who in the devil *did* Marty vote for? If she had cast her vote for Anna Ruth, Trixie was selling her part of the business and moving plumb out of Cadillac.

━━━━━━━━

Clawdy's only served breakfast and lunch. Most days the lunch rush was over and done with by two and the café cleaned up by three, but that day, it was four straight up when Marty turned off the music. When the sisters got serious about converting their parents' home into a café, they used their mother's record covers for decoration and played the old music from them all day. It made a lively conversation starter when folks heard the song and tried to find the cover hanging on the wall that went with it. Thank goodness many of the old records had been remade into CDs. After that it was just a matter of buying a fancy player that held multiple CDs and changing them every night.

Marty shucked out of her jeans right in the middle of the kitchen floor and carried them to the utility room. She peeled her shirt over her head and threw it in the basket beside the washer and found an old grease-stained sweatshirt in the dryer and a pair of gray sweatpants that were stained up just as bad.

"See y'all later. I'm off to the garage. Trixie, give me your keys and I'll get the oil changed in your car before we start on the Caddy."

Trixie fished keys from her purse and tossed them. "Thanks a bunch."

Marty caught them midair. "You've got that chamber meeting, so I'll get it done while you're over at the community center. What are you doing this evening, Cathy?"

"Soon as I get out of these clothes, I'm going to make sure my flowers are all right, prune the crape myrtles, and harvest another crop of peppers before it frosts. I've got seeds, but I swear the people coming in here to eat can put away two quarts of pepper jelly a day."

"You always plant the peppers right where your grandma and mamma did?" Trixie asked.

"Oh, yes. I'd be afraid to move them anywhere else for fear they wouldn't do as well."

"I bet the secret to raisin' them hot devils is in the soil then, not in the pepper seeds."

Cathy put a finger over her lips. "Shh. I figured that out a while back, but we can't let the Fannin County women know it or they'll be digging up my dirt. I don't know what they put in that dirt, but it grows some fine jalapeños. What are you doing until chamber time?"

"I'm going to tally up today's receipts and get a bank deposit ready to put in the night drop. After the meeting, I'm going to work on my scrapbook. Mamma's birthday will be here soon, and I'm hoping the pictures will jog her memory so she'll be herself that day," Trixie answered.

"I'll see y'all later." Marty waved from the back door. She jogged from the house to the garage, a freestanding building at the back of the lot where her vintage Caddy was kept. She inhaled deeply at the door. Oil, grease, tires, and car wax. It was the most exciting thing in the world, next to a naked cowboy in a hayloft.

"Hey, you're here!" Jack's head popped up from under the hood. He already had grease on his nose and a smear across his forehead. "Must've been one helluva busy day, but then it's not every day that Agnes almost kills me, is it?"

Jack wasn't the hunky material for a hero in her book, but he was a good-looking man. His brown hair was kept in a military cut, his shoulders were wide, and the spare tire around his waist wasn't too awfully big. His hazel eyes were kind, and he'd never, not one time, let her down when she needed a friend. Like her, he could fix anything under the hood of a car. And he was a whole hell of a lot better at body-work than she was.

"How'd you get into the story?" Marty asked.

"Mamma called Violet since you weren't answering your phone and told her that shots had been fired and I was dead. Rumor has it that Agnes was doin' the shootin' and that I got shot protecting Trixie. Trixie was the dirty culprit, and the whole thing had to do with y'all's club stuff."

"It's like that game we played when we were kids and someone whispered a sentence in your ear. By the time it got to the end of the line, it was so far removed from the original that it was just plumb crazy." Marty giggled. "We need to change the oil in Trixie's car before we start on the Caddy."

"That because you feel guilty that you voted for Anna Ruth and not Agnes or Trixie?" Jack asked.

Marty sputtered and stammered, "What did you just say?"

"Mamma said that you folded your ballot and that you came in late and was the only one who put a folded one in the bowl. Don't worry, I'm not telling, and if Mamma hadn't thought I was dead, she probably wouldn't have let it slip either. She's afraid that if any of the club members find out that she let the cat out of the bag they'll kick her out. Must be something sacred goes on at those meetings. Do y'all kill a fatted calf or what?"

Marty opened the old, rounded refrigerator with rust around the door and pulled out a beer. She jerked the tab off and guzzled a third of it before coming up with an unladylike burp.

"Not bad for a skinny-ass girl." Jack laughed. "Come look at this belt. Think we ought to replace it? You going to tell me about the fatted calf?"

"I wouldn't know. The only time I show up is to vote. We'll change the belt if it needs it. Which one?"

"The long one right here," he said.

Six months before, one of the belts had blown, and Marty lost control out on a country road. A tree stopped the car, and Marty wasn't hurt, but the Caddy suffered severe front-end damage. Jack had been helping a couple of nights a week.

She carried her beer to the pegboard where belts, small spare parts, and tools were neatly arranged. She picked out the right one and laid it on the fender.

"Where's your beer?" she asked.

"I just got here a minute before you did. Alarm didn't go off when it was supposed to. Here. You put on the belt, and I'll get one," he answered.

She took a screwdriver from his hand, deftly removed

the old belt, held it up to the light, and pointed at the split. "Another mile and we'd have had a real problem. Can't have the old girl breaking down right in the middle of the Cadillac Jalapeño Jubilee parade, can we? She's been leading the pack for more than forty years."

She was putting the new belt on when the wrench popped off and her knuckles hit the engine. She jerked her hand back, shook it, and yelled, "Son of a bitch!"

"Hurt?" Jack asked.

"What the hell do you think?"

He took her hand in his, and before she could wiggle, he poured the rest of her beer right on the open cuts. "That'll heal it. You want me to put the belt on?"

"Hell no! My hand is busted up now, and I'll make a damn believer out of it all by myself. Some friend you are, pouring beer on my poor hand."

"Bubbles will clean it out. Stop your whinin' and let's get this damn thing on."

"Soon as this belt is on, we need to change the oil in Trixie's car. Should have done it to begin with, and I might not have busted my knuckles. Wipe that grin off your face. Some friend you are," Marty said.

"Ah, you know you've loved me forever," Jack teased.

He had lived right next door his whole life and he'd moved back home two years before. He'd planned on staying with the military the full twenty years, but after that last tour in Iraq, he'd had enough.

The yards were split by a white picket fence with lantana on Cathy's side and miniature roses on Beulah's side. A gate was located right in the middle of the long expanse of fence and still squeaked on its hinges like it did when Cathy, Marty, Trixie, and Jack had run back and forth between the yards and houses all their growing-up years.

"What are we going to do in the evenings when we get the Caddy completely finished?" Jack asked.

"Well, I expect we can drink beer and just sit back and enjoy our work. Long as I can prop up my feet, talk to my friend even when he teases me, and smell oil and transmission fluid, I'm a happy woman."

That time the belt slipped on as slick as if she'd greased the posts with hot butter.

"We could go over to my house and watch movies," Jack said.

"Your house don't smell like oil and transmission fluid. And I bet Beulah would pitch a hissy if we took beer in the kitchen door."

"Yes, ma'am, she would. Speakin' of kitchens?" He waggled his eyebrows.

"There's some cold fried chicken and a plate of fried fish left."

"Any of Cathy's sweet potato pie?"

"Couple of pieces and I think there's a little bit of loaded mashed potatoes left in the refrigerator."

He nodded. "I'll have both slices of that pie and I want pepper jelly for my biscuit. Ain't nobody in the world can make pepper jelly like y'all do. It's my favorite."

"With whipped cream and lots of it on the pie, right?" Marty smiled. Jack had always liked eating at her house better than his mamma's. Beulah, bless her heart, knew her way around a kitchen, but what she produced couldn't compare to Claudia Andrews's cooking.

———————

Trixie darted upstairs, took a fast shower, and dressed in black slacks, a red shirt with black lace on the scoop neck, and black high heels. She was the chamber of commerce delegate for Miss Clawdy's Café. The chamber and the city council both helped with all the festivities in Cadillac, and that night they were discussing the craft festival, which was always held the weekend before Halloween. After that there would be the Jalapeño Jubilee in November and finally the big Christmas Ho-Ho-Ho Parade and Carnival in the middle of December. Then there was the town musical in the spring between Easter and Mother's Day and the July 4th festival. Cadillac was one busy little town.

Each partner at Miss Clawdy's had a community job. Trixie had been on the chamber roster when she worked at the bank, so she was familiar with all the members and kept that place. Cathy was a member of the club and they were always big in the Jalapeño Jubilee. Marty was the secretary of the local Kiwanis Club and they did the Christmas Ho-Ho-Ho. So they all had a holiday responsibility.

Trixie looked up at the clock. She still had fifteen minutes. She might have time for a piece of cold fried fish if she ate fast. They'd have finger foods at the committee meeting. The Lord would strike Beulah Landry dead if she didn't bring her deviled eggs to every single function and Beulah, like Violet Prescott, was one of the grand matriarchs of southern Grayson County. And Annabel would bring fancy cookies. Someone else would have those little tidbits with ham and cheese rolled up in flour tortillas and cut into bite-sized pieces. In Cadillac, folks brought food to everything. It didn't matter if it was a chamber meeting, a funeral, or a baby shower. The catch was that the food wasn't served until the function was over and Trixie would starve if someone got long-winded at the chamber meeting.

Trixie grabbed a piece of fish and was about to take a bite when Agnes pushed into the kitchen. "I'm hungry. Y'all got any fish or chicken left? And I want a piece of that sweet potato pie too."

"Got some fish and a few pieces of chicken. The pie is gone. Marty carried the last two pieces out to Jack."

"Well, shit. She's probably bribin' him to keep his mouth shut about the vote." Agnes pulled down a to-go box and loaded it with chicken strips and fish.

"How would he know anything about that stupid club?"

"His mamma talks too much. Put this on my bill. I'm still not talkin' to you."

"You would have talked to Anna Ruth if y'all were in club together, though, wouldn't you? And she's not a bit better than my mamma."

"No, she's not, and when I get into the club she'd best be married to that philanderin' son of a bitch you couldn't hang on to, or I'll vote that we kick her sorry ass out. I'm leaving now because I'm not talkin' to you."

"You going to fix the ceiling?" Trixie called out when she was on her way out.

"Hell, no! I was protecting you so you can get someone to come fix the ceiling. Besides, the twins need to update the upstairs anyway. I'll never understand why they'd sink all their money into a café, for God's sake. And namin' it such a stupid name. Don't be askin' me to bail you out when it goes belly-up in this economy. Folks ain't interested in good food. They want something fast and easy," Agnes said.

"Oh, we have a backup plan, Agnes. If the café fails, we're going to change the sign to Miss Clawdy's Brothel, and underneath it's going to say, *Y'all come on in and check out our menu.* You want a job answering the phone for us?" Trixie asked.

Agnes narrowed her eyes and clucked her tongue like a hen gathering chickens in a thunderstorm. "I knew when they let you move in here there would be trouble. I swear to God you are a bad apple, girl. Only one over here worth a dime is Cathy, and that's because she's kind like her mother was. I can't believe that Claudia took one look at those two little babies and named the wrong damn one after me. Catherine should have my name. Not Marty!"

"Why thank you, Aunty Agnes, but I disagree about the

names. Marty is just like her Aunty Martha Agnes, so I think they were named right," Trixie said.

Agnes shook her bony finger at Trixie. "I'm not your aunt and if I was, I'd take you to the river and drown you."

———————

Cathy was in the yard pulling weeds away from the sweet williams and the marigolds on the east side of the house when her phone rang. She didn't even check the ID before she pulled it out of her bib overall pocket and answered it.

"Hello," she said sweetly.

"Cathy, what was going on there last night?" Ethan said.

"Agnes thought someone was in the bedroom hurting Trixie." Cathy sat down and pulled the sleeves to her sweater down to her wrists. "I was coming home when Beulah called me. She was afraid that Jack had been shot."

"Okay, then. I just had a few minutes and wanted to check on you. I've got another campaign meeting this evening. It's a busy time with the last weeks of the election. I'll see you on Saturday night."

"I love you, Ethan," Cathy said.

"Me too," he answered.

Why was it so hard for him to actually say the words "I

love you"? He had to love her, didn't he? He had proposed and they were getting married in less than two months.

Cathy put the phone back in the bib pocket and leaned back on her elbows.

The phone rang again, and she bit back a string of cuss-words that would have scorched the hair out of a bullfrog's nostrils when she saw that it was Anna Ruth.

"Hello?" she said tersely.

Marty would have loved it if she'd lost her temper and actually said all the words about to explode in her head.

"I just had to touch base with you since we're club sisters now. Are you involved with the craft show this fall? Violet called and asked me to be at the chamber meeting tonight, and I wondered if we might get a cup of coffee afterward."

"I'm not involved with that," Cathy said.

"Marty?"

"No?"

"Don't tell me Trixie is."

Cathy sighed. "Anna Ruth, Trixie is my oldest and dearest friend. I'm not talking about her to you."

"Well, I'm your club sister, so that card trumps a friend-ship," Anna Ruth shot back.

"I don't think so."

Anna Ruth could suck the energy out of a Jehovah's Witness in thirty seconds flat.

"Well, I'm a better friend because I've worried myself sick all day that Trixie might have caused you to have a heart attack last night."

"Why would I have a heart attack? Healthy people don't have heart attacks at thirty-four," Cathy said.

"Well, you do have to deal with a drunk friend, and there is the stress of the wedding," Anna Ruth said. "I've got to go now. I'm in front of the community room. Oh, I can see you across the street. I'm waving at you. About that coffee afterward. We could still go."

"As you can see, I'm busy, so no, thank you." Cathy disconnected and put the phone back in her pocket.

A fat robin flew down from a tree and pulled a nice big juicy earthworm from the earth where Cathy had been digging. She sat very still and watched him. And then it dawned on her that Trixie had already left for the chamber meeting and Anna Ruth was on the way. She should at least warn Trixie!

She sat up so fast that it startled the robin. He flew away and dropped the worm on her bare foot. She flicked it off and grabbed the phone out of her pocket. She hit the speed dial button for Trixie and tapped her foot as she waited. On the fifth ring it went to voicemail. She tried a second time, and it went straight to voicemail.

Too late.

She couldn't get dressed in time to go support Trixie in the meeting where Anna Ruth was headed. And she sure couldn't show up at a town meeting in her overalls. Lord, Violet would stroke out right there in front of everyone.

If Trixie wasn't home in an hour, Cathy would call the police station and ask what Trixie's bail was for strangling Anna Ruth until her big blue eyes popped out of her head. Cathy would hock everything, including Miss Clawdy's and Marty's Caddy if it was necessary to get Trixie out of jail. She just wished she had had time to get cleaned up and see the fireworks.

=====

Trixie held a paper plate with three small thumbprint cookies. They weren't bad, but one bite said they weren't from Annabel's kitchen. That night Annabel had brought a dip with horseradish sauce and cream cheese, and Trixie hated horseradish. She should have volunteered for refreshments and brought Marty's pumpkin tartlets. At least people wouldn't be wrapping them in the cute little purple napkins and tossing them into the trash can like they were doing with the thumbprint cookies.

Violet Prescott, Cathy's future mother-in-law, popped the wooden gavel on the podium twice. The room went silent, and everyone proceeded to find a chair like little windup toys. Trixie turned her paper plate upside down in the trash can to cover up the cookies and the horseradish dip that had nearly sent her into a gagging fit. Violet shot a look her way that said she'd best get in her seat, so she hurriedly slid into the last chair in the front row. She looked up at the clock and got another ugly stare from Violet. No one questioned her ability to start a meeting right on time! The first thing a Cadillac citizen learned was Violet was the queen bee in Cadillac. The second was that you never ever crossed Violet. The third was that you never approached her unless she held out the golden scepter—that being her forefinger, which was, honest to God, adorned with a fourteen-carat-gold fingernail.

"If everyone is seated, we will begin our meeting." Violet's double chin wobbled like a bobblehead doll every time she moved. Trixie bit her lip to keep from giggling. Laughing at the queen could get her in big trouble. She might have to eat that horrid horseradish dip as punishment.

It wasn't until she was seated that Trixie realized she was elbow to elbow with Anna Ruth Williams. She couldn't move. She couldn't kill her. That was against the law. And her ex-husband sure wouldn't cut her any slack when he threw her in jail. Now that was an interesting idea. Sex in a jail cell with him handcuffed to the bars.

Anna Ruth realized who had sat down beside her and gasped. Trixie kept her eyes straight ahead. There was no justice in the world or it would not be a sin or against the law to shoot a cheating husband's new bimbo. Finally, curiosity got the best of her and she looked right at Anna Ruth. But the woman's eyes were on Violet as if she were God.

"This meeting is called to order. Old business?" Violet asked.

No one said a word. Someone did cough in the back row, but he cut it off when Violet gave him an evil glance.

"Okay, we'll get right on to the new business. Anna Ruth Williams is representing the city council tonight and is here to ask us to support them in a decision about zoning. Anna Ruth, honey, come right on up here. You have five minutes and then we're moving on to the next item on the agenda." The gold fingernail indicated that Anna Ruth could leave her seat and take her place behind the podium.

Anna Ruth stepped right on Trixie's toe when she stood up.

"Oh, dear. I'm so sorry. How clumsy of me."

She pranced up to the front of the room in her tight little pink skirt, matching tight sweater, and pink high heels and threw her blond hair back over her shoulder with a flick of her hand. Freshly manicured pink fingernails with cute little diamond accents glittered under the fluorescent lighting. Lord, she was another Violet Prescott in the making. When the old girl died, she'd probably leave that gold fingernail to Anna Ruth in her will.

"Hello, everyone. As you all know, there are several historically old houses on the three hundred block of Main Street. When the town was laid out, two blocks, the fourth and fifth blocks to be exact, were declared commercial lots. All others were zoned residential so that people wouldn't have cafés or coin-operated laundries right next door to their beautiful homes. The three hundred block has four houses on the south side that are at least fifty years old and five on the north side of the street that are that old or older. We need to remember that our town is steeped in history. I'm here to ask you to support the council that the old Andrews home be zoned from commercial back to residential. It's come to our attention that another business has petitioned for a rezoning on that block, and we simply cannot have our old homes being destroyed."

Trixie was on her feet in an instant. "Why would you do that? We were given a commercial zone for that corner that was supposed to be good indefinitely. We are a contributing business to Cadillac. Our café brings in tax dollars, and all three partners participate in community affairs."

"The lawyer for the council, Clayton Mason, has reviewed the papers, and he says that it does say that you have commercial zoning, but it does not state a time limit. So we either need to zone the whole block or revert your zoning. We either stop it now or pretty soon the whole town will be ruined." Anna Ruth dabbed at her blue eyes with a tissue she pulled dramatically from under the podium. "I just can't bear to see those old historical homes with businesses in them. If I'd been on the council, Miss Clawdy's…" she wrinkled her nose before going on, "would have never gotten a commercial license to ruin such an old house in our quaint little town."

"You have my support," Violet said. "I always said those old houses on that street are of historical value to the area and should not be made into businesses."

Trixie was still on her feet. "Everyone in this room eats at Clawdy's on a regular basis. Why in the hell are you all in such a tizzy about the house now?"

"You leave one bad apple in the barrel and pretty soon they're all rotten. If this keeps on, there could be a McDonald's buying up one of our precious old houses and razing it for the space to put in a fast-food place. How many of you want that right next door with that kind of noise and traffic? And we'd thank you to keep your comments clean, Trixie," Anna Ruth said.

"I want to talk after she gets her five minutes," Trixie said.

"Then get your name on the agenda for the next meeting," Violet said. "Now all of y'all be thinkin' about what Anna Ruth has proposed, and when we meet again, we'll discuss it then. I'll be expecting a vote in November. The people wanting to put a business in the old Shambles' place need an answer by then. But personally, I believe that we should rezone it back to residential."

"I should get to state my opinion if she gets to do hers," Trixie pressed on.

"You are not on the agenda. Sit down, Anna Ruth. I'll close things." Violet took over the podium again.

Trixie did not sit down. "I thought we were here to discuss the craft fair, not a zoning issue."

"That's next week, Trixie. You need to read the memo that Clayton Mason emailed everyone."

Trixie slumped back into her chair. She hoped that God would strike Violet dead before the next meeting. Hell, she might even help Agnes make her life miserable.

"Now any more new business?" Violet asked.

No one said a word.

Trixie jumped when Violet hit the gavel on the podium and said, "The next meeting will be next Thursday to discuss the craft fair, for those who don't bother to read the memos. We are adjourned."

Anna Ruth smiled smugly as she walked right in front of Trixie on her way to the refreshment table. Trixie stuck her throbbing toe out and didn't even try to catch Anna Ruth as she tumbled ass over teakettle, knocking down the chair she'd been sitting in on her way to sprawl out on the floor. Amazing! The woman wore white cotton granny panties!

"Oh, my!" Trixie bent to tug Anna Ruth's tight little skirt down over her thighs. "Those heels are demons to walk in, aren't they?"

———

The house had been occupied by the Andrews family since it was built in the 1930s. It was a charming two-story white frame house with big pillars holding up the wide porch, a driveway on the west side, and flowers blooming everywhere Cathy could plant them, but it didn't have enough parking space to support a business. That's where Darla Jean first came into the picture. She offered them the use of her parking lot right across the street for a free dinner every so often.

The first Andrewses had owned a cotton gin in town. They left the house to their son, a lawyer, who left it to his son, also a lawyer. When those folks were gone, their two daughters, Marty and Cathy, inherited the place and turned it into Miss Clawdy's Café six months later. Marty quit her job as a full-time teacher at the Grayson County College in Sherman but stayed on to teach adult basic education classes once a week. Cathy quit her job as a home economics teacher in Tom Bean, just south of Cadillac. And just before the café opened, Trixie quit her job at the Cadillac Community Bank to join them.

Getting the right zoning and all the legal papers to put in a business had taken time and money, but now it was not only up and running—it was a thriving business. The only reason Violet and Anna Ruth were so eager to shut them down was that Anna Ruth was afraid Andy would kick her out and go back with his ex-wife. Little did she know that Trixie was still way too pissed at him to take him back.

"I don't want him for anything but a romp in the hay,

Miss Granny Britches," Trixie said aloud as she angled across Main Street to the café.

She expected to go right to her room and work on her scrapbooking the rest of the evening, but Cathy was waiting on the front porch in one of the rocking chairs. One look at her said volumes. Cathy could never play poker because everything she thought showed on her face.

"Did Agnes die?" Trixie asked.

She could hope, couldn't she?

"I tried to call but you had your phone off. Was it awful?"

"What?" Trixie asked.

"Anna Ruth was at the meeting, right?" Cathy asked.

"How did you know?" Trixie asked.

"She called me on the pretense of being worried," Cathy said. "I couldn't be ugly to her. We're in the club together. She told me that she was coming to the meeting. I tried to call you but it went straight to voicemail, and I didn't want to crash the meeting by showing up out of the blue, so I kept pulling weeds and deadheading plants and worrying my head off."

"Well, you might not be in the club together very long, darlin'," Trixie said. "She was there to propose taking back our rights to a commercial zoning. Another business wants to buy the old Shambles place next to Agnes, and now the council is thinking about sending us back to a residential status."

The rest of the color drained from Cathy's face. "No!"

Trixie sat down in the other rocker. "She's just mad at me and trying to run me out of town. She's afraid Andy will come back to me for some decent sex. I can't imagine anyone as prissy as her liking sex, but I guess she does since she was able to talk him into bed in the first place."

"I don't think she did as much talking as he did, Trixie. Blame Andy. He's as guilty as she is, maybe even more so," Cathy said.

"How's that? It took both of them," Trixie asked.

"He was married and she is so young. Now tell me about the meeting. Why didn't you tell them what you think? I can't believe you didn't storm up to that podium and rant and rave."

"Sorry suckers wouldn't let me talk because I wasn't on the agenda. So I tripped Anna Ruth and enjoyed watching her fall on her face. She wears white panties."

Cathy slapped a hand over her mouth. "You didn't!"

"I did, but she deserved it. She stepped on my toe and it's still throbbing. I think it may be broke," Trixie said.

"I'm so sorry," Cathy said.

"Hey, it wasn't your fault, and it's worth the pain to get to deliver the payback. Let's go in. I need a drink."

They circled the house and went in the back door. Trixie went straight for the cabinet and grabbed the Jack Daniel's.

Cathy was still pale as a ghost when she slumped down in a chair.

Trixie poured an inch of whiskey into each of two glasses. "Tip it up, darlin', and drink it like a cowboy in an old Western movie. It'll put some color back in your face. We aren't going to lose our business. We'll put Agnes to work for us."

Cathy shook her head. "It's not you they're after. It's me. Ethan doesn't want me to work when we are married. I wouldn't tell him that I'd sell out or quit my job, so he and Violet are going after it a different way. If I sell or quit, they'll drop this thing. If I don't tell them I will, then they'll shut us down. I wouldn't even be surprised if Violet burned us out to get her way."

Trixie threw back her whiskey and poured another shot. "Could be it's both of us they're after. Remember the line in that old movie? 'They haven't seen trouble, but it's coming.' Well, they'd better not mess with us, because we've got Marty on our side."

"And Agnes. Don't forget her." Cathy picked up the glass and sipped. She shivered and said, "This stuff is vile. How do you drink it?"

Darla Jean opened the door and stopped in her tracks. "I don't believe it. I'm going out and coming back inside. Has the devil done claimed your soul, Cathy Andrews?"

"Come on in. It's just a shot to get her color back," Trixie said.

"Who died? Oh, Lord, don't tell me that Agnes done passed on," Darla Jean asked.

"No one died, but the lines have been drawn. Violet and Anna Ruth have spit on their knuckles, but we aren't afraid of them. Agnes has a gun, so there could be blood on the field." Trixie laughed. It wasn't so bad now with two shots of Jack warming her. She replayed the story for Darla Jean.

"They might come after your church next," Trixie said.

"I don't think that's possible since it was a gas station before I inherited it so it's already zoned commercial," Darla Jean said. "But if they do, they better get prepared to fight a long uphill battle, because I've got God on my side and he's got a lot more power than Violet Prescott."

Cathy put her head in her hands. "It's going to be horrible."

"Don't tell God how big the storm is. Tell the storm how big God is," Darla Jean quoted.

"You tell him for me," Cathy said.

"I'm going. I just wondered how the meeting went." Darla Jean headed for the door and met Marty halfway across the yard.

"Hey, no leftovers to take home?" Marty asked.

"Let's sit on the bench and I'll tell you what's going on. Cathy is still pale and blaming herself, and Trixie thinks it's her fault. Neither of them need to hash it out again."

Marty sat down on a bench beside the crape myrtle bushes. "Now you are scaring me."

Darla Jean told her the whole story and then added, "Marty, if you need money to beat this, I've got it."

"Thanks. If it gets deep, I might. We could move the café on the other side of your church. There are plenty of vacant buildings, but it's the principle."

"I agree," Darla Jean whispered. "So if they want war, let's load up our slingshots and take it to them."

"David and Goliath." Marty laughed.

"That's right."

"Still makes me mad as hell, though." She went on inside the house.

Darla Jean wiped the sweat from her forehead and headed over to the church. So the almighty Prescotts did not want Cathy to work at the café when she was married. What on earth Cathy, with her beauty and looks, saw in that man was a mystery for sure, and he was a big mamma's boy to boot. Cathy had to marry Ethan because she was afraid her biological clock was about to blow up in her hands. She talked more about having a baby in nine months than she did about being in love.

Twins were a strange sort. It wasn't uncommon for one to be a hellcat and the other a pious saint. And Marty and Cathy proved that point. Marty was a free spirit, a coyote running wild in the plains. Cathy was the complete other side of the coin—grounded, rooted in traditions. And yet, there was something about Marty that wanted a taste of Cathy's personality and something in Cathy's eyes that craved a taste of Marty's wildness.

Darla Jean had never had time for real friends, not until she got acquainted with Cathy, Marty, and Trixie. And even with their faults, she'd gladly give them everything in her bank account if they needed it to keep their café going. And that bank account was even bigger than Darla Jean's good heart.

Acknowledgments

We've all heard that it takes a village to raise a child, and I believe that, especially when it's applied to producing a book. Taking it from a one-paragraph pitch to a full, fleshed-out book takes a lot of effort on more than just my part in writing the original book. With that in mind, I owe lots of folks a bushel basket of gratitude.

First of all, thank you to Deb Werksman and the team at Sourcebooks Casablanca for reissuing this story and working so hard with me to bring *An Old Love's Shadow* up to date as *On the Way to Us*. At the time it was written, most folks didn't have cell phones or laptops, and looking back over a quarter of a century, I have to admit that more than that has changed. Also, thanks to my agent, Erin Niumata, and my agency, Folio Management, for continuing to believe in me; to my family for understanding the life of a writer; special thanks to my husband of more than fifty years for being my rock of support; and most of all to my readers. Without all of y'all, we authors would soon be at the top of the endangered species list.

About the Author

Carolyn Brown is a *New York Times, USA Today, Wall Street Journal, Publisher's Weekly,* and #1 Amazon and #1 *Washington Post* bestselling author. She is the author of more than 130 works of fiction. She's a recipient of the Booksellers' Best Award, Montlake Romance's prestigious Montlake Diamond Award, and a three-time recipient of the National Reader's Choice Award. Brown has been published for more than twenty-five years, and her books have been translated into twenty-one foreign languages and have sold more than ten million copies worldwide.

When she's not writing, she likes to take road trips with her husband, Mr. B., and her family, and she plots out new stories as they travel.

Website: carolynbrownbooks.com

Facebook: CarolynBrownBooks

Instagram: @carolynbrownbooks

Twitter: @thecarolynbrown

THE SISTERS CAFÉ

New York Times bestseller Carolyn Brown brings her unique voice to this poignant and hilarious novel.

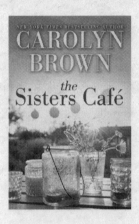

Cathy Andrew's biological clock has passed the ticking stage and is dangerously close to "blown plumb up." Cathy wants it all: the husband, the baby, and a little house right there in Cadillac, Texas. She's taken step one and gotten engaged to a reliable man, but she's beginning to question their relationship. Going through with the wedding or breaking off her engagement looks like a nightmare either way. She knows her friends will back her up, but she's the one who has to make a decision that's going to tear her apart.

> **"Fans of beloved Southern films, like *Steel Magnolias* and *Fried Green Tomatoes*, will flip for this charming small-town tale."**
> —*Woman's World*

For more info about Sourcebooks's books and authors, visit:
sourcebooks.com

THE SHOP ON MAIN STREET

New York Times bestseller Carolyn Brown brings her trademark Texas twang to this hilarious novel of love and revenge.

Carlene Lovelle, owner of Bless My Bloomers lingerie shop, has everything she's ever wanted: a loving husband, a successful small town business, and great friends who never disappoint. But that all changes when Carlene finds a pair of sexy red panties in her husband's briefcase. She knows exactly who those panties belong to—they were purchased from her very own shop.

Carlene is humiliated. But, even with her life is in a tailspin, Carlene finds she has all she needs as the ladies of this small town rally around and teach her that revenge is a dish best served red-hot.

"Will have you howling with laughter...I guarantee you will enjoy the ride."
—*Book Junkiez* for *A Heap of Texas Trouble*, 5 STARS

For more info about Sourcebooks's books and authors, visit:
sourcebooks.com

SAID NO ONE EVER

A delightful celebration of found family, rediscovery,
and being right where you belong...

Ellie Reed's self-esteem can't take any more of her family's constant
criticism and attempts to control her life. But when she rents an
Airbnb on a gorgeous farm in Montana, she encounters a whole new
set of family drama as she is caught between two handsome men
competing for control of the farm. Ellie is surprised to find herself
not only the caretaker of a barn full of farm animals, but the sudden
best friend of a spunky elderly widow whose outrageous ideas just
might change her destiny...

"A playful story with heart and teasing goodwill."
—*Publishers Weekly* for *The Unplanned Life of Josie Hale*

THE TOURIST ATTRACTION

Welcome to Moose Springs, Alaska! A laugh-out-loud romantic comedy series from Sarah Morgenthaler.

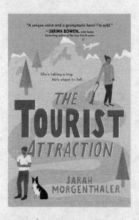

When Graham Barnett named his diner The Tourist Trap, he meant it as a joke. Now he's stuck slinging reindeer dogs to an endless parade of resort visitors who couldn't interest him less. Not even the sweet, enthusiastic tourist in the corner who blushes every time he looks her way...

Two weeks in Alaska isn't just at the top of Zoey Caldwell's bucket list—it's the whole bucket. One look at the mountain town of Moose Springs and she's smitten. But when an act of kindness brings Zoey into Graham's world, she may find there's more to the grumpy local than meets the eye...and more to love in Moose Springs than just the Alaskan wilderness.

"Fresh, fun, and romantic."
—Sarah Morgan, *USA Today* bestselling author